ANOTHER PERFECT DAY IN BIG SQUIRREL

D1736896

ANOTHER PERFECT DAY IN BIG SQUIRREL

TERRY WILLIAMS

BIG SQUIRREL PRESS

Library of Congress Catalog-in-Publication Data Available

Williams, Terry

Another Perfect Day in Big Squirrel / Terry Williams —1st United States edition 1. Fiction 2. Humor

ISBN-13: 9798386102470

1

TIFFANY AND CHAD

Chad could feel the bile rise as he turned red with anger. A woman had stopped her Honda Accord on the side of the causeway that spanned the lake connecting Chad's neighborhood of townhomes with the more expensive island on the other side. He often laughed at those who had bought over there. "They spent another three hundred thousand, and my view is better. Ha!" Chad wasn't laughing now.

She exited her Honda with a drink in a Styrofoam cup and a phone. That wasn't unusual. People from out of town often would stop to admire the views of the lake running behind Chad's house. He found that charming and validating of his choice of places to live. What she did next was less than charming.

She looked average enough. Five foot three, pudgy in a normal American way, dark auburn hair. He smiled until she emptied her cup and threw it in the lake.

Chad started to yell at her. It was an equivalent to an old man's, "Get off my lawn" admonition but for those who no longer had a lawn. "Hey you. Pick up the cup. What is the

matter with you?" She ignored him. He noticed the white
earbuds. Maybe she couldn't hear him. He used the window-
shattering whistle he'd mastered over his sixty-six years. Still,
no response. Frustrated, Chad searched for his glasses. Giving
up, he grabbed his phone, hoping to intimidate the woman by
photographing her and her car.

Still ignoring him, she returned to her Honda and left.
Chad went inside. Tiffany was in her recliner watching "90 Day
Fiancé," a show Chad loathed, and she loved. "What's going on
out there?"

"Nothing. Just some dumb slob tossing her cup in the lake. I
could not believe how deliberately she did it. Can you imagine
what her house must look like?"

"Try to let it go, Chad. You're going to give yourself a heart
attack."

"And I can't find my glasses. I'm so pissed. I was kind of
thinking about driving up in the mountains to Big Squirrel."
He'd do that sometimes when he felt he was obsessing over
small irritants. There was a greasy spoon in the town with a
delicious breakfast. The drive always calmed him down.

"They're hanging on the front of your shirt."

"Oh. Right. Thanks, Tif."

2

MASON AND DIXIE

Dixie had a Beretta 92 laid out on the kitchen table in front of her. The fancy design on the grip cost extra. A coffee cup steamed as it cooled next to her box of 9mm shells. She was cleaning and checking the pistol when Mason walked in the room.

"Jesus, Dixie. I don't have that much life insurance. I'm just not worth murdering."

She didn't look up from her work but lifted and turned the weapon as if inspecting it. "You're right about that, Mason. You are not worth it. This isn't for you."

"Well, who are you planning on killing today?"

"Anyone who threatens me. Would you prefer your wife was killed or raped?"

"When was the last time either of those things happened to anyone around here? What's gotten into you lately? You said our postal carrier looked threatening. I hope you don't take her out. I'm expecting a check in the mail any day."

The couple lived in a small town in the mountains east of Los Angeles. The last time anyone was shot there in Big Squirrel was Herb Gardner, a short, nearly blind, octogenarian gun nut. He had finished cleaning and loading a revolver that he stuck in his waistband for his evening walk. Retired for twenty-five years, he still wore polyester Jaymar Sansabelt dress slacks that he'd bought when he was still working. The elastic waistband on this pair had finally given up the ghost. The gun slipped just enough to drop to the floor and go off. The bullet missed a number of still valued though less than totally operational organs on its potential trajectory, having been stopped by his upper thigh. Herb was one lucky dude.

The wound hurt like hell. He screamed out multiple epithets as he began to bleed like a stuck pig. Still, he hesitated as he picked up the phone to call 911 due to his embarrassment. "I forgot to set the safety. Another senior moment. Oy. God, that hurts." Looking at the blood that appeared nearly black as it expanded on his favorite burgundy pants, Herb overcame his pride and called for an ambulance.

The next morning, the local paper ran the story. Once the locals knew he was okay, they had a good chuckle. Several sent flowers and visited him at the hospital. It was that kind of town. One presented Herb with a gun belt with holster and walked out laughing.

Dixie was one of those who'd sent flowers. Dixie looked up to Herb as a mentor. He was twice her age, had been around, and best of all, was a fellow gun aficionado. Herb looked down on Dixie. He thought she was as an idiot but tried to help her as best he could. Herb's wound embarrassment returned when he read the note and saw who had sent it. "Guess we're both idiots now," he thought out loud to himself.

Dixie responded to Mason after a long, quiet pause. "That postal carrier *does* look threatening. You know who doesn't? You, Mason. Remember when you tried to shoot my target and almost hit the house? The house was behind you. How do you do that? That's the only reason you don't own a gun. You know you couldn't hit a barn. I'm trained and I'll protect you, smart guy."

"You'll shoot your eye out." It was one of the few times Mason actually got the last word. He padded out their front door in his Birkenstocks, rayon Hawaiian shirt and cargo shorts with tool belt, ready to repair air conditioners. It got very hot in the summer there even though they were well up in the mountains. Nobody took care of their own HVAC systems. They just waited until they failed and then called Mason. He'd moved up here to have more time for sculpting and tried to make a go of turning his art into cash, but that hadn't proved any more profitable even with an increase in quantity. So, he fell back on his Air Force training and experience fixing large appliances and equipment and opened his own small business. It was a living.

He'd heard there was a concert in the park that afternoon and wanted to go, but he scheduled a couple of simple tune-ups for the morning, figuring his day was long enough to hold both activities comfortably.

Heading to his truck, he almost walked into Patti, the postal carrier, delivering to their rural box a little early to beat the heat. She glowered under her cap, but only because the sun was in her eyes. "She does look a bit threatening," Mason mumbled to himself. "Hi Patti, any big checks today?"

"Couldn't say, Mason. I might read your mail, but I still wouldn't say." She smiled and winked. Postal humor he guessed.

He grabbed his stack of envelopes and flyers and forged ahead. "Have a good one, Patti. Oh, and watch out for Dixie. She's armed and crazy as a loon."

"Roger that. Thanks Mason."

3

LOLITA AND MARVIN'S GHOST

Most of the residents in Big Squirrel didn't remember Marvin. Lots of new people had moved in when working from home became a trend. Those who did recalled him fondly. That was especially true of Lolita.

Her mountain-dwelling, wannabe beatnik parents, the Smiths, named her that when she was born in 1962, the year the kinky Kubrick film, *Lolita,* was released. Those familiar with the Nabokov story will understand what a peculiar, if not twisted, thing that was to do. Horrible, really. Lolita's life, thus placed on an odd path at birth, never quite recovered from its unusual beginning. It would mimic the film to an extent and go well beyond, down into a rabbit hole of her own creation.

She was just eighteen when she met Marvin, a history teacher some seventeen years older. Lolita had taken to sunning herself in a revealing swimsuit and shades in a chaise on her parent's front lawn that summer. She hadn't decided whether to go to college or just hang out in Big Squirrel. Her ambition was almost as low as her energy. Upon seeing her, most of the neighbors shook their heads in disapproval and moved on, remembering to gossip about her when they got home.

Not Marvin. Marvin stopped his car, determined to admonish the young trollop severely enough to set her on a straight-and-narrow course. That isn't what happened, of course. He started out alright. But his train of thought was derailed when he paused his lecture for a breath of oxygen and the girl interjected with, "It's too bad you're so uptight. You're kind of cute, for a weirdo. Almost sexy."

Marvin was very used to being called a "weirdo," only a bit less "uptight," but never "cute." He was clearly not cute. Stern-faced, bookish, tweedy, but certainly not cute. And sexy was out of the question. His brown suits smelled of mothballs, and his head resembled one. These were facts Marvin was familiar with, but that affected him not at all. Her description stopped him cold.

Five months later, they were married. Marvin and Lolita were hopelessly in love that day. They stayed that way for thirty-six years when Marvin suddenly died.

An old "friend" suggested at the wake that Lolita's recent and obsessive interest in conspiracy theories killed him. She threw the friend out, never to speak with her again. Lolita knew what killed Marvin. She was certain Antifa poisoned him. She was certain because Marvin told her so one day after his death. At least that was what she thought he said.

Marvin's ghost was mentally a bit different from the living Marvin. He had, of course, been through some changes. In life, Marvin was very liberal, progressive even. Post-mortem Marvin had drifted and now entertained some of the same conspiracy theories that captivated his widow, maybe.

An amateur but thorough autopsy performed by Mort Soul at the funeral parlor confirmed that Marvin had died of a cerebral hemorrhage, not poison. That fact did nothing to convince the couple. Marvin's ghost seemed confused and vague about his death. When he first appeared to her, she wasn't as surprised as most folks might be. After a few preliminary greetings, she asked, "What happened to you, Marv?" The apparition floated up and down and seemed to ponder what the question meant. He mumbled, "Antifa..." His answer was ambiguous as it wasn't at all clear if he understood the question. His speech faculties tended to go awry, as he still wasn't used to his new form.

Notwithstanding the garbled nature of the reply, Lolita seized on it as confirmation that an evil and mysterious cabal was actively engaged in destroying them and their way of life. Marvin could hang on no longer and dropped his connection with the living plane and faded into the ether. At least for a time.

4

CHAD DRIVES INTO BIG SQUIRREL

Leaving Tiffany in the valley, Chad slowly wound his Citroen 2CV up the winding and increasingly narrow road into the mountains. The little town of Big Squirrel lay just over the first crest. He loved the car and secretly loved how its ugly duckling looks provided contrast for his strikingly handsome face. Chad faintly resembled Rob Lowe, but with the addition of streaks of grey running back through his otherwise dark hair. He relished the irony that someone like him, a perennial A-Lister, would be found driving this fanatically economical vehicle the British had nicknamed "The Snail." The disadvantage was that slow was the only way his underpowered sedan could go up the mountain grade. If he'd been in a rush, he would have taken Tiffany's BMW.

Chad also secretly loved being alone for periods of time. He also loved how yucca plants along the highway gave way to manzanita, that upon reaching a little more elevation, yielded to the pines. It provided a contrast they lacked down below.

The air was cool, fresh, and blue when he passed under the banner at the entrance to the town. It announced a concert in the park that would happen that afternoon. Melody Gratch, the jazz singer, would be appearing on stage. Chad knew of Melody and really liked her voice. He wondered why she didn't change her discordant last name to something more fitting for a chanteuse. He was surprised that she was doing an afternoon outdoor gig at such a small venue. Going on around 10 pm at some dark cellar in the city would be more her usual M.O. He figured there might be an interesting story there and decided to attend the show.

Before he did, he was due for a stop at Mother's Café, his favorite old greasy spoon that served breakfast all day and into the evening. "Mother" Rue had opened the joint back in '49. She was the stereotypical café owner and waitress, with a crumpled white uniform, pencil behind her ear, cigarette dangling from her mouth, and a dose of love and sass for everyone who walked in. Passing in 1982 from lung cancer, her daughter Maisie inherited the restaurant and Rue's sass. She made cinnamon rolls from scratch every morning that were the size of the halfmoon hubcaps hot-rodders liked to add to their Chevy Bel Air coupes back in the early 60's. She also taught her short order cook to make a Denver omelet into a sandwich, pressing the egg, ham, and green bell pepper mass between two slices of white toast.

Maisie was better known around town as "Little Mother," even though she was childless herself. She could look a little matronly in her white uniform when at the café, but in civilian clothes Maisie bore a strong resemblance to Dorothy Malone when the actress played a very steamy scene as the hot owner of the Acme Book Store opposite Humphrey Bogart in the 1946 film, *The Big Sleep*. In other words, she was cute as a button and very hot.

Chad would gladly make the drive up for that sandwich alone and a cup of Mother's very hot coffee served in a classic heavy off-white porcelain cup on a chipped saucer.

"Morning, Chad. I see you forced that ugly-assed egg-beater

car of yours up the hill again," said Maisie, nodding toward the window. The Citroen was parked right out in front. "You want the regular, hon'?"

"Nah, no red-hot lovin' today, dollface," Chad joked. "I just want the Denver."

A regular down-counter from Chad chuckled at the exchange and turned back to his paper.

"You got it. It'll be up in a minute."

"Thanks." Chad looked around the café. A wire rack held some tourist flyers and real estate magazines. Among the flyers was one for today's concert. He ambled down and grabbed one from the rack. Melody Gratch would be on at 2 pm. Jeff Stickney was scheduled to accompany her on piano. Chad knew of Stickney too, but more from his work in movies as an actor, not as a musician. Now his interest was piqued. The flyer mentioned something about the event being recorded for a TV special, thus explaining why they were up in the mountains this weekend.

"Hey, Little Mother, how do you get tickets for the show? The flyer doesn't say."

"Sorry, no idea hon'. I don't go catch much live music."

"Ya' just pay at the door." The regular sitting by the register chimed in with the answer.

"Thanks buddy. I don't want to miss it."

"There's gonna be a camera crew, so if you've done any crimes you might want to lay low."

"I think I'll keep that in mind." Chad laughed. "Thanks again."

"Here's the Denver, Chad." Maisie slid Chad's order on the table.

He savored each bite of the sandwich and slurped hot coffee as he envisioned the concert in the woods.

The crowd for the show would outnumber the population of Big Squirrel by a good margin. It was a small town that used to exist to serve the loggers that worked this part of the mountains. That was until they cut down most of the large older growth trees. The company left when profits dropped due to lower production. Later in the sixties, the town became a hippie haven, complete with a commune, head shop, and spontaneous concerts in the very park that would be graced by the velvet tones of Ms. Gratch later that day. It also sported at least two marijuana grows in the woods. As those little farms contributed enough to the economy to lift the town back out of its post-lumber felling slump and didn't cause any trouble, the sheriff and his two deputies looked the other way. Eventually the hippies took over for the most part. They filled the town council seats and made several small, somewhat odd changes to town ordinances, including updating the title of the mayor to "Illustrious Mayor and Glorious Pooh-Bah." That was streamlined a bit in later years by the town's various mayors and city councils, but it still commanded attention.

Chad walked past the shops, post office, auto repair garage, and bar to get to the park with its ancient, raised bandstand under a large gazebo. He paid $20 at the gate and searched for a suitable roost on the lawn. A decent crowd had already gathered. There was a professional sound control table in the center of the lawn. A lot of action surrounded the bandstand inside an old-fashioned gazebo with both roadies and the camera crew setting up and testing. A black Steinway sat on the stage, looming like a Panzer.

Chad found a vantage point where he would be able to see both Melody and Jeff Stickney. Asking a neighbor to hold his seat, he headed back to the snack stand by the gate to grab a lemonade. He had forgotten his anger at the cup tosser back at his lake in the valley. All tension had left his body when the announcer came to the mic to introduce Melody Gratch and get the show underway.

"Good afternoon, everybody. I am your Mayor and Grand

Pooh-Bah, Kelvin Nader. Welcome one and all to the best little town in these mountains or any others, Big Squirrel. It is my honor to introduce a performance I know you will all love and remember from this day forward! Remember, there's a camera crew filming here today, so I hope you wore a clean shirt. Ladies and gentlemen, boys and girls, the fantastic Melody Gratch and the Scratchers!"

Melody burst out in the shortest fluorescent paisley retro-mini dress seen since 1972 worn over her white pleather go-go boots. "How are all you darling people doing today?" she called out to the cheering crowd. Chad and everyone else rose to their feet, whooping and whistling as they applauded madly. The small combo called the "Scratchers" took their places and started tuning in the back. "I am so happy to be back in Big Squirrel. That's right, some of you may remember I was here a few years ago. I wasn't so well known back then, but you folks sure made me feel welcome. So, when our producer asked where I wanted to film our special, you know what I said." The crowd yelled, "Big Squirrel!" and cheering resumed.

"Now I want to bring out my accompanist for this show, Mr. Jeff Stickney!" The spectators exploded once more. Some had come just to see if it would be the same Jeff Stickney they'd seen in *Monkey Island* or *Just Like Last Time*. When they realized it was, they went nuts. After air kisses and hugs with Melody, Stickney took his bench and warmed up the keys.

"I'm going to lead off with a little number that Jeff taught me in more ways than one, if you know what I mean. It's called 'The Man Who Hurt my Pride.'"

Down below, Chad was enthralled as he sucked his lemonade through a straw. Everyone was feeling pretty mellow, and the smell of grass wafted over the crowd.

A couple of numbers later, Gratch was telling a slightly off-color story to lead into the next song when a woman's voice yelled from the crowd, "Socialists! Socialists! You're trying to corrupt our kids. Just shut up and sing!" It belonged to a middle-aged blonde wearing a Tammy Faye Bakker level of make-up and a white dress. Both the blonde and the dress had seen better days.

A male voice farther back in the audience hollered back, "You shut up, Lolita! Shut up and sit down!"

The deputy on duty at the park walked up behind Lolita and whispered something to her. She sat back down and was quiet. Gratch couldn't resist, and quipped, "Hey no worries, hon'. I remember when I had my first beer."

The crowd laughed, but an embarrassed and red-faced Lolita wasn't smiling when she got up again to scream, "Bitch! Commie bitch!" at which point the deputy took her gently by the arm to escort her out of the park.

"Let's go, Lolita. You don't need to listen to them," intoned Deputy Mace. He was using his lower soothing voice, something practiced at a conflict management seminar he'd attended the previous year. She went along peacefully. Most of the audience cheered, including the now-old residual hippies. Some of the more average-looking older folks didn't. In fact, a couple of them also walked out.

Gratch, being used to hecklers and unruly crowds, took it in stride. "Where was I? Oh yeah…" She resumed her story, got a big laugh, and went on to sing, "Heavy Breathing Never Wears Me Out."

After the concert ended, Chad joined a line to meet Gratch and Stickney who were shaking hands and signing autographs after the final encore. In line, he overheard the couple in front of him discussing the heckler. It sounded like gossip, so Chad joined right in. "Excuse me, who was that rude woman and what was wrong with her?"

The older male ahead of Chad turned and said with a faint smile, "Oh, that was just Lolita. Lives down the road. She's okay but a bit flighty these days. She got a bad case of the "Q" about a year before her husband died. Hasn't been the same since. Best ignored. Where are you from, stranger?"

"I live just down in the valley. Drove up for breakfast when I noticed there was this concert. I really like Melody, don't you?"

"Yep, she's got some pipes alright. That Stickney fella plays better than I thought he would too."

The couple in front reached the point where Gratch and Stickney were signing things. Chad reached into his pocket for his flyer. He didn't collect autographs. He mostly just wanted an excuse to say hello and ogle.

5

MASON AND DIXIE GO OUT FOR DINNER AFTER THE CONCERT

"You didn't need to yell at poor Lolita like that, Mason."

Mason and Dixie had stopped at The Anvil Tavern for a beer on their way home. Sitting on the patio on a warm afternoon was one of their favorite pastimes. Mason peered at Dixie over the foamy head on his glass. "Yeah, well, that bimbo is always stirring up shit. She drives me nuts."

"I'm just glad nobody seemed to notice it was you screaming at her. I'll bet you were glad I had my little friend with me, just in case I had to defend your honor." Dixie was laughing now, and Mason joined her. A touch of alcohol always either made things better or worse. Today it was the former. "I'm mostly happy that you didn't shoot me. I wish you wouldn't carry that thing everywhere we go. You have to admit, Lolita has at least a few loose screws these days, with her insane theories on everything."

"I don't know, honey. Sometimes I think she's the only one of us who may see the complete picture. I mean, I wouldn't be surprised if some of those things actually were going down."

"Holy Moly, Dixie, don't tell me you're becoming one of

those. I don't need that crap flowing through our home. Home might be the only sanctuary left us pretty soon. Even some of the old folks who've been here since the sixties and seventies are buying into the B.S."

"Don't worry. I haven't been turned. I just don't think any of us ever has all the answers."

"Well, I'll drink to that." Mason smiled, Dixie grinned back, and they downed the last of the beer. "Another?"

"Damned right, honey. Keep 'em comin'."

6

LOLITA FUMES

Lolita had been crying into her wine. The white dress was now even more crumpled and a red drop from her glass had created a tiny stain near the hem. She didn't notice. She was still angry and embarrassed, even though Deputy Mace had been very gentle and kind with her. Why didn't everyone see things the way she did? Sure, some did, but many of them were laughing at her. They just didn't get it. Or maybe they did, and they were part of the cabal. Her mind was flipping around like a freshly landed bass on a pier.

So busily was she chewing over the recent events, she didn't even check her online conspiracy sites. She normally would have done so at least twice by now. There were new scandals and drops all the time, and she didn't want to miss anything. Obsessing over the concert experience filled the same receptor spaces in her head, at least for now.

"Marvin? Why aren't you here when I need help? You were here, then you weren't, then you came back, and now you're gone again. I can't take it. I need you, Daddy." She'd taken to calling Marvin that several years ago during another moment of feeling needy. The nickname was another facet of the twisted life that was hers.

Marvin had passed six years prior to these events, but the once too-young woman still talked to him and trusted he would reappear. Nothing like it had ever happened after the first time. But this evening was different. Upon her pronouncing the word, "daddy," a light and chilling breeze swept across the floor and Lolita's legs. Feeling a draft, she glanced around the old pine A-frame from her perch on the sofa. All the doors and windows were shut tight. Maybe it was from the fireplace. Maybe not.

"Marvin, are you there?" The lamp next to her sofa flickered for just a second. "Oh shit, oh shit, oh shit!" Lolita rose and began to pace the room. "Come on, sweetie. You can make it. Keep trying!" Then, nothing. The room began to warm back up and the lightbulb glowed. "Damn, Marvin. You were close, huh?" Lolita refilled her glass and returned to the sofa to continue ruminating.

HOMEWARD BOUND

C had retrieved his little French car and headed back toward home. The Citroen was much happier going downhill than it was going up to Big Squirrel. *That was fun,* thought Chad. *I like it there. It felt like home. We should find a way to just move up there.* He'd present that idea to Tiffany over dinner if he worked up the nerve.

He heard a loud "BANG" just as he passed under the concert banner. Fearing it was the car, he looked at the hood, then the gauges. All seemed fine. A rearview mirror check confirmed no smoke from the exhaust. Chad pulled over to check the tires. Those were okay, just a bit low on tread. Shaking off the stress, he got back in and resumed his drive.

The shock of the explosion woke Chad up. His mind started to piece together how they could move. He was an independent CPA and financial advisor with a massive list of clients for whom he worked remotely, for the most part, so he could work anywhere. The situation would be more difficult for Tiffany, who was a contracted physical therapist at a local medical center back in the valley. Commuting would be tough on the long, twisty, two-lane mountain road, especially in wet weather.

He'd have to check the stats on the area surrounding Big Squirrel. He knew the community was aged, and that was promising. Would there be enough population and demand up there to support a business for Tiffany? Would she even be interested in going out on her own?

His mental machinations were flowing full steam ahead now. Chad enjoyed problem solving and was generally pretty good at it. He felt hopeful and positive as he wound through the curves, loving the way the road felt through the goofy old car. Those good vibes would dissipate upon his return.

DIXIE LIGHTS UP THE ANVIL, SORT OF

"Holy Shit!" exclaimed Mason. The other patrons on the patio recoiled instinctively. Some dropped to the ground. Slim Jim, the hulking, somewhat rotund owner of The Anvil Tavern, peered cautiously out the back door to the deck.

A rather tipsy Dixie had been reaching in her purse searching for a lipstick to take with her to the john. Somehow, she had tripped the safety on the Beretta and the pistol went off. The slug went down through her bag and the wood deck below. Fortunately, nobody was hurt, but everyone was scared.

The gun had made quite a noise. The sound reverberating off the surrounding mountains was the explosion heard by Chad on his way out of town. Had he known about it, he might have had second thoughts about moving to Big Squirrel.

Back at The Anvil, it was enough to panic the half of the town that was there. There had been trouble at The Anvil more than once. It was just that kind of place. Deputy Mace happened to be walking back from escorting Lolita home after her demeaning concert departure and entered the patio from the sidewalk, hand on his sidearm. He hadn't drawn his weapon except for target practice for the five years he'd served in Big Squirrel. As Mason's outburst was the second loud sound on the patio, Mace looked that way to see smoke rising from Dixie's purse.

"Dixie, what the fuck is going on?" The policeman's practiced conflict management skills were slipping. The other customers froze in their seats, waiting to see what would happen.

"Oh God, deputy, I'm sorry. The thing just went off. I don't know what happened."

Mace could see the hole the bullet had made in the deck and surmised the situation was now under control. "Let me have the purse, Dixie. I'll have a look if that's okay." He had regained his composure and was back in his professional mode. Mace carefully opened the mouth of the bag and looked in. He gingerly pulled out the weapon and quickly flipped the safety back on. The hole in the bottom of the bag was still smoking when the lipstick Dixie had wanted fell through it. The sound of it hitting the deck was enough to cause a couple of the nearby customers to flinch again.

"Oh, there it is..." Dixie was feeling her beer. When she reached for the makeup on the floor, Deputy Mace said, "Let's just leave it for now. I'm going to take the gun back to the station and you two are going home. You can retrieve your weapon tomorrow morning, understood?"

Slim Jim had mustered up the courage to walk out to the table. His heavy brow furrowed when he saw the hole in his deck. "Hey, nobody leaves until this is all paid for."

Mason found his voice again. "Sorry, Slim. What do I owe you?"

"A hundred ought to do it, and you'd better leave Jaycee a hell of a tip too!" Mason handed over a small wad of twenties and said to keep it. Slim nodded while looking back down at the hole. Mace unloaded the Beretta, dropped the clip in his pocket, and tucked the weapon into his belt.

"Wait a minute. What about my second amendment rights? You can't take my gun! It's in the constitution!" Dixie was on her feet, waving her hands wildly in front of the deputy. Slim Jim and his customers gasped.

"Oh shit, Dixie." Mason was not pleased. Neither was Deputy Mace who gently cuffed Dixie, told Mason to go home again, and started to mirandize the repairman's wife as he led her across the street to his patrol vehicle.

"This is bullshit! This is bullshit!" Dixie was lathered up and giving the policeman a piece of her mind. He gently protected her head as he popped her into the backseat, and they drove off into the Big Squirrel twilight.

PEOPLE MOVIN' OUT. PEOPLE MOVIN' IN. SORT OF

"How was Mother's?" Tiffany had enjoyed her alone time too.

"Great. I love the Denver sandwich there."

"I remember. You were gone longer than usual this time. What was her name?"

"Ha! There was a concert in the park. Melody Gratch and Jeff Stickney! Can you believe it? Together on one stage, as they used to say. It was really fun. I even got to watch a crazy heckler get bounced."

"That's a lot of action for Big Squirrel. It's usually as dull as oatmeal and lacks the nutritional content. I thought Stickney was an actor."

"He is. He also plays a mean piano. I love that guy. A multi-talented man, he is."

"Please don't start talking like Yoda again. That Gratch chick has got to change her name. God that's awful."

"She sang like Ella. Didn't look so bad, either."

Tiffany seemed to be in a jovial mood. Chad thought this might be a good moment to float his moving-to-the-mountains balloon.

"You know, Tiffany, I started thinking while I was up there..."

"Oh no, here it comes." She was still smiling though, so Chad pressed on.

"We should look into moving up that way. It's so much nicer than down here."

"Let's see, oh yes, how about no?" Her smile had waned.

That was her standard reply to 97% of Chad's ideas, so he was only a tad crestfallen. Foolishly, he asked a question thinking he already knew how she would reply. He didn't. "Why?"

"I'm pregnant."

"What? You cannot be serious. At our age? What?"

Tiffany laughed, literally out loud. "Nah, I'm just kidding, ya' big palooka." Chad had no idea where Tiffany had learned so much slang from the forties. They weren't that old. Now Chad was off-center and wouldn't be able to argue as well. Making him that way was a tactic Tiffany had employed several times over the course of their relationship. It never failed. Following that, she went in for the kill.

"Seriously Chad, we can't afford to move. Plus, what about my job? They aren't going to move the med center to Big Squirrel just to make you happy. And as I said, it's dull as a box of wood." She was almost gloating with what she was sure was a coup de grâce ending to her husband's silly pipe dream.

"It's beautiful there. No traffic. There are a lot of old folks who could benefit from your expertise. We should do some market research to see if there might be enough potential demand in the general vicinity to support you hanging out your own shingle."

"You haven't thought this through, Jeremiah Johnson. Will we even qualify for a new mortgage if I leave my job? How am I going to raise the capital to open my own clinic?" Glancing at the kitchen, she continued. "Look, I kept dinner warm. Let's have a glass of wine and get back to planet earth."

He was certain the difference between what they could sell their house for in the valley and what homes probably cost up in the mountains would be sufficient to address both concerns. He was also certain he'd better make sure of that before presenting another pitch only to have it drawn-and-quartered by his girlfriend doing her locally famous Torquemada impression. Unfortunately, she was making sense, not what Chad was hoping for at all. He was an "If we build it, they will come," kind of guy. Tiffany was more like, "Look before you leap," and she never actually leapt. That made them an effective couple, but it was maddening to them both. He decided that some research was in order.

Walking into the kitchen, Chad found Tiffany had already poured two glasses and was smiling at him over the island stove. The debate was over. For now.

DIXIE GETS SPRUNG

Deputy Mace once again showed his compassion, community awareness, and professionalism when he offered Dixie a Get-Out-of-Jail-Free card. He spoke to her as she sat in her cell. "Look, you do not want to go to trial for threatening a peace officer and resisting. And I sure don't want you in here. So, here's what we're going to do. You leave the pistol with me for now and you can go home with no charges filed. I'll check in on you next week, and if I'm convinced you can handle it, I'll return your firearm. Deal?"

A night in the slammer appeared to have had a calming and humbling effect. She simply answered, "Yes, sir."

Mason was waiting in the jail lobby, hoping to bail his wife. He didn't need to. Dixie was mighty glad to see him and gave him a long hug. They were home in ten minutes, sitting at the kitchen table.

"What came over you, Dixie? Mace wasn't giving you as much trouble as he could have, given you don't even have a permit to carry that thing around concealed in your purse."

"I really don't know, Mason. I've felt really edgy lately, and sometimes it seems like the whole world is conspiring against me."

"Maybe that's why you worry about poor Patti. All she ever did was deliver the mail and you act like she's coming to kill your puppy. What can I do to help?"

"Just let me talk it out?"

"That will be easier if you don't spread out gun parts on our table here. Remember that Carole King song? You can't talk to a man with a shotgun in his hand. Seriously, sweetie, if you need to talk, I'm here, and I'll listen."

"That would be a first!" Dixie stood. "I'm going to take a shower. Jail time always makes me feel grungy."

"Wait, you've been in jail before?"

"Nope." With that, Dixie turned with a smile and left the room.

Mason's instinctively apprehensive thought quietly spilled out of his mouth. "Oh boy."

He had met Dixie at the Desdemona County fair in Groverton, some seven miles south of Big Squirrel, right after returning from his stint in the Air Force. She caught his eye when he got his two corn dogs and a Coke from the big yellow and white food truck near the carnival rides. He turned and was walking by when he heard her order, "Two of those for me too." She gave him a toothy grin when he stopped and turned to see who was ordering. While Dixie was only 5'4" tall, most of that was leg, as was amply displayed below her Daisy Dukes. The requisite yellow gingham shirt rolled up at the waist and a pair of Tony Lama cowboy boots completed her ensemble. The shirt was unbuttoned enough from the top to prove to Mason that she sported the smallish breasts he secretly preferred. She was blonde & blue, with just a hint of freckles. Her blindingly white teeth were large enough to have been transplanted from a thoroughbred. He almost dropped his hot dogs.

"The mustard's over there, cowboy."

Disarmed and stopped like a deer in the headlights, Mason coughed up his weak reply, "I'm no cowboy. I'm a sculptor."

"You get stoned a lot then?" Dixie was giggling to herself.

"Yeah," Mason quickly regained his smartass demeanor to run against hers. "You here showing your prize sheep, Rebecca?"

"Ha, my name's Dixie, not Rebecca. And I'm just here to pick up a guy."

"Oh, how's that going?"

"We'll see in a few minutes. Meet ya' at the condiment stand."

A very nervous and red-faced Mason accidentally squirted relish on one of his corn dogs. He hated relish and was wiping it off with a napkin when Dixie arrived, dogs in hand. She sounded a little like Mae West when she smiled and said, "Couldn't wait, huh, Big Boy?"

That was it. His smartass demeanor lay in tiny piles of smoking ashes on the ground, and while they were substantially opposites except for a love of corn dogs and maybe a couple of other things, he'd been hers ever since, for better or for worse.

Following Dixie's joke about having been in jail before, Mason decided he needed a break. He grabbed his rod and vest and headed over to the lower part of Murrieta Creek near the confluence with the river. The creek was a minor tributary for the lower branch of the Santa Quiteria River. It had been named after Joaquin Murrieta, although the famous gold rush era criminal had never operated around Big Squirrel, so nobody knew why it was so named.

Much of the wee bit of snow that fell in the surrounding mountains flowed down Murrieta Creek and from there down to the Santa Quiteria. Mason knew where some holes were that often held brook trout waiting for a meal to float downstream into their mouths. Very rarely he'd spot and once caught a California golden trout. Neither species was native to the area, but someone had introduced them way back, and Mason delighted in reducing their invasive population. He mainly delighted in eating them. Rainbow trout were given the catch-and-release treatment.

He carefully checked around the creek, watching for hatch. Not spotting anything, he just pulled a fly he felt good about from a patch on his vest and tied it to 4x tippet, thinking it should be good for trout. No sooner had he cast into a favorite hole where a couple of roots protruded from the opposite shoreline than he had a ferocious hit. An unusually aggressive largemouth bass leapt from the water and ripped through the light tippet making off with it and the fly, leaving a surprised Mason holding a limp line leading to nowhere. He noticed a couple other bass swimming after the aggressor and snapping at it.

"Well, that's pretty weird," he said to the surrounding woods. The bass seldom ventured from the river into the creek. Shrugging, Mason tied on another fly and cast a bit upstream from the hole. Patience was the key to success in this game, just as it was while living with Dixie.

Meanwhile, after arriving late to her receptionist job at Doc Jones office in Groverton, Dixie was secretly checking online to see how late Big Bob's Gun Shop and Ice Cream Parlor was open.

11

TIFFANY GETS THE BIG SQUIRREL BUG

T iffany had an epiphany after a lot of chardonnay-lubricated soul searching. What if Chad was right?

She'd thought about opening her own practice more than once. She loved the clinic where she had an office, was technically (but not really) an independent contractor, and the doctors there gave her all her business. But a girl needs a dream, and running her own, fully independent business was hers. Competition and cost would have made it brutal in the valley, but up in a smaller town, it just might be doable.

While she liked their home on the lake, she had never really wanted to move to Rancho Niebla Tóxica, where they now lived. They only did so because it was affordable, and they could get a cool house there. She'd grown up in Hermosa Beach and was used to a more fun-loving atmosphere where you could always enjoy the outdoors without Rancho's oppressive summer heat. But it was true what her friends said: Once you move away from the beach in Southern California, you can never afford to return. Maybe they could recapture some of that feeling in the mountains.

Coming to the same conclusion as Chad had a few days ago,

Tiffany decided some research was in order and opened her tablet. She searched "Big Squirrel" on Google maps, then medical centers near there. Nothing came up in town, but a Mortimer Jones and Thomas Stubbs, MDs, came up in a slightly larger dot on the map named Groverton, just a few miles from Big Squirrel. They were general practitioners, a semi-endangered species. "What luck!" Tiffany was getting into the chase now. She called their office number.

The call did not go into an endless and irritating menu of choices to be made by entering different numbers. A live human answered after only three rings. "The office of Doctors Jones and Stubbs. This is Dixie. How may I help you today?" Tiffany was so stunned to hear a real voice she forgot why she'd called for a red-faced moment. "Hello?"

"Oh, yes, hi, sorry. My name is Tiffany Van Pelt. I'm a physical therapist, and I'm doing a little research. Could you possibly help me?"

"Sure honey. What do you need?"

Again, Tiffany was shocked. She would have never gotten that type of response down in Rancho or L.A. "Great! I am wondering if your office refers many patients for physical therapy?"

"Are you kidding? We have a lot of retired seniors around here. They are constantly falling, pulling muscles, tearing ligaments, and breaking bones. Torn meniscus is a hobby up this way. It's a real shit-show sometimes. We had to triage them a while back."

"Wow! That's super!" Tiffany reconsidered that statement. "Well, not super for them, but good for business. Mind if I ask about how many on average and where you send them?"

Dixie shared a number that perked up Tiffany's ear, and told her, "We split it up. Most go to San Bernardino. But many of them go to a clinic down in Rancho Niebla Tóxica. I hear they have a good therapist there."

"That's me! I knew I got some who lived in the mountains, but I didn't remember that they came from your office. That's so cool!"

"Oh, that's you? Fun! Yeah, we'd send more, but the clinic in San Berdo takes Delicato-Ricotta Health Plan Senior Advantage. A lot of our oldsters use them for Medicare because of the free premiums. But boy, are they surprised when they get their pharma bills. Not so free then."

"Ah," Tiffany made a note regarding Delicato-Ricotta. Maybe she could get in their network up there. "I hear you and appreciate the referrals. What other medical offices are up your way, Dixie?"

"Doc Lopez still practices part-time. He's up the road from here. Lopez is older than most of his clients, so that won't be for much longer. Others go down to Redland or Loma Linda to Simons Wellness, near the VA. Old Stubbs retired about five years ago, so it's just Doc Jones and me at out office. Doc Jones has been seeking a replacement for Stubbs, so hopefully we'll be able to handle more in the near future right here."

"Wow, Dixie, you've been super. I owe you one. Thanks so much for taking the time to chat."

"My pleasure, sweetie. Are you thinking about heading up our way?"

"I sure am. My husband loves going up there, especially for breakfast. He wants to move there."

"Well, we sure could use a therapist who's closer. We'd make sure you got some business." As usual, Dixie was speaking out of school. "Call me if you are visiting up here. I'll meet you at Mother's Café in Big Squirrel, near where I live. They have a Denver omelet that's to die for!"

What a friendly gal, thought Tiffany. *Maybe I've already made a friend in Big Squirrel.*

After a few more calls and some math, Tiffany was feeling optimistic. She had also checked the general cost of living and was surprised to learn it was much less than around Rancho, which she had felt was very modest. This might not be such a bad idea after all. But where would she come up with the money to open and operate a few months without much income?

Chad had been doing his own research and math. He was fairly adept at that, as both were key to his work. It hadn't taken him long to calculate that the sale of their house in Rancho would cover both a new home in Big Squirrel and the capital expenses of opening an office. His ample income could cover both their living expenses and Tiffany's operating expenses at least until she began to turn a profit. All that was left was to convince her what a brilliant plan it was. The CPA put a few graphs into a PowerPoint presentation and girded his loins. They may be married, but Chad knew to get buttoned up for a meeting like the next one, as if he was seeing a client. Tiffany was no pushover. Had sales been one of his skills, Chad might have realized Tiffany had already sold herself on the concept and bought in.

12

DIXIE REARMED

That Tiffany sounds really nice, and I know she's a good therapist from our patients' results. It might be fun if she moved up and we hung out. Dixie was thinking to herself and smiling while strolling down Main Street to Big Bob's Gun Shop and Ice Cream Parlor after she got off work.

A little bell hanging from the heavy door tinkled merrily as Dixie walked into the store. A short man in a plaid flannel shirt looked up from the counter, behind which was a rack of shotguns and rifles. Under the counter glass was a refrigerated display case of ice cream, and to the right of it, a pair of shelves holding an array of pistols. Cake cones were housed on the counter in a brightly colored cardboard sleeve featuring a grinning clown face and the brand name "Loopy's Circus Cones." The owner had put it in because of his love of ice cream and the fact that it provided a profitable diversion to keep kids from interrupting their parents' gun purchases. Speaking from his perch behind the study-in-contrasts area, Robert said, "Well, what do you know? Welcome back, Dixie!" Big Bob Ziglar, the founder, had passed a few years back. The shop was now run by one of his sons, Robert. At least that is what he called himself. But everyone around Groverton and Big Squirrel knew him as "Little Bob," the sound of which he hated, perhaps due to his relatively diminutive stature.

"I heard you caused a bit of commotion at The Anvil yesterday after the show." Robert chuckled but had a warm smile for his customer, whom he really liked.

"That I did, Little Bob, that I did."

He winced a bit at the sound of his detested nickname. "I'm grateful you returned, Dixie. How can I be of help?"

"I'm glad you asked, Bob. Here's what I need…"

Robert dutifully reminded her of the ten-day waiting period after showing her the merits of a new Glock 19 he pulled from the display case.

"So, what's a girl got to do to walk out with one today, Bobby?" Dixie flashed her best melt-you-like-butter smile at Robert as she leaned wantonly over the counter. Ten minutes, not days, later she hit the street with a purse that weighed thirty ounces more than it did when she entered the shop. In the end, she hadn't actually done anything for Little Bob to get him to risk his livelihood, it was just the mere suggestion that she might that worked every time with every man. Dixie smiled as she licked her free ice cream cone and walked to her SUV.

Little Bob gathered the small wad of hundreds Dixie had withdrawn from savings along with the documents she'd left to accompany his Dealer Record of Sale report. He started the online process. If all went smoothly, he'd be out of the woods in ten days. Bob had heard gossip about the shot fired through the deck at The Anvil Tavern, but not the fact that Dixie had been arrested. If Mace had filed an arrest report, Little Bob would be toast. But he wasn't thinking things through. He was still pretty lathered up from what his own imagination had done with Dixie's suggestive behavior and comments. Mrs. Little Bob was in for a very rare surprise when he got home.

13

LOLITA ENTERTAINS A LATE-NIGHT VISITOR

After hitting sites that included Gobsmack, Living Room, and 13chan, Lolita had seen enough to be fuming and freaking out at the same time. She and Marvin had never had any kids. But she was super pissed about what the libs were doing to children if the posts could be believed. And even though they were unbelievable due to the fact that they were total bullshit conjured up and originally disseminated by trolls in a dark office building in St. Petersburg, Russia, believe them she did.

"Damn, I cannot believe what the libs are doing. They should all be locked up! Hurting and indoctrinating children like that. Then they jacked up our gas prices to send money to that rebel group in Ukraine. We have to stop them!" Lolita was on a roll, nearly foaming at the mouth and rapidly muttering to herself.

She had opened a bottle of zinfandel and kept it on an end table next to her recliner so she could refill her glass without getting up. A steady stream of fictional horror stories flowed in a narrow river of sickly blue light from laptop to cornea, coursing straight into her amygdala. The middle-aged widow was ready to fight or flee as the adrenaline rush got her heart pumping 110 beats a minute while she was sitting stock-still.

That is why she released a blood-curdling scream when, from behind her chair, Marvin whispered, "Loliiiitaaa..."

She turned to face the apparition floating translucently in the semi-darkness. Light from her computer screen appeared to diffuse into tiny rapidly disappearing starburst-like points on the shimmering ghost. "Marvin, you came back! Oh God, I am so glad to see you, honey."

"Don't believe them." Marvin's ghost spoke louder and with greater force now.

"Who, honey? The libs?"

"Don't believe them. They are lying. They are lyyyyiiiing." The gossamer face twisted into something resembling a frown complete with furrowed brow and down-turned mouth.

"I won't Marvin. I won't ever believe them again. Those libs lie like rugs. Stay this time, Marvin. I need you here. You're the only one who ever really understood me."

That wasn't exactly true. In life, the teacher never understood his dangerously young wife. Marvin assumed she suffered from at least a few neuroses. He overlooked them and even concealed that suspicion as he truly loved her unconditionally. He also loved the benefits she brought along to their home. He returned to his treasured old A-frame with a warning for Lolita. It wasn't easy. In fact, it hurt a little when he materialized, as much as a ghost can hurt. He really wanted to move along in his journey. But he fretted about Lolita and still wanted to protect her.

"It is all a lie. You must listen. Listen, Lolita, Listen!"

"Ah Marv, you really love me, don't you?"

Eventually Marvin's ghost had to let go and return to the spirit world. The bookish and spindly shade was no stronger in death than he had been in life. Before leaving, he encouraged and calmed Lolita by saying, "I'll be back. Baaaack." He flickered out. His widow smiled with the knowledge he'd return and soon passed out in her recliner with the glowing laptop still resting on her legs.

14

DIXIE FESSES UP

It was a couple of days later that, standing in the kitchen, Dixie fessed up to Mason over their morning coffee that she had acquired a new sidearm. Despite their names, Dixie's political views varied from moderate to slightly liberal, except for the second amendment. On that, she was a staunch conservative, maybe even a little extreme as demonstrated by her scoff-law shenanigans at Bob's.

Mason was the traditional conservative of the duo. He didn't buy into any of the conspiracy stuff, reasoning it was political propaganda. In spite of that, he voted along party lines, figuring smaller government was better when it came to business. Before getting into stone carving, Mason dreamed of being a rodeo rider. He'd even gotten some lessons and was strongly influenced by that crowd when he was in his teens. He held cowboy values, although as an HVAC repairman, he was all hat and no cattle.

"Damn it, Dixie! What were you thinking? Even Sgt. Sunshine is going to bust your ass and throw away the keys if he finds out."

Mason wasn't old enough to have seen the original Sgt.

Sunshine. He was a fan of the little-known Swedish rock group of that name though, and when googling them up one day, he came upon an article on Sgt. Richard "Sunshine" Bergess. Bergess was a San Francisco cop who participated in a marijuana law protest in the sixties by publicly lighting up a joint during the event. The hippies lovingly nicknamed him, "Sgt. Sunshine," and that's how he made the papers. Some of the older residents of Big Squirrel remembered Bergess fondly, so they occasionally used the nickname for Deputy Mace, whom they also dug. Mason used the term in a slightly derogatory way when referring to the Deputy.

While he appreciated that Mace had let Dixie off with a warning after her unofficial night in the jail, he mocked him for his live-and-let-live policy with the old tie-dye and boho macrame-wearing folks in the county. Mason was a little conflicted as his Libertarian side told him that was the way to go for a public official while his law-and-order traditionalism argued for the opposition. With all that, he liked Deputy Mace and did not want to end up on his bad side. He sure didn't want Dixie to get into real trouble.

"It's cool Mason. I'm just going to carry it in my purse in case I'm attacked. I think the worst that would happen to me is a fine anyhow. I'm willing to take that risk, especially with crazies like Postal Patti and Lolita out there."

"You have got to get over your problem with Patti, Dixie. And little Lolita is harmless as a butterfly. That one has been through a lot. You should show her some mercy. You proved at The Anvil Tavern that you aren't as good with those things as you think you are."

"Anyone can have an accident, Mason." Dixie stood in a posed position and swept an arm down one side of her body. "You wouldn't want anyone raping this, now would you, ya' sweet mug?" She had learned that term during a followup call from Tiffany, who was checking with her about potential office locations around Groverton. The therapist had used it to describe her husband Chad when she said, "That meshuga mug is chomping at the bit to move. He's even got me a little into it." The receptionist had filed that new-to-her term in one of her mental folders marked, "For later use."

Dixie flashed her 150,000-lumen smile and followed it with a wink while turning slightly to show off what might be raped should she not be properly armed. She was a manipulator extraordinaire, but Mason had been down this road enough times to have developed an effective, albeit weak, resistance.

"You'll end up doing hard time in the slammer, dollface." TCM movie buff Mason turned Dixie's newly learned film noir slang back on her in a verbal jujutsu move, but it was to no avail. The Glock was staying. With that settled, the couple went off to their respective jobs.

15

TIFFANY AND CHAD HOLD A MEETING

C had was testing his mini projector on a wall mounted screen when Tiffany walked into his home office. Sometimes when a longtime client wanted to meet in person, Chad would have them see him there instead of the shared rental space he'd use for those less familiar to him.

He sat at the circular conference table that held his projector. He was accessing his excruciatingly boring PowerPoint presentation from the cloud with his phone and clicking through his real estate market research graphs on the screen. She absolutely hated it when he put her through this crap, but she covered her disdain with a furtive smile. She had been holding some good news for her husband that she planned to share before this torture session went very far.

"Welcome, Tiffany," went Chad's cold opening.

"I live here, Chad." Tiffany's flippant response was still covered with a smile, so Chad took it in stride and forged ahead.

"So, I've done some research and made some discoveries I'd like to share with you tonight."

Tiffany thought, *Ugh. How does he make a living like this? Sounds like I'm in for a dose of mansplaining.* But she listened attentively.

"First, this is approximately what our house would sell for in today's market. The bottom line shows what our net proceeds would be after selling costs. Not bad, eh?"

"Not bad at all." She was warming up despite her cynical self.

"Next, here are prices for some comparable and even larger properties around Big Squirrel and Groverton. Groverton is the bigger town a few miles from Big Squirrel. As you can see, we can actually pay cash for a very nice house up there. Cool, yes?" Chad advanced to the next slide.

"Here is what is left of our Rancho Niebla Tóxica net equity after paying for the new house and moving expenses."

"I have to admit that is more than I would have guessed, Chad." Tiffany couldn't hold back any longer. "I've done some research too!" Tiffany gushed, genuinely excited. Chad braced for what he was sure was going to be yet another merciless take-down. It wasn't that at all.

"I can easily open my own clinic with that much. It isn't just home real estate. Office leases are a lot lower in Groverton as well! I can rent furniture for the place. You always said leasing was better than buying in business. I've been thinking about it, and I made a couple of calls up there. I want to go up to look around and make sure it isn't as dull as I recall, but Chad, I think this might be a good move for us."

The CPA was jonesing to show his next slide, but for once Chad didn't get in his own way. Happy shock descended on him. He walked over, picked Tiffany up, and kissed her in an urgent but loving way that he hadn't in years. "Tomorrow is Saturday. You don't have to work. How about we drive up in the morning?"

Together they cracked open a bottle of champagne that had

gathered dust in the fridge and looked up the names of some real estate offices around Big Squirrel and decided to call one named "Palatial Real Estate." The nearly giddy couple wolfed down a quick light dinner and headed up to bed, where the revelry continued.

16

EVERYONE MEETS AT MOTHER'S, OR SO THEY SAY

aisie was standing beside a booth up front, listening to a customer delivering what sounded like an animated litany of opinions about current events, when Tiffany and Chad walked in. She waved them on to sit anywhere they liked. Tiffany noticed the customer wore an unusually large amount of make-up and was speaking endlessly without taking a breath. Maisie smiled, nodded, and gave Tiffany a wink as they went by. The couple found a booth across from the end of the counter where a couple of the local oldster hippie dudes were chatting while blissfully wolfing down stacks of vegan, gluten-free pancakes dripping in warm, pure maple syrup from Vermont. Maisie knew her customers and always kept their preferred ingredients in stock. Either one of the living fossils would have been a shoo-in for the part of Grandpa Walton were auditions held today.

The door crashed open when real estate agent Penelope Fumagalli blasted in with her enormous orange Kate Spade purse. Fumagalli was imposing at six feet tall and used that to her advantage when negotiating or closing a sale. The purse contrasted with the ice blue pantsuit she wore over a pair of sensible shoes, best for showing homes. If any driver ran over her in the street, they couldn't say they hadn't seen her. Fumagalli could be recognized from space.

She immediately spotted her prey, uh, clients, and quickly walked over to their booth. Extending a hand, she said, "You must be the Joneses, yes? I'll bet everyone's trying to keep up with you, heh, heh!"

Chad ground his teeth as Tiffany smiled with a polite laugh and raised her hand to shake with Fumagalli. That joke would have fallen flat even if their name was Jones, which it was not. In fact, his surname was Burr, like the dude that killed Alexander Hamilton, and Tiffany's was Van Pelt, as in—Van Pelt. This was the kind of agent he would have expected to meet back in Rancho Niebla Tóxica, not up in idyllic Big Squirrel.

Sitting across from the couple as she swung the formidable purse over to its resting place next to her, Fumagalli went on. "Just kidding, folks. I'm Penelope Fumagalli, but everyone calls me Penney." Chad found it a little hard to believe she would be called by a diminutive name.

"It's nice to meet you, Penney. As you've already guessed, I'm Tiffany Van Pelt, and this is my husband, Chad Burr, not Jones."

"Delighted. How do you like our little not-so-best-kept-secret town so far, folks? I sense you've been here a few times, Chad."

"Well, yes Penney, I come up here a lot, mostly because I enjoy driving through the woods, and I love this café."

"You've made a great choice. The breakfast here is the best. The woods are beautiful, aren't they? I'm originally from New Jersey and..." *That explains a lot,* thought Chad. "...I fell in love with this town the first time I saw it. It's so much more charming than L.A., isn't it?"

"I think so, but I haven't spent as much time around here as Chad has." Tiffany was still smiling, not put off by Fumagalli's brusque demeanor at all. In fact, she was kind of enjoying her, figuring it was all the agent's schtick, which was true.

"Well, you are going to see a lot of it today, Mrs. Burr." Tiffany had never changed her name. But it didn't bother her today. She was on a fact-finding mission and highly focused. "I have lined up a nice group of homes that match the criteria you gave me on the phone." The couple had called her just that morning while driving up in Chad's trusty Citroen. Fumagalli worked fast.

Little Mother was finally able to escape from the clutches of her customer in the booth up front. She put in Lolita's order for chorizo and eggs and grabbed cups, utensils, and a scalding hot pot of coffee for Chad's table. Lolita was nursing another blinding hangover and this dish was her go-to remedy. She'd further turn up the heat by slathering her eggs with Sriracha and washing it all down with a glass of Clamato, a disgusting but effective combination. She had bent Maisie's ear with news of the latest online misinformation drops that provoked her ire. Maisie was grateful for the excuse to serve some customers who had just arrived.

"Well, hello Chad and Penney. Who've you brought with you today?"

"Hi Little Mother. This is my wife, Tiffany. I've been telling her about your wonderful café for years."

"This is a pleasure then, Tiffany. Welcome to Mother's. Make yourself at home. I can already see you're smarter than old Chad and can read, so here's a couple of menus. I'll come back when you're all ready to order."

Chad chuckled as the side-armed insult glanced off his oversized yet occasionally sensitive ego. This was the Big Squirrel he wanted to call home. Little Mother made sure everyone had a hot cup of coffee. She never asked, just poured at will. A steel carafe of creamer and a glass jar of sugar were in a small rack by the wall, along with the requisite blue, pink, and yellow packets.

"So, where are you two from?" Fumagalli wanted to get the couple talking and answering questions. She'd make sure her line of interrogation always led to a string of "yes" answers before the end of the tour. That was her awkward but semi-stealthy approach to the ABC method, "Always Be Closing."

"I'm originally from Pasadena, and Tiffany is from Hermosa Beach, but we live in Rancho Niebla Tóxica now."

"Oh, that is a very nice community. An awful lot of traffic down there though, isn't there? What do you do in Rancho?" The agent had asked a couple of qualifying questions on the phone. Now she moved to specifics. She didn't like wasting time on looky-loos who couldn't afford anything in her MLS.

Tiffany chimed in, "I'm a physical therapist, and Chad is a CPA and financial advisor."

The agent made a mental note and started to feel good about these clients. "How interesting! The medical profession is very lucrative these days, I hear. And you have a built-in accountant to keep the books. That's wonderful! Do you plan to commute from here?"

"No. Chad works remotely and can visit his clients in person at a Rancho office when needed. I plan to open up my own clinic."

Not so good, thought Penney. "But surely, he has a substantial income." Her ex had supported her when she was studying for her license and getting started in real estate, at least until she became successful enough to divorce him and live the life she'd dreamed of when she left the east coast, so she was used to the idea. "How long have you been an advisor, Chad?"

"Sixteen years."

"You must have a nice list of clients built up."

"I keep 137 regulars and usually have 20 or so virtual drop-in clients."

"Spoken like an accountant. I love that level of precision." Fumagalli was smelling blood. "You shared your budget with me on the phone, and I can start by running you by a couple nearby that come in real, real close, but I think Little Mother would like us to order now, and I'm starving!"

Chad was grinding his teeth again, but Tiffany was all smiles as she perused her menu. Knowing what he wanted, he looked up to see the woman with the make-up in the front booth glaring at them while apparently talking to herself and looking to the side at an imaginary friend from time to time. Chad didn't recognize her from her tirade and removal at the concert. He looked away, shook his head, and thought, "I guess you've got to expect to find a few nuts in a town called Big Squirrel." He was still stoked to be moving. Like anything good, it just took a little effort and adjustment.

Just then, Little Mother showed up tableside, order pad and pencil in hand.

Lolita carried on her conversation up in the front booth, from which she faced into the café. "Marvin, I'm glad you're here darling. Did you see those people who came in with Penney? They look like libs. Probably pedophiles. There are more showing up every day and they all have the look. They give me the creeps." The widow looked down at the eggs and chorizo Maisie had deftly and rapidly dropped off with a quick splash of warm-up coffee into her cup. Lolita covered them in cheap hot sauce, and retrieved a large, dripping forkful. Marvin spoke as she shoved the generous portion of still steaming mixture into her open, red-lined mouth.

"You must remain calm, Lolita. Don't let them catch you speaking to me. They will become suspicious." Marvin had been gaining strength and visiting more often in the last few days. The ghost acted very protectively toward Lolita, though there seemed to be little he could do to actually help. He served mostly as a sounding board and a little less so as an advisor.

That isn't to say she didn't trust him and take heed of his warnings, even though she often misinterpreted them.

She nodded in agreement and looked down the line of booths. She noticed one of the strangers staring at her and glared back at him. He looked away as the white uniformed owner-waitress walked up to their booth.

Lolita finished her meal, laid down a couple of bills, and left unnoticed by the busy trio in the back, the hangover already dissipating. The shade called Marvin alternatively ambled and floated along behind her.

Mason and Dixie moved in sideways as Fumagalli and clients went out to her black Mercedes SUV, ready to see some houses. Dixie and Tiffany didn't recognize one another as they had only spoken on the phone, but Tiffany planned to call her at home before leaving Big Squirrel that day.

After the home tour, Tiffany asked Penney if there was a bar in town where she could meet a friend. Penney suggested The Anvil Tavern as it was the only game in town. Had she mentioned it was Dixie she planned to see, Penney would have told her that her new local bestie had been temporarily banned from The Anvil. It was partially for shooting up the place, but mostly about the way she'd talked to the deputy leading up to her arrest. Slim Jim really liked Deputy Mace, and he relied on him to keep the rowdies peaceful, especially late at night. The ban wasn't permanent. Slim just wanted to send a message that he didn't put up with shenanigans like that.

They dropped into one of the middle booths. It was their regular table. Mason wanted two of Little Mother's giant cinnamon rolls, served hot and drenched in melted butter. She heated them up on the flat top commercial griddle which caused the sugar to crystalize and brown up and the butter to get very hot as it dripped into the concentric ridges in the roll. Delicious and filling. Only Mason could eat two of them at a sitting. Dixie wanted the Denver, of course.

"Hey, you two. Good to see ya' here. Now, Dixie, you're not planning to blow a hole in my floor, are you?" Little Mother was chuckling, as was Dixie.

"I suggest you do a good job on my Denver omelet, Little Mother. You never know what might happen. Is the rumor true you and Little Bob had an affair and he used to call you "Mamacita" in bed?" Dixie could take it and dish it out too. The slow-eating hippies still at the counter looked up from their plates, overhearing that one.

"Nah. Me and Bob just both have "Little" in our nicknames. I like my lovers a bit bigger, if you know what I mean." Maisie enjoyed the banter and grinned from ear to ear. Dixie was a close friend, in addition to being a regular at the café. They had gone out after work and knocked back a few together a number of times over the years. Local gossip, blue jokes, and laughter always followed.

Mason shook his head and eagerly placed his order. His mouth was already watering just thinking of those rolls.

"Hey Dixie, I've been meaning to tell you about this weird thing that happened when I went fishing the other day."

17

LOLITA AND MARVIN'S GHOST STOP TO PEE

L olita had washed her eggs down with copious amounts of hot coffee. Each cup was followed by a large glass of water. She didn't notice that Marvin's ghost grew a little clearer with each swallow. She just liked to flush the toxins from her kidneys by hydrating.

As the odd couple sauntered down Mulberry Street, anyone who could see Marvin from the back might say he walked like Charlie Chaplin's Little Tramp character. Of course, nobody could see him save Lolita. Reaching the fire station, Lolita needed to take a leak. She walked through the large gaping door and looked down the side of the fire engine to find a couple of the firefighters going over a map in the back. "Hey guys, mind if I borrow the john?"

"Go ahead, Lolita. You know the way. And you do know I'm not a guy, right?" Tenaya wasn't really angry. She was just teasing Lolita.

This was her favorite place to pee, other than home. It was open 24/7, and always clean. Marvin floated up and into the driver's seat.

"I always wanted to drive one of these when I was alive."

"That would wake 'em up around here, honey."

Tenaya wondered what Lolita meant by that but let it go. The widow headed up the ramp to the restroom. She came out a couple of minutes later shaking her well-scrubbed hands and said, "Thanks again, girls and boys!" as she sauntered back out the way she came. Marvin reluctantly drifted out of the fire engine and met her on the street.

"I like that place. I should have been a fireman."

"Oh Marvin, no. You were a wonderful teacher. Even I managed to learn things from you."

"I'm not sure I should teach you anymore, Lolita. I've felt confused since death. It really messes with your mind."

"I'll bet, sweetie. That's a lot to go through. Being left behind does a number on a girl too. I have to deal with those evil lib forces all alone. I'm so glad you're here now."

"Me too, dear. Shall we continue our walk?"

18

CHAD AND TIFFANY MAKE A MOVE

The couple sold the house in Rancho and put some things in storage. The rest was sold or given to charity. They moved into a long-term hotel used mainly by companies for their transferred employees.

Fumagalli ran the deal through at blinding speed once they made their offer on a property in Big Squirrel. She had seen things fall apart before and learned that time was of the essence. But Chad and Tiffany were ready to go.

Tiffany would soon begin working on finding a suitable location for her business. But feathering the new nest was her top priority. They had selected a move-in ready four bed, two and a half bath contemporary cabin on the edge of Big Squirrel near the road to Groverton. It was more than they needed, but Chad saw it as a good investment. He also liked being able to convert a large downstairs bedroom into his home office. The Citroen and Tiffany's BMW SUV had room to spare in the three-car garage.

They had become Big Squirrel residents almost overnight. Dixie was very happy to join Tiffany on a couple of furniture shopping expeditions. Tiffany thought Dixie to be nutty and fun, while Dixie saw Tiffany as her most sophisticated friend.

Chad set up shop in the bedroom and got back to work. He took a little mental break after putting in a few hours on his client's finances. He searched for a Rotary Club in Groverton but found none of the large service clubs there at all. It still was a small town. There was a fly-fishing club. He thought that might be fun to try. Maybe he'd give them a call and ask if they knew of anyone giving lessons. There was also a hot rod club there. Chad wondered if his 32 horsepower Citroen 2CV would qualify. Probably not. He noticed a quilting club and wondered if Tiffany might have any interest in that. She'd probably be too busy setting up her clinic to enjoy any hobbies for a while.

Finally, he happened upon an article about a group of "Clampers" that were pictured participating in a Groverton parade. They looked funny in red shirts and vests festooned with unusual looking medals. Several wore sashes. One of them appeared to be driving a motorized clawfoot bathtub while wearing an admiral's hat. Checking further, Chad found a lengthy description and history of "The Ancient and Honorable Order of E Clampus Vitus," of which Groverton had a chapter.

Chad was literally laughing out loud as he read. The more he discovered, the more he liked the sound of the satirical drinking club that graced its equally ranked members with lofty sounding titles like "Noble Grand Humbug." The organization was apparently created to come to the aid of widows and orphans. E Clampus Vitus seemed to have as members the kind of guys Chad had always wanted to know, but rarely met, save for a goofy roommate he'd shared an apartment with back in college. He'd bet Little Mother would know a Clamper or two if anyone did. He planned to ask her about it the next time he went for breakfast. The trance caused by his online revelry was broken by the sound of the front door opening and laughter pouring inside. Chad left the office to investigate.

Tiffany and her new bestie fell in and dropped a pile of pillows they'd picked up at a home décor shop in Groverton. Chad hated the nightly ritual of plowing through an enormous barrier of pillows just to crawl into bed already. He was afraid he would now need to summit a mountain of the damned things when turning in.

"Well, hello, ladies. Where are all of those headed?"

"Chad, you remember me talking about my new friend, Dixie? Dixie, this is Chad, my hubcap. Chad, Dixie."

"Hey Chad, great to meet you. I've heard a lot from Tiffany, but she left out how cute you are. And a money guy too. Quite a catch, I see."

Caught way off guard and a little flummoxed, Chad forgot about his disdain for the pillows. He extended a hand, offered up a clumsy smile and babbled, "Glad to meet you too, Dixie. Welcome to our house, uh, home. Come on in."

Dixie turned to Tiffany as she shook hands, smiled and winked, and sauntered in past Chad. "This place is beautiful. Where's the girl's room, Tif? I've had to go since we left the Paper Moon Décor Store."

"Just around the corner and on the right, Dixie." Tiffany pointed. She smiled and looked very happy. "Isn't she fun, Chad?"

He helped pick up pillows to carry to the living room. "She sure seems like it. Should I open some wine?"

"That would be great. See if we have any of those shumai left too."

Tiffany led Dixie on a tour of the house as Chad prepped in the kitchen. He poured glasses of chardonnay and laid out three plates with chopsticks and forks, just in case. He then popped the dim sum in their bamboo steamer.

The women sat around the kitchen island as Chad plated

dumplings. Dixie poured a generous helping of soy sauce over hers. "I love these things!" She proved adept with the chopsticks as the conversation ensued. Tiffany asked her to tell them everything they needed to know about life in Big Squirrel. Dixie had finished up on most of the local gossip, including some concerning the widow Lolita who could be seen around town chatting it up with her imaginary friend/deceased husband. Chad figured from the description she must have been the women in the café when they met Fumagalli. Next came her dissertation on their lawman.

"And then there's Deputy Mace, or as I think of him, what you'd get if you crossed Sherriff Andy with Barney Fife. He's a good guy, but he seems like someone who is more comfortable rescuing kittens from storm drains than he would be interrogating a suspect. You've got to be worried about crime these days. It's everywhere, even here in Big Squirrel. That's why I always carry one of these..." Dixie reached into her purse on the flower and pulled out the Glock. "I mean, a girl can't be too careful. You should get one, Tif."

A shocked Chad stepped back from the island. "Whoa there!"

"Jesus, Dixie!" Tiffany laughed. "Put that thing away. I don't want you accidentally shooting Chad. I need him to pay bills until I get the clinic going!"

Dixie complied. "Sure, sure, it's gone." She carefully placed the pistol back in her purse. The Anvil incident taught her to respect safety. "But really kids, you've got to worry about the crime. I do, all the time lately."

Remembering his research prior to moving, Chad noted, "I don't know why you would. Statistically, it's like this area doesn't have any crime at all. That's one of the benefits that caused us to move up here. The overall rate is close to the lowest in the state."

"Yeah, but California, am I right? We used to leave our

doors unlocked at night. Not anymore. Not with what you see on TV. I've worried more and more the last couple of years. Some folks say I'm paranoid, I say I'm prepared." Dixie was indeed a little paranoid recently. It stood out in contrast with her otherwise devil-may-care demeanor such that people other than Mason had begun to notice.

Tiffany was used to real crime rates, having grown up in a popular beach town. They had lots of burglaries, auto thefts, and occasional obnoxious drunks on the pier at night, but she never felt the need to arm herself. She shrugged and reasoned, perception is relative, and always based on whatever you're used to. That's why people who lived in small towns complained about their "traffic." Wanting to preserve the one friendship she'd established so far, she decided to diplomatically lighten things up. "I hear ya', Dixie and I'd get one too, but then how would I be able to pay for that cute coffee table we saw today?" Her radiant smile shined as she poured another glass for her friend.

Dixie laughed at that and said, "I didn't think we were going to tell Chad about that yet!"

Chad ignored the chatter and cleaned up while the ladies giggled and laid on the new pillows in the living room, glasses in hand. "Now, you are staying tonight, Dixie. None of us are good to drive."

"Alright sweetie, but I'd better call Mason. Let him know where I am.

Chad made and delivered a tray of sandwiches and a fresh bottle to the living room. "Oh my God, Tiffany, this guy is a keeper for sure!"

"Yeah. He'll do." Tiffany smiled at Chad as he beat a hasty exit.

Finishing in the kitchen and with a glass and sandwich in hand, Chad quietly snuck out to his beautiful new garage, his personal and beloved fief.

19

CRAZY COMES TO TOWN

At roughly the same time Chad was referring to crime statistics, something was happening down at The Anvil Tavern that would ever so slightly goose them up.

A heated argument had started between a couple of the regulars. Arguments had ensued there before; alcohol was the lead product at The Anvil after all. But something was different this time and the vibe it released raised the hairs on Slim Jim's highly tuned and sensitive intuition.

He looked up from the bar to see one of the woodchucks verbally getting into it with one of the old tie-dye guys. The woodchucks were a handful of remnants left from when Big Squirrel had a logging operation. All that was left of it was the rusty old wood scrap incinerator where the sawmill used to be and the woodchuck's resentment for losing good paying jobs. Unfortunately, one of them nicknamed, "Lefty," due to his missing right hand, lost in an industrial accident at the sawmill decades ago, overheard Stargazer, one of the leftover hippies, so called as he was heavy into astrology among other things cosmic, complaining to his friends about global warming being ignored by governments of the world.

Slim observed silently until he saw the pair turn their chairs and square off. The tavern keeper figured it was getting close to game time when Lefty accidentally knocked his beer over on the table. Turning to his bartender, Slim asked, "Hey Amber, could you call Mace? Tell him to get here quick."

"Will do, boss." Amber slipped to the end of the bar and pulled out her phone. Slim grabbed his blackjack from its home beside the ice bin. He'd never hired a bouncer figuring he didn't need one, and he'd never used the blackjack before except to practice once when he first opened The Anvil.

Things went to hell before Slim could move from behind the bar. The woodchuck turned, stood up, and yelled down at Stargazer, "You're gonna buy me a new beer, asshole!" When Stargazer stood up, he accidentally brushed against Lefty's formidable pot belly, a move Lefty in his stupor interpreted as an attack. He landed a roundhouse (with his left, of course) on the old hippie's right cheek that sent Stargazer reeling back over his chair and landing on the ground.

When one of the less pacifistic friends of the now writhing tie-dye clad guy saw that scene, he jumped up and headed toward Lefty. Lefty unleashed another punch with his one good hand, but this time the blackbelt hippie used the woodchuck's own momentum to swing him to the ground. At that point, friends and onlookers on both sides started a brawl such as had never before been seen in Big Squirrel.

Amber said, "Fuck this," and slipped out the back. Slim, now making his way into the melee, started swinging the black-jack and cracking a few heads until it whipped around somehow and delivered the owner himself a surprisingly powerful gut punch. He doubled over and coughed until his face turned red and his eyes bulged.

This was the unholy mess Deputy Mace observed when he

walked into The Anvil and that he put into his report later that night, but not before blasting his whistle and making several non-custodial arrests. One exception was Lefty, who Mace hauled into the Groverton jail after listening to Slim's description of the argument and fight. The lawman had a hell of a time figuring out how to securely cuff the monohander.

20

MASON HEARS ABOUT SOME THINGS

"**A**nyhow, doesn't it seem like there's been more weird-ass shit going down here than usual, Mason?" Tenaya had just finished filling him in on the events of the night before at The Anvil. Mason had been summoned to repair the air conditioner behind the fire station. He kept their old unit running despite having advised her that it was being held together only thanks to his ability to adapt current parts into working replicas of the obsolete ones of those that had failed, and she needed to replace it. It was rarely just a straightforward pull-and-replace job at the station.

Tenaya kept the fire engine running the same way. She loved to chat it up with the truck mechanic and Mason when they were making repairs. She got lonely having nobody to talk to but her crew during her long shifts. They were great and everyone was close, but she had to maintain a little professional distance.

Fire Captain Tenaya Murphy had been ambitious and smart, working extra hard to overcome the oppression her Miwok, African American, and Irish forebears and indeed, she herself, lived through. She started at the bottom and worked/studied her way to her current rank and job, leading the Big Squirrel Fire Department. The name was a holdover from the old days. The department was part of Desdemona County these days. Her team covered Groverton, which never had its own full-time fire department, and the unincorporated parts of the county as well. She was strong and tough as shoe leather and knew how to dish it out when she had to. Today she was loving being able to peacefully gossip with Mason. She didn't need to expend any energy supervising him. Mason knew what he was doing and just handled it, always to her satisfaction. He worked like she did, albeit alone rather than with a crew, and a number of area residents owed the salvation of their homes to both of them. Mutual respect was their watch-word. This moment was fun for her.

"Yep. I've noticed a thing or two myself."

Tenaya leaned back and laughed. "Yourself? I'll bet. Wasn't it your wife who blasted the deck at The Anvil? You two were substantial contributors to the weird shit I was talking about!"

"Yeah, guilty I guess, Cap'n." Mason was laughing with her. "I sure hope she wasn't down there again last night. She said she was staying over with that new couple on the edge of town. I took off early this morning when you called, so I didn't see her get back. I think she's made it through Slim's banishment period."

"Oh, I think you would have heard if she hadn't. Folks around here love delivering bad news. Her little slip with the Beretta was just an accident, from what I understand. But other people seem to be more agitated than usual, don't they? A dude out on Shakey Jake Road in the county got so pissed off watching the news on his old cathode-ray tube TV, he threw a beer bottle at it, and it burst into flames. We managed to save most of the place, but he had a lot of repairs and cleanup to do after that little tantrum. And that Looney-Tunes Lolita seems more lathered up than ever when she stops to be here to pee and babbles nonsense to herself when she leaves."

"Lolita's alright. She's a little wound up and talks to her dead husband, that's all. I think she sees him too. People see what they want to see."

Mason thought about how Dixie was a little edgier lately too. The idea of her sharing any traits with Lolita gave him the heebie-jeebies, and it was something he'd prefer others remained unaware of, so he kept that part to himself and finished up.

"Okay, that ought to do it. Let's head inside and give her a test, Tenaya. You know, you can get a rebate from Southern California Edison if you just break down and write a P.O. for a new unit. I can arrange government pricing for you too. It'll use less juice, saving the department money." He knew she'd heard it all before because he'd said it to her all before. The silver lining was, they'd be switching from air conditioning to heating pretty soon, so his repair would last at least through the next summer. She also hated the idea of dealing with the onerous county procurement process. The county board of supervisors would probably tell her that firefighters should be able to deal with a little heat anyhow.

Tenaya smiled and nodded without answering as they walked back into the station. She was confident the thing was good for another season now that Mason had fixed it. "Waste not, want not." Tenaya had listened to her mom growing up. She flipped the switch on the wall and heard the compressor outside the door kick on. A minute later, cool air flowed from the register above their heads. "Thanks, Mason. What do we owe you?"

21

DIXIE GETS NERVOUS

"Doggone it, Dixie. You're late again. We had patients waiting. I had to check them in myself." Doctor Jones was trying to act suitably peeved.

"Sorry boss, tough night." What she might have said was, "...fun night," but that wouldn't cut it as an excuse.

"What am I going to do with you, Dixie?"

Dixie smiled up at Doc and used her Shirley Temple voice as she batted her eyelashes exaggeratedly. "Tell me I've been a bad girl, but it's okay, and to never-ever do it again?"

"Hopeless." The doctor went back into his office as the next patient entered the waiting room.

"Well, good morning, Mrs. Call. Right on time. Nice to see you. How are you feeling today?"

"Hi Dixie. Not too bad. Same as ever, aches and pains. Don't ever get old."

Dixie always wondered why senior citizens used that expression. Didn't they understand that it literally amounted to "Die young?" Mrs. Call handed over her insurance and credit cards. She knew the drill.

"So, you're here for your physical, right? Have a seat and relax while I get your paperwork rolling. Doctor Jones will be ready shortly."

Mrs. Call picked up a Cosmopolitan magazine to read. She also grabbed a copy of Good Housekeeping, in which she wrapped her Cosmo to keep Dixie and any other patients from seeing what she was really reading. Dixie always found that little quirk amusing and smiled as she ran the cards and pulled Mrs. Call's record from the computer for the doctor.

The patient looked up after a minute. "So, Dixie, have you heard about the big fracas down at The Anvil Tavern last night?"

Dixie grew visibly nervous as she listened to the now fourth-hand tale recounted with a tad more embellishment by the older woman.

"Isn't that just awful? Oh no, Dixie, I've upset you, I see. I'm so sorry."

Dixie dropped her hands behind the desk and shook off her nerves. "No, no, I'm fine, Mrs. Call. Thanks for letting me know. The doctor will see you now." She led the patient in and handed Doc Jones her chart on a clipboard. They did things the old way in this office.

Dixie went back to her desk and shook her head angrily while thinking, *See, smarty-pants man? The crime rate's rising as we speak. That stuff on TV, it's happening in Big Squirrel now. Violent crime! You can't be too careful.* She was ruminating about her chat with Chad the night before and wondering why she felt so much anxiety. She knew she was perfectly safe in the office, and of course she was still "packin' a Roscoe" (gun in noir-speak), just in case. The news about crime troubled her, nevertheless. She pinched her upper lip gently and rhythmically, frowning at her computer screen as her eyes darted about. She felt the chill of a cold sweat on her back and her pulse was pounding. She jumped a little when the next patient walked in.

"Oh, oh, Mr. Walker," she said with a big smile. "Good morning. Right on time. Nice to see you. How are you feeling?" Her hands were shaking out of sight under her desk.

"Hey Dixie! Well, I'm here because my shoulder's been hurting like the Dickens. I tell ya' kiddo, don't ever get old!"

22

TIFFANY LOOKS FOR AN OFFICE

Tiffany was already bored with buying and arranging décor items. She met with Chad in his home office to see what they could afford to move into the capital fund for her new business. Together, they developed a budget, including an income projection that Tiffany had worked up. She had done her homework and backed up her first draft business plan with some solid market research. Chad was impressed, and he only suggested a couple of tweaks.

The first items on her to-do list were to find a location and come up with some names for the clinic that she could test out with an informal focus group. She checked online, but after a while reluctantly decided to call Penney Fumagalli. Penney answered after only one ring.

"Hi, this is Penney. How may I be of service today?"

"Hi Penney, this is Tiffany Van Pelt."

"Tiffany! So good to hear from you. How are you loving the house?"

"It's great, and we're almost all moved in."

Penney breathed an inaudible sigh of relief. Disappointed

clients had little recourse once a deal closed, but it was her experience that they could make life miserable for a while.

"Wonderful, and I'm not surprised to hear it. It's a fabulous property, and I got it for you for a song, as you know. So, what can I do for you two lovebirds, Tiffany?"

"Well, I was wondering if you also handled commercial leases. I'm looking for office space in Groverton."

"Yes. Of course, I can help. You're a chiropractor, right?"

"Physical therapist. I'm really hoping to find something in or near the medical office complexes there, like the one Doctor Jones' office is in."

"You've come to the right woman, Tiffany! If it's on the ground or *is* the ground, I handle it. When can we meet?"

Tiffany swallowed to tamp down her gag reflex from that last bit of self-promotion. "I'm available anytime, Penney. I want to get this moving along as soon as possible."

"Will Chad be joining us too?"

Another irritant. Why did even women assume you'd need to bring along your husband? "Nope. This is all my thing. He's busy enough with his own work."

"That sounds fine. Mind if I ask your budget and square footage needs?"

Tiffany shared her ranges with Penney.

"I see. Well, I'll be honest, it's going to be a little tight, but let's see what I can do."

Tiffany knew Penney wasn't being totally honest. Her research indicated her budget was more than adequate. But she also realized the statement was just part of the agent's tactic to manage expectations. She needed Fumagalli's help, so she played along.

Ultimately, she settled in the same building that housed Doc Jones' office, guaranteeing easy access for referrals from there. The other tenants included a dentist, a chiropractor, and a place called Cosmic Pilates, a combination Pilates/Yoga studio-gift shop that smelled of patchouli oil and sold crystals, incense, and small books. She figured the Pilates studio might feed her some injury business via Doc Jones given the aging clientele base that appeared to frequent the studio, as might the chiropractor.

There was room for Tiffany, a small waiting room, and even one more therapist should she ever want to expand. The office got afternoon sun through the windows, making it nice and cheery for patients hoping to recover some flexibility.

Dixie was thrilled to welcome her new neighbor. They decided a celebratory cocktail was called for and invited Little Mother to join them. Tiffany suggested The Anvil, and even though Slim Jim's brief suspension of Dixie had ended, she said, "Too much crime there now. There's a steak house called the Branding Iron with a nice bar right here in Groverton. How about you call Little Mother and the two of you can get the Ride-Share there? I'll meet you after work." She said "the" Ride-Share as there was only one driver in the whole county. Raymond "the Teetotaler" Maxwell. Ray T, as he was better known, had tired of getting nothing out of being everyone's go-to designated driver. He applied at the top two ride share companies, but both rejected him, for reasons that would remain publicly undisclosed. When Ride-Share, Inc. started up, he jumped on it. The less discerning and generically named company signed him at once. He loved to drive and chat. He also loved getting paid for it. The app didn't always work in the more remote parts of Desdemona County, but Ray T knew the area as well as any London cabbie knew Kensington.

23

THE HAPPY TRIO GETS BRANDED

Dixie walked into the steakhouse before the others arrived. Calvin Kenigstein, the owner, was tending bar. Calvin was originally from Brooklyn, but when he moved west and opened The Branding Iron, he gave himself the nickname, "Tex," and started wearing cowboy boots and shirts. He was never able to shake the New York accent though he kept trying to do a John Wayne impression. People saw right through his act. Tex was friendly, generous when slinging shots, and knew how to reverse-sear bone-in ribeyes over a mesquite fire to sizzling perfection, so local folks happily overlooked his giggle-inducing manner of speaking and made his place successful.

"Howdy, Dixie! It's been too long, little lady. How ya' been doin'?"

"Good Tex, good. I'm bringing you some business tonight. Little Mother and a new friend are meeting me soon."

"Get ya' a table out back?"

"We're going to start and maybe finish right here. My friend is opening up a clinic in Groverton right by our office, so we're celebrating."

"Wonderful. What can I start you with?"

Dixie ordered a beer and looked around the bar. From her table, she could see out into the dining area with the dance floor out in the middle. The place had a total country-western vibe. There were fake game trophies hanging on the knotty pine paneled wall in the bar that included a cross-eyed buffalo. Dollar bills stuck on darts hung from the ceiling. It was meant to appear that customers had thrown them, but in reality, Tex had placed them there from a ladder. Once one of those fell and impaled a customer's outstretched hand much as the opposing mob had once done to Luca Brasi's paw in a different bar. Fortunately, the wounded patron lived, didn't sue, and The Branding Iron treated him to free beer for a month, which he happily hoisted with his unharmed hand.

The bottoms of men's neckties were tacked on the wall that led from the hostess station into the bar and dining room. Tex had seen that done at the old Trail Dust Steakhouse in Mesquite, Texas, before that legendary place went under. Those had been cut from ties worn by Trail Dust patrons, but Tex was in a hurry, in addition to the fact that nobody wore neckties anymore in Desdemona County. He ordered a couple dozen to cut and hang on the wall himself. He wanted to emulate the Texas restaurant further and build a mezzanine with a slide down to his dance floor, but he couldn't quite handle the construction and increased insurance costs. He satisfied his desire to knock them off by naming his ribeyes "Cowboy Steaks," on the menu and covering his picnic tables with red & white checkered tablecloths, plastic of course.

The dining room was already filling up. As Dixie sipped her Shiner Bock waiting for the others, waitresses in straw cowboy hats flitted among the tables, carrying pitchers of beer and slabs of sizzling meat overflowing with onion rings.

Tiffany and Little Mother arrived shortly, and after being

greeted by Tex, took their places at the table. There were smiles all around.

"Hey Dixie, how's it hangin'?" Maisie loved this place and got right into the vibe.

"Good, Mother, really good. How are you two doing?"

Tex came up to take their order and Dixie asked, "Beers for you two? Should we get a pitcher?"

Tiffany happily answered in the affirmative. Little Mother had another idea. "Yeah, let's get the pitcher, but I want to start with a White Russian tonight."

Tex smiled. "Ah yes, the mother abides."

"Shut up, Donny!" Little Mother and Tex chuckled at their references. Dixie understood the joke, but Tiffany just shrugged and smiled as she decided to ignore it and move on.

Maisie turned to Tiffany. "Where did your husband get his weird little car?"

"It was a barn-find of sorts. Not from a barn, really, a pizza joint that had burned down and went out of business. They'd been using it for deliveries because it's so easy on gas. It's so slow, the guys who owned the pizza parlor figured the delivery kids wouldn't get in any trouble making the rounds."

"Don't the cooks make the rounds at pizza joints, Tif?" Dixie couldn't resist the opening.

Little mother chuckled, "Ha ha, very punny, Dixieness."

Tiffany continued, "So Chad brought it home, and when he took me out to the garage to show it to me, I almost barfed. It looked like a big metal insect covered in rust and dirt. But he labored for months at night, ordering parts and restoring it to whatever its former glory had been back in the day. I hated the thing for a long time, but now it's kind of grown on me, like Chad. Or a goiter."

Everyone laughed at that one.

Little Mother chimed in, "Actually, I think it's kind of cute. I could do without the smoke cloud when he backs it away from the café, though."

"Oh yeah, it belches and backfires sometimes too. Once when driving up here, black smoke started to come in through the heater vents and filled the car. We almost choked."

The drinks came and Little Mother ordered a "Dale Evans, still mooing," which translated to the 22-ounce Cowboy Steak served blood rare. A "Roy Rogers" was a 32-ouncer, while the monstrous 48-ounce "Andy Devine" was the king of the bunch. Dixie said, "Make it two, Tex, and bring some onion rings, baked beans, and slaw."

Tiffany peered at them over her menu. "Oh, it's to me? I'll just have a salad."

Everyone guffawed, and Dixie responded with, "Fuck you, Tif!"

Tiffany laughed, "Just kidding, ya'll. Rustle me up one of them thar Dale Evans too, Tex, and burn it!" She liked hers medium well. Little Mother was pleased with Tiffany's grasp of short-order lingo.

As Tex put in their order, the ladies settled in for an evening of gab, laughter, and meat sweats. Ray T took them all home after they turned down the peach cobbler dessert special and paid their tab. Tiffany arranged to take Dixie to work the next day, where she'd left her car. Dixie said that would be great, but to please drive her BMW, not Chad's little beast.

Meanwhile, back in Big Squirrel, Lolita was getting worked up while watching the news on TV. She had been fuming and swearing listening to a report by a popular pundit, Aiden Lognerenson who was saying Bashar Al-Assad, the president of Syria, was really a good guy and a victim of unfair character assassination by the libs. Some of her French onion soup dribbled down her chin as she mumbled in response. The room was dark other than the shifting and sickly blue beam that emanated from the TV to light the sofa.

Marvin's translucent presence was sitting next to her and patted her hand. Suddenly he started singing the chorus from "Let it Go" from "Frozen," the animated movie about sisters. He had no idea where he had heard and learned the tune. It just came to him in the moment.

"Oh Marvin. You're the one who keeps me sane through all of this."

24

GONE FISHING

Tiffany picked up Dixie for work the next morning. She had borrowed Chad's Citroen as a joke. Dixie leaned down to get in. "Great, are we going to make it to Groverton?"

"You bet! Jump in. It'll be just like Mr. Toad's Wild Ride at Disneyland."

"That's what I'm afraid of. Well, you only live once." Dixie squirmed uncomfortably in the unusually thin and hard passenger seat. "What did your husband use to restore this thing, parts from a stagecoach?"

Tiffany turned on to the road and made for Groverton.

"So, Dixie, I was thinking about Mason."

"Why on earth would anyone think about Mason?" Dixie laughed.

"Didn't you say he likes to fish?"

"Yep, he sure does. Especially when I'm winning an argument and he wants to get away."

"I'm asking as Chad expressed an interest in learning fly-fishing. Is that what Mason does? Chad could use a good buddy up here, like the one I've found."

"Aww, that's sweet. I feel the same way. Mason does use a fly. But he's just as happy with a spinning reel too if he catches fish. He likes anything that works. Then he tosses most of them back in the creek. Seems like a huge waste of time, if you ask me."

"Cool, cool. I used to use a baitcaster from the pier when I was growing up. I did alright with it, but I sort of left the hobby behind when we moved out to Rancho. Do you think Mason would mind teaching Chad the ropes?"

"You kidding? That mug is always looking for someone to fish with. I'll talk to him tonight."

"Oh, that's swell. You're a pal!" Tiffany was trying to adopt a little noir slang to blend with Dixie's, but she was still falling a little short of the mark.

"You're not so bad yourself, for a beach dame! You heading to your new office today?"

"I'm stopping there to do some more measuring, but then I'm going down to San Berdo to an office furniture store."

"Better go home and get your BMW. You aren't going to haul much in this frog flivver, sister!"

Dixie was true to her word and brought up Chad's fly-fishing desire with Mason. He rang up Chad that night.

"Hello, is this Chad? This is Mason, Dixie's husband. Yeah, hi. Dixie tells me you want to learn to fly fish."

"Yeah, I sure do. You know anyone who gives lessons around here?"

"Nope, but I'd be happy to take you if you'd like. Are you available Saturday morning?"

Chad had to set his alarm for the first Saturday in years. Mason wanted to pick him up at 6:00 a.m. to reach Santa Quiteria River while the fish were biting. Mason decided to start there as Chad might have a tough time casting into and through the heavy cover in Murrieta Creek. It would have been ideal if there had been a lake or sizable pond around, but you had to fish the cards you were dealt. They would be just below the confluence of the creek and river, so if Chad proved to be a quick study, they could choose to move upstream into the tributary.

Tiffany was already awake and smiled when the alarm went off. She was glad Chad was going fishing with Mason. She loved Dixie and was happy with her husband too when she spoke to Mason. She was absolutely stoked with the prospect of having a couple friendship in their new town.

Chad quickly went downstairs for coffee. He would be taking plenty more with him in his Yeti thermos. He had picked up a new fly set and waders. He was also bringing his spinning rod and reel. While not having a clue about what he was doing, he felt confident that he was as prepared as possible.

He answered the door and greeted Mason, who was precisely on time thanks to Air Force training.

"Chad! I'm Mason Cadwallader." Chad thought, *Even his name sounds like a fish.* The guys shook hands. "Ready to surprise some fish?"

"You bet! And it's real nice to meet you, Mason. Thanks for picking me up." Chad grabbed his coffee and fishing gear.

They jumped in Mason's truck and took off. "Have you done much fishing?"

"I've done a little," Chad said. "I'm not much good at it. There aren't too many places to go around Pasadena or Rancho Niebla Tóxica, where I'm from. I've never fly fished before, so maybe that will change my luck."

"Probably will, but it does take a while to get the hang of it. Once you do, you'll love it."

They reached the river a few minutes later. Mason showed Chad how to look around to see what the fish were feeding on and select a fly to match, then taught him to tie an improved cinch knot. They donned their waders and walked a short way into the river. The next lesson was casting.

Chad's first cast got caught short on the back of his cap

where the hook stuck. "Oh shit. I already screwed up here, Mason."

Mason got a pretty good laugh out of that and said he did something like that on his first few casts too.

The next one plopped into the water only a few feet from where he was standing. Mason told him to aim slightly upstream on the next one, which floated across the river and started to drift down. Mason demonstrated rolling the line over to keep it from dragging the fly. Finally, they watched Chad's line drift and stop a few yards to their left. Following further instructions, Chad succeeded in pulling the line up by moving his rod parallel with the shore and casting from the high point. The experienced fisherman explained that was a cool trick if there was a lot of foliage behind him. It was solid preparation for a potential slog up Murrieta Creek one day.

They relaxed for a while as Mason just let Chad practice casting, only stopping to fill up coffee cups.

"I can tell you're going to do alright at this, Chad."

"How?"

"You're watching the fly on the river, not just looking around. Some guys miss a hit because they're not being mindful. That won't be you."

Chad smiled. He hadn't thought he'd be alright at this when they were driving to the river. But Mason had built his confidence. He was ready to learn more, but Mason said to just keep practicing for now. That was fine, and he settled in. It was a brisk but beautiful morning.

During the next coffee break, Chad pointed to the little tributary he'd spotted upstream from where they were. "What's that creek coming into the river there?"

"That's Murrieta Creek. There are often some trout to be found there. We'll give it a go later this morning, or maybe next time." Chad was glad to hear there'd be a next time. Mason then recounted how the creek got its name.

"Back in 1853, the California Rangers killed a couple of bad guys, Joaquin Murrieta and his accomplice, Three Fingered Jack, in a gunfight. There was a reward for them, but they had to prove they'd got them. So, they cut off Murrieta's head and Jack's hand, then preserved both in a vat of whisky and took it down to Stockton to collect the money.

That all happened way north of here, but some of the Clampers that found it thought it would be funny to name the creek after them, so they called it "Joaquin Murrieta & Three Fingered Jack Memorial Creek". Then, just a couple of years ago, some of the newbies told Mayor Nader they thought that was insensitive, so he changed it to just "Murrieta Creek," and that was the deal. Some of the older maps still show the original name. It does take a lot of space, I guess."

Chad thought that was a great story, and it made him like the area even more. "I like the old name. They should have left it alone."

Mason thought Chad might be OK. "Yep, same here. You got an extra sandwich in that sack, brother?"

They chowed down quickly, then moved upstream to fish a bit more.

On his fourth cast, Chad saw something large jump up to his fly and hit it with force. When the thing dropped back in the water, it jerked the line so suddenly Chad lost his grip. Rod and reel dropped into the water and got dragged a foot or two. Chad quickly leaned down to grab the rod as it moved away and, forgetting how Mason had instructed him to pull any catch in sideways, yanked the rod overhead. The tippet broke off the fly line and was lost to the fish as it swam rapidly downstream. From nowhere, an even larger fish snapped its teeth around the tail of the first one and whipped it to the right. Blood spread across the water and flowed with the current. There was splashing, and then everything just disappeared except the disembodied tail that bobbed and floated downstream.

"Whoa, what the hell was that?" Chad was marching back to shore, where Mason had been watching.

"That's some crazy stuff, man." Mason explained how he'd had something similar happen not long ago up Murrieta Creek. "The one that got mine wasn't as big, but he was also chased by his cousins. Those fish must be starving or something to act like that."

25

THINGS HEAT UP IN TOWN

Ray T was driving to the edge of Big Squirrel to pick up a fare. The early evening was hazy from the multiple wood fires folks had stocked on their hearths. It was Autumn, and the temperatures bounced up and down frequently. Today was a bit more on the chilly side. As he rounded the last corner, he swerved suddenly to avoid crashing into two guys he saw at the last second who were having a fist-fight in the middle of the road. His old black SUV was top heavy and swayed over a bit to the right. The vehicle smashed into an oak tree, climbing part way up the trunk, where the airbag discharged from the steering wheel.

A delirious Ray T managed to push open his door and unbuckle his seat belt. He dropped heavily onto a small boulder, breaking his left leg. The boxers forgot their argument and came over to help. One of them called 911.

A very old ambulance was dispatched from the fire department. When the department had received some grant money for the purchase of a new one, Tenaya had figured it would go further and buy more gear if they refurbished a used one instead of buying something brand new. The captain could pinch a penny until Lincoln screamed. She arrived with some of her crew on the fire engine to ensure any leaking fuel or oil was handled safely. Deputy Mace showed up to investigate the accident and take statements from the boxers.

The paramedics retrieved Ray and hauled him over to Doc Jones, lights and sirens going. Doc Jones felt and moved Ray's leg in the office until Ray saw stars and yelped in pain. Doc asked if he had anyone who could give him a ride to San Bernardino to get an X-ray to verify his suspicion that the leg was broken. "I *am* the ride around here, Doc!" Doc asked Dixie, who was assisting him, if she might be able to give him a lift. She said sure, it would be fun to get out of the office for a while. Doc shook his head at that too-honest response, then applied a temporary splint to the leg. Dixie grabbed a cane from the closet and gave Ray that, three aspirin, and a cup of water. She unfolded a wheelchair, helped him out to her car, and together they left for the hospital.

That event marked the end of Ride-Share service in Desdemona County for the foreseeable future, much to the dismay of both Slim Jim and Tex, who counted on Ray T to shepherd some of their more buzzed patrons home.

Late the next afternoon, Mace got a call from a very stoned Stargazer. "Hi Sergeant Sunshine, this is Stargazer. I'm out at the farm." Stargazer lived with a couple of old female hippies, Ethel and Poppy, on a small farm. They were all that was left of a much more highly populated commune that existed there back in the early seventies. "We've been vandalized."

"I'm sorry to hear that, Stargazer. What was damaged?"

"Could you come over? I'll show you."

"Sure. I'll be there in twenty minutes."

"Thanks, man!"

He arrived to find the three farmers out front by the road holding hands in a circle and chanting to attract positive vibes and drive out the evil spirits that had obviously caused the damage. They wore feathered headbands and flowered leis.

Here we go. Mace remembered to take three deep cleansing breaths as he drove in and parked.

Stargazer broke off and walked over to meet Mace.

"Hey, thanks for coming over so soon."

"Happy to be of service, Stargazer. Would you like to show me what happened?"

Stargazer guided him over to the barn. The old man pointed up to the roof. "Someone killed my weathervane."

The deputy looked up to see a black cast iron structure dangling from a long pole that protruded from the center of the roof, swinging slightly with the gentle breeze. It appeared to be constructed of some odd shapes that seemed vaguely familiar. The typical arrow was still on one end, but the tail feather was gone.

"That was my zodiac-vane, sergeant. The Blue Meanies blew it apart."

"Who are the Blue Meanies?"

"I don't know. I just use that name to describe very negative, hostile people. The kind that would do a mean trick like this."

The original Blue Meanies were the nasty antagonists in the Beatles animated film, *Yellow Submarine.* Young Deputy Mace had never heard of them, as the movie was released in 1968.

Mace looked down and noticed the Sagittarian arrow had pierced the hole in the bottom of the Taurus symbol and stuck in the dirt when they had both plunged to earth. One of the horns had a crescent-shaped hole in the end, possibly an entry wound from a bullet. Mace reached into his pocket and planted a yellow flag in the ground next to it.

The men went inside to grab Stargazer's ladder. Mace purposefully ignored the possibly illegal mushrooms that he noticed growing in a dark, dank corner. The old barn was very tall. Beams of sunlight flowed in through knotholes and spaces between the boards. Straw covered the ground, but there were no animals. The barn smelled of the straw, dry rot, and pot. Another corner held a blacksmith shop.

The forge was covered by a corrugated tin roof with a heavy round metal chimney that ran partway up a wall where it exited to continue to a point well above the roof. Bellows and several tools hung from a cross member above a very beaten anvil. The deputy thought of Wile E Coyote, and wondered if the brand name, "ACME" might be stamped on the side.

There was a second-floor loft, and a wooden extension ladder with rope and hooks was leaning on the edge of it. They took the ladder outside and extended it up just past the eaves. The deputy climbed up and walked gingerly across the roof to have a closer look at the ruined zodiac-vane. Sure enough, he spotted more holes, one in a flange that held the base of the vane. As the flange didn't rotate like the weathervane, the bullet appeared to have come from the direction of the road, as Mace expected.

Back on the ground, Mace asked Stargazer if he'd heard anything loud and, if so, when he'd heard it. "Well, last night we heard a few boomers, but we assumed it was lightning. We were pretty high, so I'm not sure we really heard them, but I thought so at the time."

"Do you recall what time it was?"

"Oh wow, man. I don't know. Late. Real late. Maybe 8:30."

Mace smiled. Stargazer was an old guy, after all. "Did you see anything unusual?"

"Nope, we were inside listening to a Firesign Theater album before bed. Those dudes are still hilarious after all this time."

Mace made a mental note to google Firesign Theater at some point. "When did you first notice that your weathervane had been damaged?"

"This morning."

"Why did you wait so long to call me?"

"Did I? I guess it slipped my mind for a while. You know."

"Yep, I do. That happens. Mind if I look around the grounds a bit?"

"Nah, sergeant. Make yourself at home. Would you like some tea? It's a chilly afternoon."

Mace flashed on the mushrooms in the barn. "I'm good for now, but thanks for asking."

Stargazer headed into the house where the others had already gone. Mace slowly walked through the raised gardens toward the road.

He scanned from side to side as he did, looking for casings. He finally spotted them just before he reached the road. There were four of them all in a neat little group. They looked like 30-30 ammo. Mace thought that might help narrow the list of suspects down. He planted a small yellow flag in the ground near them and took a photo. Then he donned some blue latex gloves, opened a Ziploc bag into which he dropped the evidence.

Mace was chapped. Most such calls in the rural areas involved nothing more than Groverton kids doing a little cow tipping or someone blasting a road sign or mailbox. Firing toward a barn and house was a notch up from that and very dangerous. After making a couple of notes and photographing the barn, weathervane, and the symbolic parts stuck on the ground, he went up to the house.

Mace asked the ladies if they had heard or seen anything. They corroborated the booming sounds but hadn't looked outside as they too assumed it was thunder. Stargazer followed as he left to get back in his vehicle.

Mace noticed the old guy had a tear in one eye when he turned to say goodbye. "It's a sad day on the farm, Sergeant Sunshine. I forged our zodiac-vane myself in our little black-smith shop about thirty, no forty, years ago. It was the best job I ever did."

"I'm sorry you're going through this, Stargazer. Do you think you can fix it?"

"I'm sure going to try. Smithing is hard work, and I haven't done it for a while. But I have to try."

Mace put his arm on the crime victim's shoulder and gave him a pat. "I understand. I'll do my best to get to the bottom of this. I'll be in touch if I learn anything. That will probably be the end of it, but call me right away if anything else happens."

"Thanks, Deputy. Don't hurt 'em when you catch 'em. We don't want to enter their dark circle." The old farmer flashed a peace symbol and smiled. Mace nodded, flashed one back, and left the scene.

While driving back, Mace thought about Lefty and the brawl he'd had with Stargazer, but reasoned he probably wouldn't have had good enough aim with a long gun to hit the weathervane from that far. He would still check in with Lefty, just to be thorough. But something else was afoot, and he didn't like it.

26

GET OUT OF HERE, BEAR!

The enforcement day stretched into the evening for Mace. He was used to practically being on 24/7. It didn't leave much time to have a personal life, though he tried.

Driving back through residential Big Squirrel from the farm as twilight gave in to the dark that settled over the quiet town, he was thinking about how his dating apps profile failed to attract the kind of women he liked. That may have been because he didn't really know what kind that was. But there he was, a genuinely nice, responsible single guy with a good job and a reasonably handsome face, and he was lonely as hell.

He was feeling unusually burned out and a little melancholy as he turned a corner and heard a sharp explosion to his right. Screeching to a halt and firing up his spotlight, Mace lit up a yard and picket fence with faded, cracked paint. He jumped out of the driver's side and looked from behind the vehicle for the source of the sound. He grabbed his service pistol but left it holstered.

The first thing he saw was a black bear running pell-mell across the yard, knocking out a portion of the dilapidated fence.

The next thing was a petite, pretty, young woman in a bathrobe and slippers chasing it and yelling, "Get out of here, bear!" Her voice was high like Minnie Mouse, yet still authoritative. She stopped to light something she'd pulled from the robe pocket that she threw at the bear. The object exploded thunderously with a flash of light in mid-air. The bear took off down the street at full speed and into the dark. The woman gave up the chase and leaned on her knees, gasping to catch her breath.

The deputy didn't move for a few beats. He was enraptured. He was impressed. He was entertained. When he snapped out of his brief mental revelry, he more professionally assessed what he had seen and announced, "Police, ma'am. Please hold on there. Ma'am, could you please drop the lighter and any remaining firecrackers on the ground in front of you?"

She dropped her lighter on the ground and held up her hands. "I don't have any more M80s on me, Deputy Mace."

He realized it was Amber, the bartender at The Anvil. He walked up to her and angrily demanded, "Amber! What the hell did you think you're doing?" He'd been scared he'd have to shoot the bear if it had turned on her.

"I was chasing that bear out of here. I caught him rooting in my garbage for the eighth time this month." Black bears would load up on chow in the month before they started their brief hibernation period. Most homes in Big Squirrel had bear boxes, strong steel structures that protected garbage cans from pillaging. Amber's was one of the few left without one. Her landlord was a skinflint who made as few improvements as possible. He treated the property as a cash cow that supported his OxyContin habit.

Amber had grown up hard, and didn't put up with much, especially if it involved gathering up scraps of strewn trash every night. She tried yelling at the bear and banging pots together. That had always worked in prior years, but now the bear just stared at her and went back to his feast or behaved aggressively. She'd driven down to San Berdo after that to score the heavy-duty firecrackers. Tonight was one of her two nights off from The Anvil and she did not appreciate any disturbances. Hence the chase.

She explained this to Deputy Mace, who took notes and shook his head disapprovingly. When she rubbed her arms together to warm up, he noticed a Care Bear tattoo on her right forearm.

"Well, that's ironic." The words slipped out.

"What? What's ironic?" She looked puzzled by his non sequitur.

"Oh, oh, nothing. I was just thinking about something."

"Am I free to go then?"

"Why? I mean, yes, yes. But no more bear chasing, especially with fireworks. Both are very dangerous. Those M8os have blown off some hands, not to mention they're illegal. And you know what bears can do."

"I'll be careful. Thanks, Deputy. Goodnight." Amber smiled, turned, and started to walk home.

"Uh, hey hang on a second. Amber, uh, would you like to go out to dinner sometime?" Mace's hands were shaking a little.

Amber had never thought of the deputy that way. But now that she looked at him, she noticed he wasn't at all bad looking. Tall. And he was really nice. "Sure. Any place but The Anvil, OK? When? I'm off Mondays and Tuesdays."

"Oh, great! Well, how about next Monday then? I can pick you up."

"In that? That might be a little over the top. But Monday's fine. I live in the second house. It's the white one. Well, sort of white. You'll recognize it by the cracked paint."

Mace was red with embarrassment, but feeling quite positive otherwise. "I have a truck. I can drive that. So, does about six sound OK?" Amber smiled and nodded. "Great, I'll see you then. Night."

"Goodnight." Amber walked off and realized she didn't even know Deputy Mace's first name.

Mace didn't share that information with many people. It was Mike. Mike Beauregard Mace. His mother, who hailed from Baton Rouge, Louisiana, called him "Mikey Bo Pooh" when he was little, which he always abhorred. The thought still made him shiver and gag. Amber would learn his first name soon enough, and she would like it a lot.

The deputy drove away smiling for a change. His very few attempts at asking someone out had typically met with failure. Rejection was a bitter pill, and Mace was unusually risk averse for a cop. This felt different. Would the date go well? It seemed possible, but time would tell. When he reached the jail in Groverton he was feeling a little giddy. Lefty's interview could wait until morning. He decided that he'd take Amber to The Branding Iron for their dinner date. He also decided to forget to enter the bear incident in his report that night.

27

LITTLE BOB WELCOMES A NEW CUSTOMER

T he next day, as Mace was visiting Lefty at work to inquire about his knowledge of the zodiac-vane shooting, Little Bob received a new customer as signaled by the little bell on the door. Increasing reports of public hostility drove up the fear factor in Desdemona County, motivating some residents to arm up. Business was brisk at Big Bob's Gun Shop and Ice Cream Parlor, so Little Bob was getting used to seeing some new faces there.

Most of those hadn't shot before, or at least hadn't in a very long time. The proprietor didn't need to sell them. Instead, he spent a lot of time teaching.

The customer looked around the store. He noticed a poster of a man holding a rifle above his head and looking out with an expression of disdain below the words, "You can have my gun when you pry it from my cold dead hands," that was in a frame hung on the white bat-and-board paneled wall. "Hmmm," was all the soon-to-be client said. Next to the poster was loosely tacked an out-of-date campaign poster advertising a candidate for sheriff wearing a Yogi Bear ranger hat and aviator sunglasses. Next, he turned to face the ice cream and pistol counter behind which stood the shop keeper.

Little Bob Ziglar moved through the greetings quickly and then came to the point.

"So, what did you have in mind today?"

"I want to find a pistol for self-defense. Something I can carry every day."

The newbie was a thirty-something male, a bit taller and slimmer than Little Bob. The shop owner sized him up quickly and decided he wasn't the type that could handle a Dirty Harry model. He'd guide him to one of the lower caliber sidearms that wouldn't break his elbow with recoil.

"Good idea. You can't be too careful these days, what with all that's going on. We have a number of quality products that will nicely fill your needs. Have you done much shooting?"

"Nope, none. I'd like to get lessons too."

"You were wise to choose an independent shop instead of one of the big box places. We are full service. The shop even owns a small practice range out in the country that is free to use for our customers. We'll have you up and shooting in no time. Are you familiar with the difference between semi-auto and revolver?"

"I think so. I've heard that semi-auto guns jam more frequently."

"That used to be the case, but today's technology has improved on that. Both have merits and some downsides. Let me walk you through them..." Little Bob went into educational mode and showed his customer some examples.

While the customer liked the 9mm semi-auto, Bob steered him toward a Smith & Wesson 38 special. It was better for concealed carry and very easy to use. His client asked how to load the two. Little Bob started with the 38 and let the client load a shell himself. Next came the 9mm. Bob told him how to make sure the safety was on and to insert the clip, and he followed suit.

Somehow, the weapon went off as the customer held it. Fortunately, the shot missed Little Bob. A bullet flew through an open door and into the shop's water heater that was housed in the small office behind the shotgun and rifle racks. Scalding hot water blasted in a hissing jet right into the freshly filled ice cream case. Steam rose from the display, shrouding the shop in a dense fog. All the flavors began to melt, run, and mix in psychedelic swirls of color. Only the cardboard Loopy's Circus Cones dispenser on top of the glass remained in proper order with its image of Loopy the Clown smiling ironically over the scene of chaotic devastation.

"Holy shit," exclaimed Bob. "Daddy told me to never let a customer load a gun in the store. Damn it! Okay, buddy, give me back the weapon."

An odd fiendish grin expanded across the shooter's face. "Hand me some more clips, little man." His head was lowered, and his darkened eyes stared menacingly at Little Bob. He now resembled young Alex in a Clockwork Orange. In all his years in the business, Bob had never had anyone point a gun at him. He thought a pistol in his hand looked very different from the current barrel-first perspective. He felt a chill run down his back and cold sweat break out on his forehead. He froze, but recovered just enough to comply. He glanced at the alarm button to his left and his personal shotgun under the counter to his right. Finally, he decided to reach directly behind him and grab a handful of clips to give to his robber.

"You touch your alarm, I'll come back and put a slug in your forehead! You understand what I'm saying?" With that, the robber dashed out the front door.

Little Bob grabbed the shotgun and hit the alarm, but his customer was on the run, heading down Main Street to his waiting car.

"Son of a bitch!" Little Bob felt something wet and warm run down his right leg. "Son of a bitch!"

"No Lefty, I'm not accusing you of anything. Let's just say you're a person of interest, one of many. Don't worry. I just have to work my way down the list, okay?"

"You expect me to believe any of that, Deputy Mace? Look, Stargazer and I got into it at The Anvil that night. But that was it. I have nothing against him except that he's a dirtbag hippie. But that's no big deal. There's a bunch of them around here. And I don't go around shooting at people's barns."

Mace sensed he was being truthful. The interview had confirmed what Mace had thought from the beginning: Lefty wasn't the one who shot up Stargazer's weathervane.

"I understand, Lefty. I'm trying to help. Can anyone corroborate where you were that evening?"

"Well, actually I was back at The Anvil for most of it. Until I went home and went to bed. Nobody was with me then, I'm sorry to say. But Slim or Amber could tell ya' that I was there if you ask them. I have a tab there, so there's a record."

"Okay, I will. Thanks, Lefty."

"So, is that it?"

That was when the call came in from the 911 operator. She filled Mace in on what had gone down at Big Bob's.

"Roger that, Becky. I'll get over there right away." Mace grimaced as he answered and turned away from Lefty. "When it rains, it pours, right?" They hung up.

"Sorry, Lefty. I have to run. Thanks for your cooperation."

"Oh gee, that's a shame, Deputy. I was enjoying our chat." Lefty allowed himself a crooked grin. "Hope to see you back here one day. Not too soon, though."

The deputy jumped in the SUV and took off for Groverton.

28

THE HUNT

L olita was driving south through Groverton on Main with Marvin riding along, sort of, in the passenger seat. She had fastened the seat belt for him, but it passed through his translucent waist to the back of the seat. Lolita dutifully buckled it anyhow. She didn't want a ticket because Marvin wasn't wearing a seat belt.

She slammed on the brakes when crossing Pine Street as a black Honda Accord went flying through a stop sign into traffic. It screeched to the right in front of them and headed out of town. Her bumper had narrowly averted t-boning the Honda as she jerked to a stop. Lolita instinctively protected Marvin by using her "mom arm" move.

"Are you alright, honey?"

"I'm fine Lolita. You can only die once. How about you, my love?"

"Yes, yes, just shaken. That was close. What was with that idiot?"

"He appeared to want to get somewhere fast."

"Where are the cops when something like that happens?

They're Johnny-on-the-Spot when a poor woman is talking a little loudly at a concert."

"I sense Deputy Mace is out of town right now."

"Worthless, that's what he is. We were almost killed!"

"Not me, darling. *You* were almost killed."

"Oh yeah. Sorry, dear."

Two other people who had been walking down the sidewalk noticed the black Honda. It was unusual for someone to exhibit reckless driving in Groverton, so it got people's attention. All the witnesses would be questioned by Deputy Mace later that afternoon.

But first he needed to stop at Big Bob's Gun Shop and Ice Cream Parlor. The little bell rang cheerily as Deputy Mace stepped through the door. Little Bob Ziglar came out from behind the counter. After shutting down the water heater, he'd been holding his shotgun there just in case the robber returned. Fortunately, he saw it was Mace and left the weapon there when he stepped out.

"Thanks for coming, Deputy."

"Sorry it took so long, Bob. I was in Big Squirrel. So, you want to tell me what happened here?"

Little Bob described the events and the person who stole his Glock.

"Did you see his vehicle?"

"Nope, I stayed inside."

"Good call, Bob. I'm glad. Things could have gotten worse. Okay, I'm going to get in touch with the neighboring law enforcement offices to alert them, then I'll check to see if anyone saw anything outside. Take care. I'll be back a little later."

Mace left the shop and got back in his SUV. He contacted the sheriff offices in the neighboring counties and the police in San Bernardino. He drove around town in concentric circles just in case the thief might still be around. Seeing a pair of women coming out of the housewares shop, Mace pulled over and got out.

"Excuse me, ladies. I am investigating a robbery and was wondering if you may have seen anything unusual around here in the last hour or so."

"Hello Deputy. I'm glad you stopped. Someone in a black Honda went speeding through here about an hour ago."

"Main Street? Which way were they headed?"

The witness pointed south. That meant they headed out of town through the mountains.

"Was there just the driver or anyone else in the vehicle?"

"Just the driver, as far as we could see. It was a terribly dirty car, so we couldn't see in very well."

He asked them a few more questions, including if they'd noted the license number (they had not), and thanked them.

Lolita appeared out of nowhere and yelled at Mace, "Hey, Deputy, where've you been? Getting donuts? I was almost clobbered by some goon in a little sedan. You know how people drive those things; they think they're sports cars."

"Hey Lolita. Was it a black Honda, by any chance?"

"I think so, yes."

"Did you get the license?"

"He was going pretty fast..." Marvin, who had been hovering right behind Lolita, whispered the Honda license number in her ear, which she robotically parroted to Mace.

"You're sure that's it?"

"Hell yeah, Mace. So, what are you going to do about that guy?"

Returning to his car, he thought about where the robber might have headed. Several old dirt logging trails intersected the highway south of town. Beyond most of those, there was a short road that led to a small park owned and operated by the county. There was a semi-rustic campground there, but no full-time ranger. It was managed by a couple of elderly campground hosts who showed up for a few days a week to clean, collect fees from the pipe, and ensure the toilets were stocked and operational.

He radioed the description of the vehicle and occupant around in case the robber kept going south as the road ultimately led out of the mountains and Desdemona County.

Mace just had a feeling about the campground, so he headed that way. He glanced at each logging trail as he passed slowly but didn't note any signs of recent use.

The campground hosts weren't on duty when he drove into the small compound. The report came back on the Honda. It was registered to a Phineas T. Burton, of Rancho Niebla Tóxica, and it€ had not been reported stolen.

A large wooden sign featuring a map of the campground showed twenty individual sites arranged in an ellipsis. His current position was indicated by a red star that contained the words, "You are here," at about 5 o'clock. He slid the SUV behind the host's trailer and got out to walk.

He left the camp road to circle counterclockwise through the woods. Mace had come here often to camp and fish when he was a boy, so he knew his way around. He also knew how to approach stealthily. The first three sites were empty, but the fourth housed a black Honda Accord. A poorly made khaki-colored pop-up tent lay beyond the car, next to a fire ring. Mace noted that the Honda was covered in dust. He scanned the area for its owner and jotted down the vehicle's license number. Moving farther back in the woods, Mace called in for backup. The sheriff was otherwise occupied, a chronic state that Mace had gotten used to over the past couple of years. So, the call went to a retired Desdemona County deputy who was still available on-call, and the San Bernardino County Sheriff's office. If his former coworker was available, they'd go in without San Berdo, as it would take them a good forty minutes or more to arrive.

Still watching the camp site for signs of life from his position of cover, Mace finally spotted the suspect crawling out of the tent and heading toward the trunk of the Honda. He was tempted to make the bust right then, but this was an armed robber who didn't appear to be going anywhere, and they were alone, so the deputy stuck to his disciplined plan.

A few minutes later, Mace received a text that his backup had arrived at the campground host trailer. He silently texted back the location of the site, the suspect, and himself.

Sheriff's Deputy, retired, Mark McPherson had taken Mace under his wing when the younger lawman first started. McPherson had been around the corner more than once and knew his stuff. Before heading into the mountains, the now retired deputy had been a big city detective until he got undone due to his obsession with a woman he referred to as "that inconveniently deceased dame." It wasn't the first time a femme fatale had massively screwed up some guy's life by dropping dead at a bad time. But that was another story.

What was important to Mace now was that McPherson was here, and he was familiar with Mace's ways, having taught him many of them. That made it easy for McPherson to find Mace in the woods without giving away their position. They nodded, and Mace pointed to the tent where the suspect had returned with something he'd removed from the car. Mace had also caught a glimpse of the Glock tucked into the suspect's belt.

The pair pulled their weapons and silently padded toward the tent while staying ten paces apart. Mace stood behind the Honda facing the tent flap, with McPherson partially behind a tree covering him from a forty-five-degree angle.

"You in the tent! Police! You are surrounded. Come out of

there slowly with your hands where I can see them." They drew aim as the tent ruffled for a couple of beats, but soon the suspect extended both empty hands through the cloth and shuffled out on his knees, looking terrified. Mace didn't see the Glock now.

"Come out all the way, then lie face down with your hands spread out on the ground in front of you. Where's your weapon?"

"I left it in the tent. Don't shoot me."

"Keep moving ahead on your knees, slowly." The suspect complied.

McPherson holstered his revolver and pulled out his cuffs. Once done, he put on a pair of latex gloves and frisked the man.

"What's your name?"

"Phineas T. Burton."

"Don't mess with me, son. It won't go well for you." Mace hadn't had time to fill McPherson in on the auto registration.

"Really, sir. It's a family name."

"Where's your ID?"

"In my back pocket. Wallet."

"Anything else in that pocket, Mr. Phineas T. Burton?"

"No, sir."

"Better not be."

McPherson mirandized Burton as he pulled the wallet from his pocket.

The name on his driver's license confirmed he was being truthful, at least about his name. It showed an address in Rancho Niebla Tóxica.

"Okay, up on your feet. You still live in Rancho?"

"Yes, sir. Well, actually, I just got evicted. I've been living in my car up here for two weeks." He didn't go into the reason he'd ended up homeless. Burton had been living off a cryptocurrency investment he'd made and seen run up beyond anything he could imagine in the prior year. He'd quit his job and was living the good life in an upscale Rancho apartment while shopping for a Porsche when the blockchain coin crashed and burned. Phineas T. Burton lost everything.

"Why'd you come up here to rob Big Bob's shop?"

"That isn't why I came. But after I was here awhile, it seemed like a good idea. I thought it would be easier than knocking over a store in the valley."

"Uh huh. And how'd that turn out?"

"Not so good."

"Not so good. Not so good. That's right. What were you planning on doing with the weapon, son?"

"I figured I'd rob a bank. They're the ones that took my money, right? Look, I've never done anything like this before. I was desperate. I'm sorry. Can't we just return the gun and call it even?"

"Give it up, kid. A fully signed confession is the only thing that's going to help you now. We'll collect that down at the jail."

Mace broke away to search the tent and car. "You got it, McPherson?"

"Yep. Go ahead."

The deputy quickly found the gun in the tent. He took photos and put on his gloves. The rest went according to Hoyle, so they walked Burton down the campground road to Mace's SUV.

Mace helped Burton into the vehicle and strapped him in. Once he closed the door, he turned to the retired deputy. "Why would he stop here for the night instead of just going on? He might have made it to the border and been gone."

McPherson smiled wisely and shook his head. "It's like I told ya' when you were first starting up here, Mace. Most criminals are stupid. That's why we catch 'em."

The report on Phineas T. Burton's ID came back. No priors. He'd been clean—until now. He made bail the next day on the condition that he stay in the county. The judge agreed to have the county pay for him to remain in the camp.

Mace released him back onto the street. "You'd better stick around, Mr. Burton, and stay out of trouble. I'll be coming by to check on you."

"Yes sir, Deputy. Thank you, sir."

29

LOLITA'S CHAPPED

The episode with the maniac in the Honda pushed Lolita over the mental cliff upon which she'd been teetering since Marvin's demise. She forgot all about clothes shopping and made a beeline for Big Bob's Gun Shop and Ice Cream Parlor. The lady was not looking for a Loopy's Circus Cone full of Rocky Road.

The tiny bell on the door made Little Bob jump out of his skin. He was still shaking from his encounter with the first criminal he'd ever met, other than himself, of course. Bob had just finished restoring order to his ice cream case. He set the open carton of pistachio ice cream he'd been shoveling into his mouth to steady his nerves down in the display case with the spoon stuck and dangling on the side like an ice ax.

"Jesus, Lolita!"

"What's wrong, Little Bob?"

"Oh, nothing. Everything is fine. Sorry. How are you doing today? Come for a cone?"

"I need a gun, Little Bob. I'm thinking about a shotgun." Marvin was floating next to her, eyeing the ice cream case enviably. When he heard Lolita say, "gun," he grimaced and shook his head—what there was of it—back and forth slowly.

"I see, Lolita. Why do you need a shotgun?"

"Some idiot in a little black car damn near t-boned Marvin and me just today. Crazy crap is happening around here lately, Bob. And that damned deputy was nowhere to be found until much later. I need to protect myself."

Little Bob decided to ignore her reference to her deceased husband and do a bit of mansplaining, "Lolita, you know I think the world of you, and I'd love to help you out. And I try to never pass up a sale. But the whole town knows what you went through after losing Marvin. That includes the treatment you received. There's just no way you'd pass the background check given the state you're in."

"State I'm in? What the hell state do you think I'm in, Little Napoléon complex creep? I'm just as sane as you."

"No, Lolita, not your state of mind. I was referring to the State of California. The rules here are pretty stringent. After that stint you did in the mental health center, I don't see how you'd qualify for gun ownership here. Florida, Texas, sure, they'll sell a weapon to anyone with cash. But not here. I'm so sorry."

"Word on the street is you helped out Dixie after she shot up The Anvil deck. Why can't you just help me too?"

"Look, I don't know what you're talking about, and neither do you. You want some ice cream? There's nothing else in here I can sell you. It's on the house." Marvin smiled at Lolita and pointed eagerly at the dark chocolate almond mocha flavor. He did the closest thing to jumping up and down that a spirit can do.

Lolita's shoulders relaxed, and she smiled at Little Bob. "I'm sorry, Little Bob. I didn't mean to call you names. I was over-wrought from our near accident. Sure, I'll have a scoop of that." Marvin's apparition did a quick little jig and laughed. Robert

Ziglar, proprietor, smiled and produced a double scoop in a Loopy's waffle cone.

The widow took her ice cream and a napkin and gave the top scoop a quick lick. "Mmmm, delicious. Thanks, Little Bob." As she and Marvin left the shop, the tiny bell on the door tinkled cheerfully. Marvin couldn't resist giving it a flick before he exited, causing it to ring a little longer than normal. Nobody noticed.

"Take care, Lolita." Little Bob prepared to shut down for the day.

Later that evening, Amber was taking an after-dinner walk before starting her shift at The Anvil. Thoughts of the handsome deputy went along with her. She strolled by Lolita and Marvin's house and heard something beautiful coming from the piano inside. She had no way of knowing that the piece was Bach's Invention Number 2 in C minor. She definitely had no way of knowing that the piece had not been played on that piano since Marvin had passed. Amber felt warm and peaceful inside as she turned at the corner to head down to the tavern.

Marvin sat at the piano as Lolita listened and sipped wine in her recliner. He knew that particular tune always calmed his young wife when she grew agitated. Tonight was no exception and what with the ice cream she enjoyed earlier, the wine this evening, and the music, Lolita forgot all thoughts of acquiring a firearm. He turned from the piano while playing and shared a little information he decided she could use.

"Darling, when I said 'Antifa' when I first appeared to you in this form, I didn't mean that Antifa had killed me. I meant I *was* Antifa. I'd been secretly dropping down to L.A. for months to participate in protests with like-minded people and stand up to the militia types. I told you I was meeting with colleagues so you wouldn't worry. I just thought you should know." Lolita didn't know what to do with this revelation. It didn't jibe with what she believed to be true, and hearing it made her feel very uncomfortable. It was too confusing. After ruminating for a few moments, she simply ignored the news and pushed it out of her mind.

The apparition cruised through a couple more of the brief inventions until his audience rose to fetch a glass of water from the kitchen faucet. He left the bench to light on the sofa that could still be seen through his legs. When his widow returned, he asked, "Are you feeling better now, dear?"

"Oh yes. I think I'm ready to catch up on a little news now."

The ghost quietly shook his head but didn't reply. Lolita recorded the national news on her DVR so she could watch it when the mood struck. One of her favorite pundits was presenting his highly biased report about recent events in Hungary and how commie protestors were making life difficult for their poor, oppressed, semi-fascist president there. It only took three minutes for Lolita to go from calm and sanguine to outraged, angry, and depressed. Her face turned red, and she started rocking from side to side in her chair. On the sofa, Marvin shuddered and faded in and out, "Oh boy, here we go."

"Those damned libtard, dirtbags, harassing that poor man! He's just trying to do his job. It's just like here, what they did to our beloved president. Damn them all!!!" With that Lolita reached for her candy dish, but rather than selecting an M&M, she hurled it at the TV.

Marvin had pretty good reflexes for being dead. He saw what was happening and instantly reached out to block the projectile. He was visibly shocked and dismayed when the dish flew straight through his hand and smacked into the screen.

Maybe some of his ectoplasm stuck to the dish, because something odd happened when it hit the TV. Not only did the screen shatter and spark, but a hissing blue electric arc also streamed from it to the shade that covered the lamp next to it. The lamp burst into sparks and smoke and all the lights went out as the breakers shut off electricity. The room was lit only by sparks and the apparition. Lolita screamed in terror, and Marvin whispered, "Better call 911, dear."

Chief Murphy led her crew to the call. They arrived in only five minutes due to the proximity of Lolita and Marvin's place to the firehouse. First step was to assess the situation and make sure all the occupants were evacuated. Lolita emerged from the front door with a firefighter.

The Chief approached her. "Is anyone else inside?"

"Marvin is still in there."

"Marvin? Oh, yes, Lolita. We'll make sure he gets out."

"It isn't really on fire, there are just sparks all over the living room."

"Got it. Don't worry. We'll protect your home. You're okay now."

Deputy Mace pulled up and jumped out to see if he could help. Tenaya went inside to inspect the damage. Fortunately, when the power shut off, the fire danger became very low. The sparking had subsided, and all that was left were a few glowing parts in what had been Lolita's TV set. A crystal dish lay nearby. M&Ms, some melted, were all over the floor and even in the ruins of the TV. A floor lamp with a blackened lampshade had fallen over the sofa.

As the fire team went about their business, Mace ushered a group of neighbors that had gathered out front to a safe place across the street. He created a perimeter around the property with yellow tape. Finally, he checked in on Lolita. "Hi, Lolita. Are you okay?"

"I'm fine, Mace. I just hope Marvin got out of there."

Mace didn't contradict her. "It looks like the fire department has everything under control. I'm sure everyone is safe and sound now. Where was the fire?"

The deputy bit his lip when she got to the part about the candy dish. Was she getting worse? She'd had a tough time of it since losing Marvin. He was feeling a lot of empathy toward the widow and didn't want to see her hurt herself with stunts like this one.

"How can I help?"

"I hope I can stay home tonight. Otherwise, I don't know where I can go."

"Well, if push comes to shove, I can call the reverend. She's let folks sleep in the church before. Do you have any relatives or close friends nearby?"

The widow looked a little crestfallen at the last question. She thought about it for a few seconds and teared up. Marvin was the only real friend she had, and he didn't seem to be around right now.

"Don't worry about it, Lolita. We'll find you a place. It'll be okay." He broke with departmental protocol and gave her a quick side hug. She offered up a brave smile.

Tenaya came out and joined them. "Hey Mace. Thanks for coming. Good news, Lolita. No major fire damage. Everything is secure inside, so I called the power company. They'll have somebody out shortly to restore power. Meanwhile, it's messy but safe, so you can stay at home. Do you have a flashlight?"

"Somewhere, yeah, I'm sure we do."

"I'll lend you one of mine. Return it to the station tomorrow, okay?"

"Yep. Thanks so much, Chief Murphy. You guys are great. You too, Mace."

"You're welcome. Now the hard part. You need to tell me how this started."

Lolita explained taking out the news commentator with a crystal dish one more time. Tenaya stifled a laugh as best she could, but it wasn't easy.

"Fine, Lolita. I think I understand what happened. Don't forget to call your insurer. We're going to head back to the firehouse, but I'll leave a team member out here to wait for the power company. Have a good night, and no more dish tossing, right?"

"Yes, ma'am." Lolita went back inside.

Turning to the lawman, Tenaya shared her other similar incident. "You know, Mace, we had one just like this out on Shaky Jake Road not long ago. That guy burned up his drapes and charred his ceiling before we arrived. But we stopped it, and everything was okay there too. That's two lucky nuts. This town is really living up to its name lately, isn't it?"

"How's that, Tenaya?"

"It's getting squirrely as hell."

"Roger that, Chief."

Lolita used her borrowed flashlight to inspect the damage she had caused. She picked up the candy dish and the remaining unmelted M&Ms and popped a red one in her mouth. She saw what was left of her TV and decided to leave that at least until the lights were back on. She put the lamp upright. It looked okay except for the shade and bulb. She could replace those in the morning.

There was still no sign of Marvin. The little widow thought about her conversation with Mace and started to cry. "What happened to me? I used to have friends. Making them used to come easy to me. I made friends with Marvin, didn't I?" Thinking that over, she realized the pouty, flirtatious looks she gave him and the daisy dukes she wore that day wouldn't work for attracting the more platonic relationship she needed now with a woman or man. Her cutoffs wouldn't fit anymore anyhow, even if she knew where they were.

"I have to make a friend."

Lolita sat on the sofa and waited for the power company to show up.

30

LITTLE MOTHER HITS A HOMER

The next morning, all was going normally at Mother's Café. A couple of the regulars were there. Chad was digging into yet another Denver sandwich, washing it down with a V8 juice and coffee. Little Mother was engaged in a whispered conversation with the fire chief. Chad figured that meant gossip, and he ignored it.

Tenaya was chowing down on the Blue Plate Special that included generous helpings of eggs, link sausages, sliced tomatoes, hashbrowns, two pancakes, toast, coffee and juice. Most of the woodchucks couldn't even make their way through the locally famous feast, but Chief Murphy would easily cause it to disappear while Little Mother talked.

"Order up," called the cook. Little Mother excused herself to pick up breakfast for a sullen stranger in a camo vest who was sitting at the counter. She brought it over with a fresh pot of Joe. "There ya' go, sir. Warm that up for you?"

"Yeah," was all he said.

She poured the coffee. "Let me know if you need anything," she said before walking over to Chad's table with the pot. She didn't need to ask Chad. She simply refilled his cup. "So how are you and Tiffany enjoying living in Big Squirrel, Chad? I sure had a nice time with her and Dixie at the Branding Iron the other night."

"Oh, it's great. I love being in such close proximity to your café, and everyone in town has been welcoming and friendly. The house is really coming along, and Tiffany has her therapy business set up already. Dixie called some doctors in other towns on her behalf, and it sounds like Tiffany will soon be doing more business than I am! Anyhow, she really enjoyed going out too, if her hangover was any measure. It was nice of you to invite her."

"That was all Dixie's doing. I don't get out much, so she thought we'd make a good trio, and we sure did. Get you anything else?"

"Nope, I have to finish this up and get home and back to work. Not even Tiffany's job is going to be enough to cover her home improvement hobby!"

"Well, thanks for coming in. Have a super day." Little Mother gently placed the bill on the table and headed back behind the counter. She returned the pot to its warmer.

She approached the stranger. "How's everything tasting, friend?"

"I'm not your friend and it tastes like a soggy newspaper. This isn't even edible. I'm not paying for it."

Mother was surprised. The omelet was one of the most popular items on the menu, and her cook had been with her for years. "I'm so sorry to hear that, sir." She noticed more than half the meal had already been eaten, but ignored that little fact in the interest of customer service. "Of course, you don't have to pay for that. Satisfaction is guaranteed at Mother's. Can I offer you a replacement? It'll be on the house."

The stranger stood up and menacingly leaned over the counter. "I don't want any more of your garbage. You probably poisoned me."

With that, he pushed his plate off the counter onto the floor and pushed Little Mother hard in the chest. She reeled back two steps toward the back wall. Behind her was a shelf of decorative knickknacks on which she almost cracked her skull. But instead, she reached up between the ceramic rooster and the set of squirrel shaped salt and pepper shakers and grabbed the old but still serviceable cast iron skillet that had been placed there by original Mother to convey that real home cooking was available here. She brought the skillet down and straight out to connect with the belligerent diner's forehead. He dropped to the ground like a sack of potatoes, out cold and probably concussed.

Chief Murphy had already phoned Deputy Mace to report the disturbance and came over to see if Little Mother needed a hand. The cook returned the meat clever she'd grabbed when the customer pushed Little Mother to its hook and resumed her duties over the flat top.

"You okay, Little Mother? Mace is on his way. It looks like this idiot is going to need some ice when he comes to."

"Well, he's not getting any of mine. And I'm better than he is! I'm fine, fine, Tenaya. Thanks for the assist. It doesn't happen often, but this guy isn't our first trip to the rodeo. Cookie and I know how to handle it. What a jerk. Does seem like we're getting a lot more of them than usual, though."

"I hear that Little Mother. At least he didn't catch anything on fire. I thought maybe I was off the hook for a while after last night's fun fest." She then went ahead to share what had happened to the TV at Lolita's place without mentioning the widow by name. It was the first actual gossip she and her café proprietor friend had engaged in that morning. The earlier friendly conversation that Chad had seen them having was about something else entirely.

A rather tired looking Deputy Mace walked in at that point, looked around, and asked Tenaya if everyone was okay.

"Everyone is fine, except for that jerk." She pointed to the still unconscious man crumpled on the floor. "Little Mother here has the situation under control for you, Mace."

He looked over the perp to make sure he was breathing. "Yeah, I can see that alright. Little Mother, you want to tell me what happened here?"

Murphy dropped a twenty on the counter next to the register and made to leave. "I'd better get to the firehouse. Take it easy, Little Mother. Let me know if you need help with anything. I'll see you soon. Let me know if you need a witness. Have a good day, Deputy."

"We're good for now. You gave me your report on the phone. Thanks, Chief. You have a good day too."

Mace noticed Chad sitting at his table, still holding his steaming hot cup of coffee. "Hi Mr. Burr. Did you see what happened?"

"I sure did. Caught it all from here. That guy threw his food on the ground and pushed Little Mother."

"Please stay here for a little bit. I may need to ask you some questions. Go ahead, Little Mother. I'll listen while I check him out some more. Looks like I'll need to get him over to Doc Jones before I book him." Mace rolled him over and woke him up. He then cuffed his hands behind his back. He pulled his wallet from a back pocket and read his I.D. as Little Mother recounted the event of the last few minutes.

"Here's what happened…"

31

DATE NIGHT AT THE BRANDING
IRON

The doors swung open at the steakhouse to reveal Tex holding some menus and instructing his new hostess. The place was jumping, and laughter and loud Little Feat music spilled out. The band was playing a cover of Dixie Chicken.

"Howdy kids! Why it's Deputy Mace and Amber Bärnsten, fastest mixologist west of the Pecos! Welcome to the Branding Iron. How are you two doing tonight?" Tex let that flow out slowly but cheerfully loud in his odd Jersey-laced faux-western drawl.

Amber wore a short burgundy long sleeve dress with a little bit of silvery embellishment around the collar and cuffs that sparkled and reflected the colorful and rapidly changing lights from the bar area. The same material shimmered in a curvi-linear design on her burgundy heels. Her hair, usually tied in a braid or ponytail for work, was flowing tonight. It was a warm tawny brown with a couple of dark red streaks that nearly matched the dress. It was draped over her right shoulder and went halfway down her back. The deputy arrived in khakis, a brown plaid western shirt, and a dark brown western suede jacket. A nice pair of Tecova cowboy boots completed his outfit. Amber wondered if the boots were brand new. They were.

Mace replied, "Hi Tex. How's it going? Hope you can find a table for two."

"Why sure, good buddy. We've always got a place for a lawman and his lovely date. Nice to see you two out in your civvies. And Amber, it's nice to see you out of The Anvil for once. You know you'd be making more if you took my offer to put you behind our bar."

"I know, Tex, but I like being able to walk to work. Besides, Slim would be lost without me. I'm just in for one of your awesome steaks and maybe a dance if Mike here turns out to be as nice as I think he is."

Tex looked dumbfounded. "Who's Mike?"

"Me, Tex. I have a name other than Mace."

"Well, I'll be sheep-dipped. Don't that beat all," Tex drawled, unfortunately sounding more like Tony Soprano that Slim Pickens. "Right this way, folks. I'll get you two wonderful young folks a beautiful table even if'n I have to 86 a couple of cowpokes with my trusty lasso. Come along, Crystal, and learn something." He handed the menus to his new hostess to carry as he led the way. Mike and Amber rolled their eyes at each other and chuckled softly.

Tex took them to a quieter and partially sheltered table in a slightly darker corner where conversation could happen more easily. "I'll send your waiter over. You two enjoy your dinner, and Amber, don't forget my offer."

Mace answered, "Thanks Tex."

"He's sweet, but a bit much with the cowboy talk. Doesn't that accent just kill you?" Amber smiled at her date. Mike noticed for the first time that she had something in her hair that sparkled just like her collar and that her eyes were a warm brown with tiny flecks of emerald. He took a breath and pressed his feet down in his boots to steady himself.

"Yep, he's a hoot. All hat, no cattle. He sure does run a successful steakhouse though. Look at this place. It's slammed. Have you ever considered working for him?"

"Nah. I'm happy at The Anvil, and I like Slim. And I meant what I said about him being lost without me. The poor man couldn't correctly pour a shot of bourbon let alone mix an actual cocktail. I think he just sells beer and margaritas from the machine on my nights off."

Mike Mace caught a whiff of fragrance that barely made it across the table from Amber. He had no way of knowing it was Chanel Coco Mademoiselle and that Amber had driven rapidly to the mall in San Bernardino that very morning to drop the most money she ever had for perfume just for this one date. It did have an effect that meant she got her money's worth, and once again, Mike pressed his toes painfully into his boots to keep from losing what little cool he had.

"So, enough about Tex. Let's talk about you. How long have you been at The Anvil?"

"Is this an official interrogation, officer? Maybe you should read me my rights." Amber smiled mischievously at Mike.

"Yes, it is. And you gave up those rights when you agreed to dinner at your competitor's place." He grinned back, and Amber laughed.

"Okay, well, with that established, I've been there for seven years, ever since I graduated college."

"You did? What was your major?"

"Child psychology."

"That's great. So why are you tending bar in Big Squirrel?"

"As it turns out, I can't deal with children. They make me nervous."

"Why did you study it then?"

"It was my mom's idea. She's a child psychologist in Santa Rosa, where I grew up. You know that new woman in town, Tiffany Van Pelt? She told me her sister Lucy is a shrink up there and knows my mom. Small world, huh?" Amber omitted any reference to her dad and the spousal abuse that led to her parents' divorce. Way too heavy for first date conversation. "Anyhow, I didn't really know how I felt about kids until I interned at a clinic. A couple of the young patients got to me on a personal level once they started talking. I couldn't help it. I felt so much empathy that it tore me apart. I realized that the professional detachment that I needed wasn't a part of my nature. There was no way I could emotionally do the work. I finished school since most of it was paid for by then and set out to decide what to do next that was not child psychology."

"Wow. You went through a lot, Amber. And that led you to Big Squirrel?"

"Indirectly. Remember that big music festival held up here about eight years back? I came up for that with a friend from school and fell in love with the place. I remembered it and thought Big Squirrel might be a good spot to chill for a while and figure out what to do with my life. Got a job waiting tables at The Anvil, then barback, was promoted to bartender, and I've been there ever since. At least my education taught me how to handle our customers."

"No doubt. How'd you learn to bartend?"

"I did it when I was in school. I bs'd my way through the interview to get the job because it paid better than waiting tables. I was able to do that because I mixed drinks for my parents from an old bartender's guide they had. I made every drink in the book and memorized them all. I'm a quick study, so I observed what the outgoing bartender would do to prep and make everything efficient, and I copied him. Fake it 'til you make it, right? I think they were on to me from the start, but they were desperate for a replacement. So how does one become a deputy sheriff, Mike?"

"I'm actually a superhero, but Marvel didn't have any openings, so I went to work in Desdemona County instead." Mike felt his face redden after his lame attempt at a witty response. Amber thought that was cute and smiled. She was also fighting a nervous urge to play with her hair. "No, actually, I love helping and protecting people. My uncle used to be sheriff up here, and he was a hero to me, especially after my dad died. So, I went to school and studied criminology. I went to a couple of preliminary interviews for a job in L.A. after I got my degree, and I received an offer, but Big Squirrel was home, and I wanted to give back. They needed a deputy up here, so I applied. Sounds kind of silly when I say it out loud."

"No, no Mike. It's a sweet story, not to mention the fact that we both studied psychology, albeit for different reasons. And all this time I didn't want to like you." They both smiled across the table. It was Amber's turn to press her feet into her shoes to keep from losing what little cool she still had. She quickly changed the subject to something that would prove less endearing. "Do you live here in Groverton?"

"Nope. I sort of keep it secret, given that some people don't care for me after I bust them for something, but I'll tell you. I live in a little farmhouse just outside Big Squirrel. It used to be my uncle's, but he gave it to me as a graduation present. Said I deserved it as the first college grad in the family."

"Does he live there with you?"

"Nope. He moved to Redondo Beach after he retired. Said he never liked the mountains and always loved the ocean. He took surfing lessons there, plays beach volleyball, and fishes. He never tells anyone what he did for a living. His new friends all think he's an old rocker or actor or something like that because he seems crusty, and a bit burned out."

"You're all alone out there then?"

"I have a one-eyed goldfish. I call him Popeye. He's always happy to see me when I get home, and that isn't much."

"I know you work all the time. Where do you stay when you don't go home?"

"Sometimes I'm so beat or have so little time, I just bunk in a cell in the jail."

"That sounds like the life, man!"

"Livin' the dream, right? Glamour, glamour, glamour. Yep, that's me."

The waiter arrived, and they ordered drinks and some guac and queso with chips. "Maybe we'd better check the menus, Deputy."

"Yeah, I don't want to take up the table and have Tex yelling at us. He'll make it sound like it's a threat coming from the New Jersey mob and Roy Rogers all at once."

Amber smiled to herself and pretended to read her menu. She knew what she wanted when she walked in the door. Right now, she just needed to come up for air. Against all her trepidations about going out with a cop, she found she really liked this guy. A lot.

Drinks and dinner went equally well. After the check arrived, Mike asked, "May I have the next dance?"

Mike left a generous tip, which Amber found even more endearing, and they walked over to the dance floor hand-in-hand. The band finished playing the Cotton Eye Joe, and moved into a slow rendition of "Crazy," the old romantic song written by Willie Nelson and made famous by Patsy Cline. The couple became entwined and lost themselves on the floor as a whisper light Chanel scent, a tickle of soft, tawny waves against his cheek, and the feel of this sweet, warm young woman moving gently under silky taffeta he lightly grazed with his fingertips almost made the tough-as-nails lawman buckle at the knees. And she was having exactly the same feelings about him.

He decided to lessen the pressure by asking another work question he'd forgotten earlier. "Do you have any idea why the Tavern is called 'The Anvil?' I know there is an actual anvil in the entry, but that's only been there a couple of years."

"Yeah, that anvil was a found object. Not sure where it was found. Slim told me the origin story a while back. He named it when he was first building it out. He was searching for a good name that would speak to what the bar was about. One night he was randomly channel surfing at home and stopped to watch a Road Runner cartoon. Wile E. Coyote had set a trap for Road Runner with an ACME anvil, but the bird ran right past it. When Wile tested it, it fell on his head and flattened him to the ground. That triggered something in Slim's mind. He said he named it 'The Anvil' because it's a place you go to get hammered."

Much later, Mace safely deposited Amber back on her doorstep after using his flashlight to make sure her bear hadn't returned. He gave Amber a polite kiss on the cheek and said, "Well, that's goodnight then, I guess."

"It is, but you aren't getting off quite that easy, Mister." Amber pulled him to her by his lapels and they shared their first kiss.

For some reason, he awkwardly asked her, "Why'd you do that?"

Amber looked up at him slyly. "I wanted to see if I'd like it."

"And did you?"

"I don't know yet." She kissed him again and this time he lost himself in the act of kissing her back.

After several seconds, Amber leaned back, smacked her lips, and said, "Mmm. It's even better when you help." Mike knew he'd heard this dialogue or something like it before, but he couldn't place where or when. One day Amber would confess she had been reciting lines from "To Have and Have Not," but this wasn't that day. She smiled and turned to unlock her door. "Good night, Mike. That was fun. Let's do it again real soon."

"You can count on it. I'll call you very soon. Good night, Amber." She went inside, bolted the door, and their very wonderful first date was over. There would be others to follow. Mace headed back to his truck, whistling "Crazy." He felt light on his feet and better than he had in years. As he opened the driver's side door, the bear bolted noisily from behind Amber's trash cans and sprinted into the woods. Mike laughed and drove home.

Before heading into work the next day, Amber had the borrowed dress cleaned and returned it with the matching shoes to Tiffany, whom she had met only a few nights before at The Anvil where they had been introduced by Dixie.

"So, how did your date go with Deputy Mace, Amber?"

"It was awesome! No, that's not the right word. It was, uh, how can I put it? It was—dreamy. Yeah, that's it. Dreamy."

The two women smiled and hugged. Tiffany replied with a simple, "Awww. That's sweet."

32

THE ANVIL, REVISITED

"Sweet are the uses of adversity which, like the toad, ugly and venomous, wears yet a precious jewel in his head."—William Shakespeare

T hey called themselves the "Nefarious Bards M.C.," wherein "M.C." stood for Motorcycle Club. There were three of them.

Their black leather vests matched the custom Harleys that were out in the parking lot in a row. The vests had full sets of patches across the back. The top patch read the name of the club. The bottom said "Arcadia, CA." In the middle was an embroidered skull, the forehead of which was emblazoned with the name "Yorick." They generally looked like typical biker gang outlaws; except this bunch each had a tattoo of a Shakespearian female character on their right arm. One sported Cordelia from King Lear, another Lady MacBeth, while the last had Miranda from The Tempest. The one with

Miranda had a line of hers tattooed in a Gothic script that ran up his left arm, "O brave new world, that has such people in't."

Jaycee was cocktail waitressing that night and took their order. She headed up to the bar. "Hey Amber, I need a pint of Sierra Nevada and a Campfire Stout. This is for those bikers at table four. One of them said he wanted a flagon of "mead." Do you have any of that?"

"Yeah, it's that honey drink. It'll knock ya' on your ass and you won't even notice it. There's a couple of bottles left over from that Renaissance Faire promo Slim ran a couple of years ago. I'm not sure it's still good though. I guess he will let you know. And I don't have a flagon, so he'll get it in a regular pint glass."

Stargazer and a couple of his buds were at table three. Jaycee had strategically located eight of the woodchucks well away from them at table seven when they came in. The bikers were placed in between the two groups, hiding one from the other. Conversation hushed to a whispered fury among the woodchucks when the Bards were seated. Jaycee served the beer and mead to the Bards. She asked Lady MacBeth to take a sip of the mead and let her know if it was OK. He answered with "Ah yes, nectar of the gods!" He thanked her and asked "So, my sweet young serving wench, what news of your fair hamlet today?"

Jaycee cocked her blonde head to one side and jutted out a hip. "There isn't usually much news here in Big Squirrel, mister." She smiled and asked if they wanted to open a tab.

"Aye, that's the rub. Yes, fair maiden, a tab if you please."

She walked over to another table, muttering under her breath, "Weirdo."

Meanwhile, the woodchucks were growing more agitated around their back-of-the-room table. Their mostly white faces were frowning even more than usual and multiple conversations were getting louder. Both Slim's and Amber's ears perked up and they could smell trouble. "Amber, could you give Mace a call, please?"

"On it boss." The bartender had already hit his number in her phone's memory. Mace picked up after one ring.

"Hi sweet girl, how's it going?"

"Hey Mike, we may be a little jumpy, but Slim and I think something may be brewing here that isn't beer. Do you have time to pop by for a visit?"

"I'm on my way. Ten minutes."

Amber waved Jaycee over to the bar. "Stick around with me for a minute, 'kay?"

"Sure, Amber. What's up?"

"Hopefully nothing."

One of the woodchucks stood and asked another if he'd like to step outside to back up what he said. The target of this inquiry rose and said, "Why bother?" and punched his challenger in the face.

The old hippies had drilled on the eventuality that violence might return to The Anvil. They quickly rose and filed out the front door to form a circle by holding hands in the parking lot and proceeded to chant for peace.

The Nefarious Bards at table four knew that they'd get blamed for anything that went down in the tavern, whether they were involved or not. Lady Macbeth dropped a hundred-dollar bill under his empty glass of mead, and the bikers followed the hippies out the front door. Within seconds, they were helmeted, fired up, and headed down the highway, looking for adventure. One of them called out to the chanting hippies as he rode out, "Fare thee well, vagabonds; We must away!"

Inside, Amber flopped the service bar open, grabbed Jaycee by the arm, and dragged her out the back door. They ran together toward Amber's house.

At the moment they escaped, a muffled shot went off and a

bullet narrowly missed Slim's right ear. It plunged into a photo
of Ronald and Nancy Reagan smiling broadly in front of Mother's Café during a visit they made to Big Squirrel back in the
sixties when he was governor of California. The .22 slug shattered the glass and lodged in the wall behind the frame,
creating a hole in the space between the Reagans' heads. Slim
ducked behind the bar and grabbed his blackjack.

Mace showed up a couple of minutes later and pulled the
first hippie he spotted out of the chanting circle. "What's going
on in there?"

"It's a fight, Sergeant Sunshine. We heard a shot coming
from inside. We're praying for peace."

The deputy took hold of his holstered pistol and opened
the door. When he saw the woodchucks had stopped boxing
and stood with their mouths hanging open when the gun went
off, he blew a small airhorn and told everyone to freeze. They
basically already had, so they simply continued to do so.

"Mace, it's me, Slim. I'm coming up behind the bar." Slim
stood up, leaving the blackjack in its place.

"Where's Amber?"

"She's fine. She and my waitress ducked out the back door
when the fighting started. They're either outside behind the
tavern or headed for home."

"Good. What's going on here?"

Slim explained and pointed to the newly perforated photo
on the wall. Mace pulled his weapon and told the woodchucks
to put their hands up. "Who has the gun?"

One of them in a red plaid flannel shirt stood on tiptoes to
raise one of his hands a little higher. "Me, it's mine."

"Put it down on the table in front of you and then everyone
take two steps back and stop." The woodchucks complied as
McPherson entered, taking cover behind the decorative anvil
up front. "Police! Everybody freeze!" The men continued to
remain frozen.

"Hey, McPherson. Thanks for coming." Mace had called him for backup when he was driving over.

"What's up, Mace? I thought I was retired."

"Sorry, buddy. Lots going down all of a sudden." Mace grabbed the pistol, emptied it, and placed it on the bar. "Keep an eye on that, Slim."

The deputy turned back to the woodchucks and asked, "What were you fighting about?"

A beard in green plaid flannel answered, "We were arguing over who would get to go tell those bikers they weren't welcome here. We don't like their kind, spreading drugs and raping our women."

Both lawmen looked at each other and shook their heads. Slim let out a "Holy shit, man." He sighed and looked down at the .22 on his bar, thinking of how it barely missed him.

Mace cuffed Mr. red plaid and read him his rights. He then zip-tied two of them that Slim identified as having started the fracas. Mace then took names and other information from his prisoners. "Can you get IDs on the rest, Mac?"

"No problem, Mace. You hauling those miscreants into Groverton?"

"Yep. Slim, could you let Amber know I'll call her when these boys are locked up?"

"Yeah, Mace. Will do. Thanks for getting here so quickly."

"Okay, you three. March."

McPherson addressed the remaining five woodchucks. "Alright you schmucks. I was watching a game at home, and I am not in a good mood. Sit down, pull out your wallets, and hand me your identification. Keep your mouths shut unless I ask you something. This party is officially over."

Mace walked Red Plaid and his bloodied friends through the front doors, past the still-chanting hippies, and deposited them in the back of his SUV.

He knew they'd be bailed out by morning.

He called Amber after depositing the busted woodchucks in cells.

"Hello?"

"Hi Amber, it's Mace, I mean, Mike. Are you okay?"

"I'm fine, Mike. I'm at home with Jaycee. Are you and Slim okay? I thought I heard a popping noise as we ran off. Was that a gun?"

"Slim's fine. One of them drew a pistol and accidentally fired a shot into the wall. It busted a picture. Nobody is seriously hurt, although a few woodchucks are bruised and bloody from the fist fight. Three of them are guests here at my bed-and-breakfast tonight. I just wanted to make sure nothing bad happened to you."

"Nope. All good. Thanks for getting there so fast, Mike. I'm glad you're OK."

"I better get going. I'll call you soon, assuming you'd still like to go out again."

"I'd love that. Can't wait. Take care, Mike."

"You too, Amber. Bye."

One of the prisoners overheard the conversation and called out mockingly from his cell, "Awww. Isn't that sweet?"

Mace just leaned back in his chair, smiled, and thought, *Yes. Yes, it was.*

The Nefarious Bards were all back in Arcadia by then and the next morning would be off to their respective jobs: corporate attorney, bank vice-president, and insurance adjuster.

33

HOW TO GET AHEAD IN THE WORLD
WITHOUT REALLY TRYING

Mace's overnight guests were granted bail and checked out the next day, as he knew they would be. He kindly gave them all a ride back to The Anvil so they could pick up their trucks. The deputy decided to surprise Amber at her place and ask her to the second date they'd already agreed upon.

Meanwhile, Mason was out in his truck heading to an installation job when his phone rang. "Hello, Mason's Heating and Air, this is Mason."

"Hi Mason, it's Chad. Thought I'd give you a call and see if you were up for some more fishing."

"Always, man, always. How's Saturday morning sound? We can traipse up Murrieta Creek this time. I almost always get hits from trout up there and the crazy bass don't go that far upstream cuz' it gets pretty narrow in spots. It's a bit of a hike."

"Sounds perfect. I'll come by your place about 6:30 then."

"Make it 6:00, Mason. We'll need some walking time."

"Got it. See ya'."

Fifteen minutes later, Dixie flew through the door of

Tiffany's physical therapy business with the shiny new brass nameplate on it that read:

Tiffany Van Pelt

Physical Therapist

"Hey girl, you busy?" Dixie stopped and smiled at Tiffany's new receptionist. "Wait, oh, I forgot you started work here today, Jen. How's it going so far?"

"Hi Dixie. Great! Tiffany is awesome and seemed so happy that I'd done this before."

"That's why I recommended you, kid. Is she with a patient?"

"One just left. Her next one is running late. I'll get her for you."

The new receptionist walked to Tiffany's office and followed her back to the waiting room. "Dixie! Hi. What's up?"

"How'd Amber's date go with Barney Fife?"

"She had a wonderful time. It's nice to see a girl so happy. She said he was really sweet, a perfect gentleman."

"Ah, that's great. It was nice of you to loan her your killer party dress and shoes. So, it looks like the boys are going fishing on Saturday. I thought it might be fun to drive down to Temecula for brunch and a little wine tasting."

"I'd love to go! Sounds fun. What time?"

"Meet me at my place when you wake up and we'll see how early my hangover goes away. Later."

Tiffany's next patient walked in as Dixie was heading out. Dixie greeting him with "Hi there. Nice to see you again." He was one of the woodchucks, wearing a blue and black plaid flannel shirt and a tractor cap with a patch in the front that read "State of Jackson." He'd hurt his rotator cuff in the latest brawl at The Anvil. Doc Jones had prescribed steroids and sent him to Tiffany for therapy.

"Good morning, sir. How may I help you today?" Jen was cheerful and efficient. Tiffany went back to her office as she checked the rotator cuff in for his appointment.

Stargazer had finished his early chores out on the farm and was walking down to the road to pick up mail from the day before as Jen checked in the patient in Groverton. He noticed something odd-looking lying in the gravel driveway on his side of the gate he'd put in after the zodiac-vane shooting incident.

The old farmer slowly walked a little a little closer to the object. It looked like some kind of animal. When he got his eyes in focus, he was startled to see it was a decapitated horse's head. Bright red blood appeared to have oozed under it and spread across the gravel.

Stargazer beat a hasty retreat up to the house while reciting his mantra repeatedly. He placed a call and met the ladies who were working in the barn to meditate. They all sat down in the lotus position next to the mushrooms the women had been tending and hummed a low "Ommmmm."

Mace figured he knew what was going on when the call came in. He'd heard from a store in town that a fake horse head was missing. Dahlia's Cleaning Service was sanitizing the cells, which is to say, Dahlia, so he asked her if she'd please lock up when she was done as he had to go out.

"No problem, Mace. I'll only be about an hour or so."

The deputy was surprised to find the new gate at the entrance to the farm. It was locked, so he called Stargazer who took a few moments to answer. The farmer walked down, giving the bloody head a wide berth as he did, and unlocked the gate. "Hi Sergeant Sunshine. I found the head right over here. It looks like something from The Godfather, man. Freaky deaky."

Mace went over and kicked the hard plastic neck. He turned it over and could see the "blood" was actually just paint.

"That's from Millers Feed & Seed, Stargazer. I got a call

from them right before yours saying somebody had vandalized the horse statue in their parking lot the night before."

"Whoa, that's a trip. Do you think it was one of those wood-chucks? They're sort of hostile toward us lately, as you know. Maybe it was them that shot my zodiac vane too."

"Probably not. My bet is it's somebody else. Know anyone who would want to scare you or the ladies?"

"Nope. I can't think of any reason anyone would want to do that. Maybe it's just kids. Have you had any leads on the shooter?"

Mace felt guilty that he hadn't devoted as much time and energy to investigating the zodiac vane shooter as he should have. "Not yet. Sorry, Stargazer. I'll step it up now. Actually, this incident might help me figure it out."

"Okay, Deputy. We're not quite ready to return to Mother Gaia yet. There's a lot to do around the farm."

"I'll get to the bottom of this and make it stop. You take care and keep an eye out until I do. Have you ever thought about getting a dog?"

"I'm not good at holding animals captive. But maybe it could be a good thing. We'd be sure to treat him with respect and love."

"I know you would. The shelter would love to help you with that. Meanwhile, I'll let you know what I find."

"Vaya con Dios, brother."

"You too, Stargazer." Mace picked up the horse's head and put it in the back of the SUV. He still felt bad about neglecting the farmers, but he knew what to do. He drove back down to Groverton to visit Little Bob. He was feeling burned out again.

Along the way, he did something he rarely did these days and phoned the sheriff at home. A gravelly voice answered, "Hi Mace. How's it going?"

"Only fair, Sheriff. How are you doing?"

"As well as can be expected. No real change." Sheriff George had a rough time during the pandemic. He caught Covid early in the game and was isolated at home. Physical recovery had occurred on its own, and he improved, but something had changed inside the man. He had panic attacks simply walking out his front door. The shrink called it "agoraphobia" and gave him a prescription after their Zoom visit to steady his nerves. That didn't help at all. Neither did the cognitive behavioral therapy he had tried for a few months. The sheriff turned out to be one of those exceptions for whom nothing worked.

"Sorry to hear that, Sheriff. I know you loved being out in the community. That brings me to the reason for my call. I need some help. There's a lot more going on lately than usual, as you are aware. I can't cover it all, and McPherson really wants to limit his on-call time."

"You know I can't go out yet, Mace. What do you want me to do?"

"I know, I know. I thought maybe we could hire another deputy. It would be an added strain to get him onboarded, but it would be worth it if I could just see some light at the end of the tunnel. I'd really like to try to start a life, if that's still possible."

"Yeah, Little Mother told me you'd started dating Amber from The Anvil. That's great. Listen, I hear you, Mace. You're a good man. Those jerks on the board of supervisors cut our budget after McPherson retired. So, we can't afford a new hire until I can get them to replace the funding. Sorry, buddy. You're just going to have to muddle through for a while."

"OK. I'll do my best, sir. Hope you feel better soon."

"Thanks for the call, Mace. Be safe out there."

They hung up. Mace felt dejected, but not wholly out of options. His next call was to Chief Tenaya Murphy.

The little bell on the door rang when Mace walked into Big Bob's Gun Shop and Ice Cream Parlor. Little Bob came out from the stockroom where he'd been taking an inventory.

"Hi Mace. Hey, I heard my robber was out on bail."

"Hi Little Bob. Yes, that's true. That's how it works these days. I'm keeping an eye on him. It turns out he's really a paper tiger, so you don't need to worry."

"What about my Glock?"

"It's in the evidence locker until the trial. Sorry about that. How are you doing?"

"Busier than ever, deputy. I have to order more stock every week now. People are pretty anxious lately. That's really good for business."

"That's good. And I'm sure you're following protocol and getting your background checks before you turn over any firearms, right?"

"Wouldn't have it any other way, deputy." Bob was starting to feel a bit nervous.

"I know, Little Bob. I need some information. Have you sold any 30-30s in the past couple of months?"

"Yep, two of them. The first was to a guy named Martin out on County Road 4. He hunts deer and also uses it to shoot rattlers he encounters on the trails. He picked up a Hornady American Whitetail as a replacement for one he dropped into a ravine and broke."

"And the other?"

"That one went to Ray T., the Ride-Share driver. He wanted one for personal defense."

"But a 30-30 is a hunting rifle."

"I told him that. He should have bought a shotgun. But he was dead set on having a rifle. He popped for a beautiful Winchester, and you know what he did?"

"What?"

"He sawed off the back of the stock for some reason. I told him that was a nutso move and a terrible thing to do to such a beautiful firearm and would hurt the accuracy. But like I said, his mind was set, and nothing would stop him."

Mace was intrigued by what he was hearing. "Anything else?"

"Not that I can recall. Oh, he did buy a lot of ammo. Wiped out my supply of 30-30 for a while. You want a copy of the paperwork?"

"Sure, Little Bob. That would be helpful."

Nothing in the background check indicated that Ray T. had been in trouble or had mental health issues. Mace thought of how the Ride-Share driver often wore a long parka on cool days. Could he conceal the shortened rifle in that? Probably.

"Okay, Little Bob. I'll be going. Thanks for your help."

"Don't mention it. You want an ice cream for the road?"

"Sure. How about a scoop of coffee?"

"You got it."

34

CHAD, MASON, AND ONE MORE GO FISHING

A tinny sounding horn blasted out front. "So long, Dixie. Chad is here."

"Okay, bye hon. Have fun. I'll be late getting home with Tiffany, so take your time."

Mason emerged from the house with rods, waders, boots, and a thermos in hand.

"Morning Chad. I brought coffee if you want some."

"Thanks Mason. I have a cup, but I may take you up on that later. Should I go back to where you parked the last time?"

"Nope. I'll show you. There's another dirt road that will get us upstream without all the slogging."

"Dirt road" turned out to be a bit grandiose a title for the ruts, potholes, and rocks they bumped over. Chad regretted driving the little Citroen as he wasn't sure they'd make it, but Mason said it would be no problem, that the rough part was short. The 2CV was light and did have surprisingly adequate ground clearance for such a tiny car, so they cleared the bumpy patch without a problem.

Chad reached into the backseat and came up with a bag of

donuts upon reaching Murietta Creek. "Breakfast of champions, huh?"

Mason laughed and took one as they got into waders and boots.

"We still have to walk upstream a piece from here."

"How far is it?"

"About 200 yards farther."

Chad stared up the narrow, rocky stream overhung with branches and thought about stumbling that far in his rubber boots. "Jesus, can't trout swim downstream?"

Mason chuckled at that. "There are a couple of funny shaped boulders in the creek up that way. They like to hide just below them and wait for their lunch to float down to them. They're smart but lazy. Ready to go?"

"Yep. Let's do it."

Mason led the way. He hadn't mentioned the steep grade they had to walk up through the creek. Partway up, Chad was huffing and puffing.

"You OK there, buddy?"

Chad stopped to take a few breaths. "Yeah, I'm OK. I can't die here. There wouldn't be any way to recover my body."

"True enough. Ignore the skeleton on the side of the creek. It's just some fisherman who hadn't figured that part out."

"Ha, ha."

They finally arrived at the spot Mason had described with two oddly shaped rocks in the middle of the creek. One looked like a miniature Half Dome, the famous rock in Yosemite. The water cascaded over the top and dropped a few inches past the flat side of the rock.

The other was formed with a flat top and slide-like back. If the trout positioned themselves well, bugs floating downstream would simply drop into their mouths. It was like Door Dash for fish.

They watched to see what was floating down before

choosing their flies. Chad noticed at least two fish jumping for bugs behind one of the rocks. The water behind Half Dome was churning so madly, he couldn't see what if anything was there.

They both dropped in their flies and within seconds Chad had a fish on. He brought it in by pulling the rod sideways, as Mason had instructed him their first time out. Chad kept the writhing fish in the water as he pulled the hook from its mouth with a set of small pliers. He gently released it back into the creek, and it swam for safer regions.

"That was a nice one. I'm glad you released him. Maybe I'll get him when he is old and fat."

"He seemed hefty already. I may have to bring one back just to prove to Tiffany that we didn't spend the day at a strip club."

"You ever go to those joints?"

"Nope. You?"

"Not unless I have a hazmat suit on. I had to do a furnace installation at one in Redlands once. Trust me, you never want to see what a strip club looks like with all the lights on."

"That bad, huh?"

"Worse. Hey, you catch that Philly/Atlanta game on Monday?"

"Yeah, what a shit show that was."

"Caulfield was throwing like a third grader."

"Sad. Is there any of that coffee left?"

The conversation went on, but very quietly. They brought in three more trout before 10 am. As Mason had predicted, there were no psycho bass up here to gum up the works.

It was a beautiful Fall day. The air was crisp but not freezing, no wind, and only a couple of wispy clouds floating by. The leaves had just started to turn, and the trees shimmered with an orange and red glow. The guys fishing below didn't notice that one of the networks of leaves and bark in the canopy overhead glowed more intensely than the others. Had one of them looked up, they would have noticed the branches seemed to be flowing in time with the creek, and the leaves on them were going in and out of focus. One of the trees seemed to bend over and bloat.

Had they noticed that unusual visual, they may not have been quite so shocked when the ghostly figure of a man appeared, sitting on one of the oddly shaped rocks with its feet and lower legs dangling in the water. Trout jumped up and swam downstream in what seemed to be a panic. The apparition was speaking, or at least trying to.

Chad dropped the thermos and cup, and Mason tripped over the rod that was perched in the gravel as Chad exclaimed, "What the hell is that?"

Mason looked closely at the grey shimmering shape. The mouth was moving as though forming words, but no sound was coming out. He thought for a moment that it looked something like Lolita's dead husband, Marvin.

Chad answered his own question. "It's a ghost! A real ghost!" He called out to the apparition. "Are you Joaquin Murrieta? Three Fingered Jack? Who are you? Or rather, who *were* you?"

Mason was certain they'd both lost their minds. *What was in those donuts?*

"The water..." The apparition was becoming more solid and managed to get those words out.

"Yes, you're in the water. Did you drown?" Chad was trying to speak to the ghost the way he had seen people do in movies.

"The water. It's the water." Mason thought of the old Olympia beer logo. His dad used to buy that stuff by the case. The figure on the rock was really starting to look like Marvin.

"Lolita was telling the truth," Mason said. "Either she isn't nuts, or I am, or we all are. Holy smokes."

Chad had no idea what Mason meant by that. He turned back to the ghost, who was now casually leaning back on one arm. He seemed to be wearing some kind of tweed blazer and flannel slacks. He lifted one of his wet feet onto the rock, revealing a desert boot. Mason thought that was a bad choice for wading in the creek.

"It's the water."

"What about the water?" Chad was the lead inquisitor in their chat with Marvin.

"Drugs."

"Drugs? Are you saying there are drugs in the water?" Chad stepped back on the beach. Mason followed suit. "What kind of drugs?"

Marvin was now fully present. "The recreational variety, nitwit. That's why the bass down in the river have been acting out. Have it tested."

Chad turned to Mason. "You know what he's talking about?"

"Maybe." Chad then used a stage whisper. "We need to get out of here right now."

"Why?"

"He is right," Marvin roared, "GO!" The sudden 120 decibel command shook the leaves and freaked the fishermen out.

Mason grabbed his rod. The pair turned to leave when the ghost said, "Chad."

They stopped and faced him. "Yes?"

"You forgot your fishing rod."

Chad looked at the rod on the gravel. "Oh, you're right. Thanks." He picked it up with the thermos and cup.

"GO NOW!"

They started slogging down Murrieta Creek faster than they had walked up. Part way down, Mason asked, "How'd he know your name?"

"I've no idea."

"Jesus."

"Yep."

Chad continued to ponder what the deal was with the water. Focusing on that enabled him to compartmentalize the fact that he had just seen and had a conversation with a ghost. He couldn't fully process that information quite yet.

Mason, on the other hand, was quietly freaking out about it. He clearly understood the impact, but didn't know what to do about it. He knew it was Marvin, or at least a shade of Marvin. That was at least sort of familiar. He hadn't really known him in life, but he'd been to his home a few times to extend the life of their ancient furnace. Marvin had steadfastly refused to replace the unit as he should have, until he couldn't bear listening to Lolita whine about being cold all the time. Why would such a person, a dead person, spend energy, if that's what it was, to warn them about drugs in the water? And he had seen a ghost. A ghost! He'd always believed that reports of such things were total B.S. Now he believed something else, but he wasn't sure what that was. None of this fit his view of the world. That feeling began with fear, but as so often happens, quickly evolved into anger.

After a long and distracted tromp down the creek, they made it back to the Citroen. By then, Mason was pretty agitated. "Why'd that S.O.B. Marvin have to come back from the dead to screw with *our* heads? I could have lived my whole life without this and died happy. I do NOT want to be one of those weirdos that's all into paranormal crap. That's not who I am. I don't need this right now."

"I think he chose us because we have been wading in the water," Chad suggested. "He told us to test it. How do we do that? Get a swimming pool or aquarium test kit?"

A little earthbound technical problem solving broke the spell and helped Mason calm down about seeing a real apparition. "I don't think that would help. Those just test for things like chlorine, pH, and hardness. Aquarium kits are similar but more sensitive. We might want to check in with the County

Water Reclamation guys. They might already be checking the water for drugs. I read an article in The Acorn Times that they were testing wastewater for coronavirus during the pandemic. But why do I say we want the water tested for drugs? I can't explain we're on a mission from a ghost."

"Do you know anyone with the water bureau?"

Mason shook his head. "Nope. Not really. But I'll bet Chief Murphy at the firehouse does. It's called the Big Squirrel Fire Department, but it's really run by the county with some of their money coming from Groverton and Big Squirrel, just like the sheriff's office. They do more than put out fires. They deal with hazardous waste spills and check businesses for chemical storage problems, things like that. I'll bet they work with the water people sometimes."

"Sounds likely. Do you know him very well?"

"Her. Yes, really well. I do a lot of work there. Another tight-wad. But she's good people. I trust her."

"What about Deputy Mace? I'm sure he deals with drugs in his line of work."

"One mention of Marvin the ghost and he'll have us both committed. We should stick with Tenaya for now. That's Chief Murphy's first name."

"Okay," Chad said. "You know these people. I'll follow your lead. There's a better chance we'll be believed if we both report it together."

"That's the plan then. Let's get out of these waders and head to the firehouse."

"Any donuts left?"

Mason checked the bag on the dashboard. "Hell yeah! You scored, man. Let's eat 'em on the road. I want to put a few miles between me and Murrieta Creek. Marvin, can you believe that?"

35

RAY T. DID NOT GET A FIVE STAR RATING

"Where's the rifle, Ray?"

"Out in my SUV. You want me to go get it?"

"No, Ray. You stay put and don't move. Where exactly?"

"Under the dash. You pull a latch in the middle to release it."

"Loaded?"

"Of course."

"Wait here." Mace went from Ray T's front porch over to the SUV with the small Ride-Share logo in the lower right side of the windshield. He kept an eye on Ray T. as he opened the passenger door, found the latch, and removed the weapon. "You have any more guns around here?"

"Nope. That's it. So, what's wrong anyway?"

Mace removed the shells from the rifle. They matched the 30-30 casings he'd picked up on Stargazer's farm. "Why did you carry a loaded gun in the SUV, Ray T.?"

"Self-defense, Mace. There's been a lot of crazy stuff going on around here lately. I don't know every one of my passengers."

"Some of that crazy stuff includes you shooting up a weathervane on Stargazer's barn. You got anything to say about that?"

Raymond "the Teetotaler" Maxwell wanted to lie and say he didn't know anything about that, but something in the way Mason stared at him caused him to realize the jig was up. There was no way he could talk his way out of this.

"Those hippies piss me off. They just slouch around that farm and do some kind of weird pagan circle jerk. They don't do any real work, those lazy, dirtbag hippies. Get a job! Am I right, Mace? And when that damned Stargazer wants to go drinking with his hippie buds, he uses the app to get me to drive him. Where do they get their money?"

"They're retired, Ray. They have their savings and social security. Get back to telling me about shooting at the barn."

"Thought my warning shots might help 'em decide there are other places to lie around. I was hoping they'd just pack it in and move out. I didn't mean any harm."

"Not only did you break the law, what you did was dangerous. You could have killed somebody. By the way, it is also a crime to keep a loaded weapon in the driver's compartment of a vehicle. I plan to charge you with both. I suggest you cooperate as I am asking you these questions. I'm going to read your rights now, and then I want to know what was up with the horse's head, got it?"

"Yeah, go ahead." Ray T. was looking more pissed off than scared as Mace read him his rights, but he was plenty scared inside. He'd been in trouble a few years back, did some time. He knew that was going to come out pretty soon. He thought about demanding an attorney but still thought he might be able to get off on his own. That wasn't a smart move.

"So, those are your rights. Any questions? Nope, good, moving on. Tell me about the head in the driveway."

"That was something I'd seen in The Godfather. Remember when the movie producer finds a bloody head in his bed after chasing off Tom? Anyhow, I was giving that real estate gal, Penney, a lift back from The Branding Iron and complaining about these hippies. She informed me of what the property was worth and told me if they ever decided to sell, she would get me a deal on it before the listing went public. I could flip it and make a fortune on it. I got to thinking about it, and I figured maybe I could scare them enough that they'd want to leave Desdemona County for good. When I passed Miller's Feed & Seed and saw the horse statue out front, I knew what to do. I already had some red paint at home. The rest is history. Are they planning to move?"

"Congratulations, Ray. That is one of the top three dumbest criminal plots I have ever heard. And it is indeed criminal. What were you thinking? I'll be charging you for that one too. Turn around and place your hands behind your back. We're going to Groverton, and I'll be doing the driving this time."

Mace helped the freshly handcuffed Ray get in the back of his SUV and then shut the door. As he made his way to open the driver's door after ensuring Ray's front door was locked, he muttered, "What a colossal moron." He shut the dividing panel between the front and rear seats and called Tenaya. He explained what had been going on, and what kind of help he needed.

Down at the firehouse, Chief Murphy asked Firefighter Jimmy "Wheezer" Collins to come to her office. He figured he was in some kind of trouble, so he entered contritely.

"I'm here, Chief. How are you?"

"Fine, Jimmy. Listen, I have a special assignment for you. I just got off the phone with Deputy Mace over in Groverton. He's on his way over here right now. He's looking for a tempo-rary assistant, and I couldn't think of anyone better than you. I told him I'd lend you to his department for a couple of weeks as long as he made sure you weren't going to get into any heavy cop action. Are you up for it?"

"Cool! Yes, Chief. Does this mean I'll get a to crack a couple of skulls?"

"It absolutely does NOT mean you will crack anybody's skull. You're to stay out of any violent situations, and Deputy Mace knows that. Otherwise, you just do whatever he tells you to. Understood?"

"Yes, ma'am." Jimmy looked down dejectedly and kicked his feet around like a little kid.

"The job involves watching the jail and guarding prisoners when he is out. You'll also answer the phone and run any errands he needs done. He'll tell you the rest when he picks you up. Okay?"

"Yes, ma'am. I'm looking forward to it, and I'll make you proud. Thanks for the opportunity."

"You've earned it, Jimmy. Go grab your civvies and gear. You should continue to wear your uniform while you're working there."

"Will do." Jimmy headed upstairs to gather his stuff.

Mace arrived a short time later and got out of the SUV. He left Ray in the backseat. Tenaya met him at the garage entrance.

"Hi Mace. What did *he* do, overcharge a fare?" She pointed to Ray in the vehicle.

"Remember the horse's head that was missing from Millers Feed & Seed? He left it out at Stargazer's farm covered in red paint to look like blood. He was trying to the scare those old folks into selling the place. He also took a couple of shots at their barn. I'm trying to decide whether to charge him with vandalism, illegally discharging a weapon, trespass, theft, or domestic terrorism. I wish I could just book him for being an asshole."

"Well, I have some good news that should cheer you up. One of our finest has volunteered to help you out for a couple of weeks. His name is Jimmy Collins, but everyone calls him 'Wheezer.'"

"Great!" Mace said. "Why do you call him Wheezer?"

"He sounds like a diesel locomotive when he climbs ladders. Plus, he snores. Poor kid has a mild case of asthma."

"But he still passes the physicals?"

"He has a lot of heart. He won't allow himself to fail. You'll like him."

"I can't thank you enough. I sure do hope we'll find a way to return the favor."

"Don't worry, Mace. I won't forget. Consider yourself indebted."

Wheezer came down with his gear, ready to go. Tenaya did the introductions. Wheezer said, "Chief, I do have a question. What if there's a big fire?"

"Good question, Jimmy. Deputy Mace agreed that if we needed you, he would bring you out to the scene. He usually comes out anyway, as you know."

Wheezer seemed satisfied and went to drop his stuff in Mace's trunk. "Whoa, who's that dude in the back?"

"That's a prisoner, Jimmy. We're going to take him to the jail in Groverton. Then you're going to keep an eye on him," Mace replied.

"Cool! I won't let him go, you can be sure of that!"

"Remember, Jimmy, no shenanigans," the chief warned. "You aren't getting deputized. You're admin only."

"I'll remember."

"I'll bring him up to speed on the procedures on the way over," Mace said.

"I trust you. I need him back in one piece. He's one of the good ones."

As Mace was preparing to head out, the Citroen drove right up to the garage and stopped in front of the open bay door.

"Hey, you guys can't park there. Move it onto the street." Chief Tenaya didn't like anyone blocking her truck. They backed out, parked, and ran back up to the firehouse.

"We gotta talk, Chief. Can we go somewhere private?" Mason was out of breath.

"Unless you two are here to report a fire, you look like I might want a witness or two for our conversation. Whatever you have to say to me, you can say to Mace too."

Tenaya pointed at Chad. "I suppose you're Tiffany's husband. She said you were nice. What are you doing hanging around with this guy?" She motioned to Mason and smiled.

"Oh, we're both pretty nice," Chad replied. "We aren't here to report a fire, but it is important and urgent."

Tenaya turned to Mason. "Why don't *you* tell us what is going on?"

Mason and Chad looked at Deputy Mace, then at each other. They both shrugged to say, "We don't have much choice."

"So, there's a problem with the water," Mace began. "We don't know how big a problem it is, but it might be a lot. We need to get some tests run."

"Whoa there, Mason. Slow down. What water are we talking about?"

"In the river. The Santa Quiteria River. We fished there, near the confluence of Murrieta Creek, and the bass were going nuts. They were stealing our catch from each other and biting one another."

"For that you came here?" Chief Murphy looked both skeptical and perturbed. She enjoyed the goofy people in the community but did not like her work time wasted.

Chad piped up, "There's more. A lot more."

"Okay, why don't you tell it?"

Chad looked uncomfortably at Mason, who shrugged and said, "Go ahead. That's why we're here."

"So, we drove up along above the river Murrieta Creek. When we reached the end of the dirt trail, we walked on about 200 yards more."

Chad went on to share the entire tale and did a pretty fair

job reporting it as it happened, including that they were warned about the drugs by Marvin the ghost.

Mason added that he had an experience with unusually aggressive bass before ever fishing with Chad.

The tough part for Tenaya was that it happened to be unbelievable. "Have you two been hanging around with the widow Lolita? You're telling me you were warned about the water by her dead husband? Listen guys, why don't you go to the café and grab some hot coffee? I've seen hypothermia cause delusions like this. You walked quite a way in the water. Maybe you just need to warm up."

"I don't think we would both suffer the same delusion," Mason pointed out. "How likely is that?"

"At least as likely as the ghost sitting on the rock in Murrieta Creek." Tenaya was now losing patience. "Look guys, I don't know why you came to me with this. What do you want me to do?"

"We thought maybe you knew somebody at the water reclamation department and could convince them to test the water for drugs." Mason felt he was pretty far out on a limb with his reputation. He began to regret starting this scene.

"You not only want me to accept that a ghost warned you about drugs in the water, but you also want me to bother people in another department with your story and request? I'm sorry, gentlemen. Unless you have a more rational explanation, I think we're done here."

Deputy Mace, who had been leaning in and listening intently, now spoke up. "Chief, do you mind if I ask a couple of questions? Mason, how were the trout acting up on the creek?"

"Pretty normal. Lazy and hungry."

"No signs of aggression, like the bass?"

"Nope, they were just acting like trout, at least until the ghost showed up."

"Any bass around today?"

"Nope, they don't go as far up the creek as the trout do."

"So, all the unusual fish behavior was only in the river. Interesting. Chad, what did Marvin look like?" Chad described him as thin or maybe even gaunt, tall, bookish, well dressed except for dripping wet desert boots, and translucent. His description of facial features matched up with those of the Marvin that Mace remembered.

"And what kind of drugs was he warning you about?"

"He said recreational when I asked him that."

"Any specifics, marijuana, cocaine?"

"No, he didn't get into details. He told us that and then told us to leave, which we did."

"Well, we'll have to narrow the list of possible types down. When you test for drugs, you have to know which ones you are looking for. The tests are specific, only one type for each kind. We can't ask the water department to run tests for everything. There are too many kinds. Right, Chief?"

"You'd know more about drug tests than me, Mace."

"You guys should take Chief Murphy's advice and go get warmed up. Here's my card. Call me if you think of anything else."

Mason asked, "What are you going to do?"

"I have a few ideas. Let me work on it. I'll contact you if I need anything. Thanks for reporting the incident and let me know if anything else happens."

"Our pleasure, deputy." Mason turned to Chad. "Let's go to Mother's. I know you like that Denver Sandwich she makes."

The fishermen got in the Citroen and headed off for the café, leaving a black pall of exhaust behind for the firefighters and deputy to choke on. When it cleared and the coughing stopped, Tenaya asked Mace, "You aren't taking what they said seriously, are you? I'd say any drugs are most likely to be found inside them, not the river."

"I hear ya', Tenaya. I didn't always pay attention to my dad, but he did teach me a couple of useful things about police work. One was, "Never automatically dismiss a lead just because it sounds ridiculous. The world is a ridiculous place."

"Okay, so like you said, you'd need to know what drugs to test for. How are you going to decide that?"

"Around here, the most likely culprits are opioids and methamphetamines. I think we could start with those two and go from there."

"Oh man, Mace, it sounds like you're really going to follow up on this."

"I've heard a lot about drugs leaching into the water supply. That's one of the reasons why we have a Turn in Your Drugs Day once a year. But most folks still flush them down the toilet. Some more goes that way when they urinate. If it's enough to affect the fish, could it be enough to affect people? I don't know, but it would sure explain some of the wacko behavior we've seen around here lately."

"Well, if you're going to accept a ghost as an informant, maybe you better add an annual séance day to your calendar too. Good luck, Mace. Jimmy, stay away from the ghosts, OK?"

"Yes ma'am. Will do." The young firefighter was grinning from ear to ear. Inside his head, Wheezer was stoked and silently thinking, "Cool! I'm gonna do some ghostbusting!" He and Mace jumped in the SUV and headed for the jail. Ray T. spoke up from the backseat. "What took so long? I don't want to miss lunch."

Mace and Wheezer laughed up front. Mace closed the acrylic partition and ignored the handcuffed prisoner in the back. It looked like Desdemona County would have to live without Ride-Share service again.

Mace filled Wheezer in on some of the needs he had. Wheezer was amenable to helping with everything and told Mace it would be a nice change of pace. He was still sorry he wouldn't get to bust heads though. Mace told him that wasn't the way they conducted police work in Desdemona County. He also shared some very good and even some personal reasons as to why that was.

Wheezer said he was sure he could watch their prisoner when Mace mentioned he might need to go out for a while.

After they got Ray T. settled in and fed a lunch delivered from Mother's, Mace ensured Wheezer knew what was expected and how to contact him at once if there were any problems.

Wheezer was a quick study. The Deputy felt confident enough to go.

Mace got back in the SUV to drive back to Big Squirrel. He had a certain someone he wanted to ask out for a hike and picnic, and he wanted to do it in person before she had to go to work. He could call the county water people on the way.

36

DINNER CONVERSATION

The fishermen drove over to Chad's place to commiserate a bit more about the events of the day. Chad turned on college football, and they used alternately yelling and cheering at the TV and downing beer with chips as a tonic to soothe their ghost-rattled nerves.

Seeing and hearing Marvin had been a heck of a shock. They didn't know it, but letting their subconscious minds do the processing was the best course of action for both of them. They'd done what they could do with the information and needed to wait while the creaky wheels of bureaucracy rolled along and solved the riddle. Or not. Maybe they were nuts, as Chief Murphy appeared to think.

When the game was over, Cal had been defeated by three points, one lousy field goal. Mason, who had a little money riding on them, was dejected. Chad, a UCLA grad was elated even though the winning team was the Oregon Ducks, not his alma mater. The guys began to realize that they'd pounded more than the usual number of beers for either of them.

"Mason, I don't know about you, but I don't think I'm in any shape to drive you home. If you are, you're welcome to take the

Snail. Tiffany can run me to your place to retrieve it in the morning. Or maybe you can get a Ride-Share."

"Nah, there's a DUI with my name on it, and I can't afford it. And I don't think Ride-Share is going to be available for a while. I'm pretty sure I saw Ray T. locked in the back of Mace's cruiser when we were leaving the firehouse. He's the only Ride-Share driver up this way. I'll call Dixie. She can take me home from here after they get back from Temecula."

"Good call. Hey, I've got four prime ribeyes in the fridge. Why don't you two stay for dinner?"

"It has always been my policy to never turn down red meat, especially if it's of the free variety. I'll check with Dixie, but I bet she'll feel the same way. That girl never met a steak she didn't like."

"Great, I'll get my secret rub on them while you make your call. Tell Tiffany I caught a marlin."

"Ha will do. Are we going to tell them about what happened up the creek today?"

"Let's figure that out before they get here. That should give us just enough time to weigh the options and determine if they can have us committed."

Chad applied the rub on the steaks, chopped some broccoli, and started chopping veggies and tuna for a salad. Mason made it into the kitchen. "As predicted, she said she'd love to stay for dinner. The way she said it made me realize that they definitely did some wine tasting, which is what Dixie calls knockin' 'em back."

"You can be sure Tif is under the legal limit, at least for now. She wouldn't risk that BMW for anything. Well, then maybe you'll both end spending the night. We have two spare rooms, so it's no prob Bob. You guys can take your pick. I can get you back in time for church tomorrow, so don't worry." The last was said with a smile.

"Heh, yeah, so we were in my church this morning. Maybe that's why we were seeing ghosts."

"You mean you saw more than one?"

"Nah, just Marvin. He was a lot all by himself. By the way, we now need to decide if we're going to tell the girls about him."

"I was chewing that over while chopping broccoli." They both sang a few lines of "Chopping Broccoli," the Dana Carvey song from Saturday Night Live, and laughed hysterically. "Seriously, it looks like Mace may be planning to follow up on the water thing. That means it's going to get out sooner or later. I'd rather Tif heard it from me than somebody else. I say we tell them tonight."

"Excellent reasoning there, Ace. I'm in. You can start."

"Great, thanks."

They went over it again to make sure they had it straight after the beers.

A few minutes later, the BMW rolled into the driveway.

"So, Tif," Dixie said, "Mason sounded like he was already pretty well lubed when he called. I'm not certain what we're going to walk into."

"I'm not worried. Knowing Chad, they probably watched college football and had a few belts. And you are at least a point or two over the legal limit, so you'll just fit right in. It sounds like I'll have some catching up to do. Why don't you two stay over tonight? We have plenty of room and it would be fun."

"Hell yeah, Tif. Then I don't have to clean up all the crap I left back at our house. No, really, this has been a great day, and I'd love to keep it going. Thanks so much. We can cook fish. Mason told me Chad caught a marlin because he thinks I'm an idiot."

"Maybe we'll call for a pizza. If Chad caught any fish today, you could bet it was in the supermarket, and there is no way he went there."

The girls walked into the kitchen, laughing arm-in-arm. Tiffany gave Chad a smooch on her way to open the chardonnay they brought. Dixie turned to Mason and asked, "So, did ya' miss me, big boy?"

"Yep, but my aim is improving."

"Ha, you only get to tell dad jokes if you have kids, Mason. That's the law. Come over here and we'll get started on making some." She gave him a bigger smooch than Chad had received.

"How was Temecula?"

"It was awesome and expensive. For you." Chad noticed they both were holding a lot of shopping bags. A lot.

"Ah. Great."

Tiffany dropped the bags and poured wine for Dixie and herself as Chad continued with food prep. She replaced the guys' empty cans with frosty mugs, each with a perfect head. For a physical therapist, she really knew how to pour. "What's cooking, Chef?"

"We'll be starting with a Niçoise salad followed by beautiful ribeyes, roasted broccoli, and sautéed mushrooms."

"That's it? What's for dessert?"

"White Russians."

Tiffany looked at Dixie. "You two will definitely be spending the night."

"But I haven't anything to wear. I'll have to sleep in the nude." She was laughing as she looked at Chad to see if he'd blush.

Tiffany replied, "I have some nice, baggy flannel PJs I can lend you. So only Mason will be running around nude. I'll turn the heat on."

Chad asked, "How do you like your steak, Dixie?"

"Still mooing."

"My kind of girl. Mason?"

"Same. What can I help with?"

"See if Tif can find you something to wear to bed. I don't

want to bump into you naked, running to the bathroom in the middle of the night."

"How about a board game after dinner?" Tiffany suggested. Everyone agreed it sounded like a fun idea.

"How was the fishing on Murrieta today, hun'?"

"It was an interesting morning, Dixie. Chad's going to share our experiences with everyone over dinner."

Chad glared at Mason and started violently slicing mushrooms. "Tiffany, would you mind tossing some coals and wood in the grill and firing it up?"

"On it. Be right back."

"One little factoid I can share now is we saw the Ride-Share driver locked up in the back of the deputy's cop cruiser."

Dixie looked up. "Really? First, he breaks his leg, now he's murdered someone. That boy is a bucket of bad luck. What was the rap?"

"No idea."

Mason weighed in. "We don't know, Dixie. We didn't notice him until we were leaving."

"Leaving where? Were you in jail too?"

"Long story. We'll explain that during dinner. I can't walk and chew gum, so cooking takes all my efforts of concentration."

"I can't wait to hear this one. Well, we went to La Lavasse Vineyards for a little wine tasting. They serve a lovely brunch there on weekends. Mason, I ran into Judy and Daryl there. She said they might need a new furnace, so give them a ring, okay? Then we went shopping after brunch. They have more cute shops there since the pandemic ended. Come to think of it, I do have something to sleep in. It's in one of my bags, but I don't think Tif would like me parading around in front of Chad in it." Dixie giggled. "I even found you something, Mason."

"Really?"

She pulled out a carved, garishly painted wooden sign

depicting a man fishing and bringing in a jumping trout. It was inscribed with the words, "World's Best Fisherman."

"What do you think?"

"Ah, it's great, honey. I'll put it up over the mantle. Thanks." He gave Dixie a kiss, turned around to Chad and rolled his eyes while shaking his head "no."

Chad stifled a laugh and looked down at his work as Tiffany came back in. "It's fired up and will be ready to go in ten minutes. I brought some oak chips to soak. Those add a lot of nice smoke, Dixie."

Chad was grateful for the diversion. "Super, thanks, Tif." He took the finished salad out in a bowl that he placed on the table with a tall pepper mill.

Tiffany asked Dixie, "Did you give it to him?"

"Yes."

"What did he think?"

"He loved it! Didn't you, Mason?"

"Absolutely! It's very well done. "

"I saw it and thought it would bring you good luck."

Mason thought it would be lucky if she used it for target practice, but he smiled and nodded, the key to their successful marriage.

Finally, with the steaks done, dinner was on and so was the conversation about the fishing trip.

Tiffany settled in with another glass of chardonnay. "Okay, Chad. Mason said you were going to tell us about fishing today."

"Yeah, well, Mason knows those waters so much better than I do. Mason, maybe you should start."

"Okay, but only because I don't want to piss off the chef. These steaks are amazing!" Everyone agreed, and they toasted Chad. "So, today we went a ways up Murrieta Creek."

"Isn't that where you went the first time?" Tiffany was starting to get the lay of the land.

"We got close to it but spent that time fishing the Santa Quiteria River. That's where the bass went nuts on Chad here."

"Got it."

Mason continued on about the march up the creek to his remote fishing hole. He then turned to Chad and said, "So now that you know where we went, Chad can tell you what happened there."

"Great. Thanks Mason." Chad described the scene with Marvin's ghost and what he had said about the water.

"We drove into town to talk to Chief Murphy about asking the county to test the water. She thought we were nuts. But Mace was there, and he seemed much more open to the idea."

"Maybe you should follow up with him and see if he contacted the county." Tiffany had enough to drink to be open to the idea that Lolita's dead husband would show up to warn them about the water while they were trying to fish.

Dixie was a little more skeptical, but not as much as the fire chief had been. "Sounds like a crock to me. Are you two pulling our legs? I am not going to get suckered into another of your pranks, Mason."

"Cross my heart and hope the Dodgers lose if we aren't telling the truth, hun'. Listen, I know how weird it all sounds, but it happened and all we can do is tell it like it is."

"I've heard of drugs getting into the water supply. There are commercials telling us not to flush them down the toilet sometimes. But I'll bet people still do it."

Dixie was chuckling a bit. "Was Marvin naked? I heard he used to wander around their house naked with the shutters opened all the time."

"No, Dixie, he wasn't naked. He was pretty well dressed, in fact, which was odd for someone sitting in the middle of a creek. Looked like an English college professor."

"How would you know anything about professors in England, Mason?"

"I've seen them in movies. Anyway, he wasn't naked. Are you getting lathered up about the ghost? I don't think he's your type, Dixie."

"You know as much about my type as you do about professors, dear."

Chad jumped back in. "Maybe I'll give Deputy Mace a call on Monday. See where we're at."

"I think that's a great idea, Chad. Okay, enough ghost talk. I'm not worried. We aren't drinking water anyway, right? Who wants to play a game?"

Dixie answered first. "How about Clue? It seems appropriate."

"Perfect! I'll go get it."

37

MIKE MACE ASKS FOR A SECOND DATE

"Hello, this is Deputy Mace calling for Steven Hewitt." Mace had called the contact at the county water department Tenaya gave him with reservations. She said he was the most likely to know about water testing."

"This is Hewitt."

"Hi Mr. Hewitt. Deputy Mace here. Would you mind helping me out with a couple of questions about the drinking water?"

"Of course, deputy. I'm happy to help. We don't get many calls here, so I really am happy." Hewitt took pride in the work done by their department and felt everyone just took it for granted.

"Wonderful. Thanks. First of all, do you currently test the water for opioids or methamphetamines?"

"No. I know we probably should given the high use in rural areas like Desdemona County. But we haven't had any requests from your department yet. Even if we found it, it would likely be trace amounts, unlikely to cause any harm. It would also cost a fortune to remove, and you know how the supervisors are."

"I sure do. Is there any chance you could run some tests?"

"Yeah, we can do that, especially with a law enforcement request. I have a form for you to fill out. You haven't had anyone confessing to trying to spike the water supply, have you?"

"No, no, nothing like that. We just have heard from a couple of concerned citizens, so I thought I'd follow up, mainly to put their minds at ease. In addition to the treatment facility, I am hoping you might be able to take samples from the Santa Quiteria, up near Murrieta Creek."

"Sure, but I can tell you now that water is snow and spring fed from our own mountains. It's so pure we wouldn't have to treat it at all if it weren't for animals spreading giardia or cryptosporidium. We have another treatment facility upstream just below Grey Lock that handles all the water that's used by the unincorporated areas before it flows down our way. It does a great job."

"I have no doubt. So, how long do the tests take?"

"Those are very specific tests. I'll have to order the test kits, which will take a week or so, and then we'll get results rapidly. I don't get the sense you are dealing with an emergency."

"Right. That should be fine. I really appreciate your help."

"Anything for our boys in blue."

"Our uniforms are green, but thanks. Please email me the form and I'll get it right back to you."

"I'll call you when we get the results, deputy. Have a safe day out there!"

"Thank you, Mr. Hewitt. You too. Bye."

Mace was in a good mood. With that out of the way, he was free to spend a little time with Amber. He thought about using his lights and siren but decided to just goose the accelerator a bit. She wouldn't have to be to work until five, but he'd already cut into the afternoon a bit.

The plan was to ask her on a hike and picnic on one of their days off. He made it to Big Squirrel in record time and turned onto her street. He could feel his heart pounding and the breaths getting a little shorter. "Calm down. You're going to give yourself a heart attack before you can ask her."

All his nervousness subsided when she opened the door, squealed, and jumped into his arms. "I'm so happy you're here! Come on in."

She led him by the hand into her living room and swept an arm around. "Welcome to my McMansion, Mike! Isn't it grand?" Amber laughed and smiled. He thought it was the prettiest smile he'd ever seen. "Have a seat. Can I get you a drink?"

"No, I'm fine. And I like your place."

"No? Okay. So, what brings you here in the middle of the day, officer?"

The nerves came back, but only a little. "I wanted to see if you might like to go on a hike and have a picnic with me next Monday. There's a beautiful spot just a couple of miles up the trail I want to show you."

"I'd love to! I like hiking and never have anyone to go with."

"Great, can I pick you up around nine?"

Amber stood and pulled his hand to stand. "You can pick me up anytime you'd like, Mike. Let me show your around the place. There's something I'd like to show you too." Amber kissed him deep and hard, and he kissed her back.

She led, he followed, and they disappeared into the back of the one-bedroom house.

Much later, a tired but beaming Amber looked at Mace in her big brass bed and said, "I've got to get dressed for work. I don't want to be late."

"Aw, stay just a little bit longer. Is Slim going to dock your pay?"

"Ha. No, much worse. He'll have a nervous breakdown

thinking he might have to cover my shift himself. You don't want to see him that way. It's really sad."

His new girlfriend ("girlfriend!") stood up. As he gazed upon her, Mace thought she was the most beautiful thing he had ever seen, and he was the luckiest man on the planet. He was afraid to say anything and ruin it.

Amber smiled down at him for a moment. "You know, Mace, you look great out of uniform. Even better than in my fantasies." She turned to her dresser and Mace checked her mirror to make sure he wasn't blushing. Amber grabbed a few things from there and the closet and headed into the bathroom.

Mike Mace was relaxed enough that he could have fallen asleep in her sheets, but he shook it off. He looked around the room from her bed. It was small and old, but she'd done a great job fixing it up with a couple of antiques and white lace curtains. He thought it looked sweet, just like her. The only thing that seemed out of place was his black gun belt, wrapped around a spindle on a white chair by the dresser. He got up to gather his stuff. Everything he'd worn in was strewn around the floor where Amber had dropped it. Her clothes were mixed and mingled with his. He chuckled at the memory of that and smiled. *Don't screw this up, smart guy.* The boy was on cloud nine and rising.

Amber emerged ready for work just as he finished dressing. Mace complimented her look. "You are as beautiful in clothes as without."

"Thanks, I think. This is my idea of a uniform. Just work-like enough to not give guys the wrong idea, just tight enough to ensure good tips. Pretty sexy, huh?"

"With you wearing it, an old burlap sack would be sexy. I wish you didn't have to go so soon."

"Me too, Mike. But I'll see you Monday, or sooner if I'm lucky."

"I'm looking forward to it. I should check back on Wheezer

anyhow. He's watching Ray T. back at the jail."

"Ray is in jail? What did he do?"

"Long story. I'll tell you all about it on Monday."

They walked to the front door and shared a last kiss of the day. "I really, really like you, Amber."

She smiled. "I feel the same way about you, Mike."

Mace got into the SUV to drive back to Groverton with a huge grin on his face. He knew he had come dangerously close to saying he loved her.

When another heated argument started to get loud at The Anvil that night, and two guys stood to face each other, there was a bit different Amber behind the bar. Rather than ducking out the back door and leaving the dirty work to Slim, she turned off the TV and yelled across the room at the top of her lungs, "There'll be no fighting here tonight. You two lunkheads can take it out to the street if you have to and don't come back. Otherwise, sit down and shut up or I'll cut you and your friends off, understood?"

The two penitents hung their heads and together said, "Yes ma'am," and immediately took their seats. Amber turned the TV set back on, and cheerful conversations resumed.

She looked over at Slim, who was standing in the corner, blackjack in hand. He simply smiled and gave her a quick head nod. Jaycee, who was taking an order from table 4 when the scuffle-that-didn't-happen almost broke out, grinned, shook her head up and down and pumped her fist while lifting her knee and mouthing, "Yeah!" She had never felt better as she turned to an old couple who were sitting at the bar, now with their mouths still hanging open from the outburst that occurred right over their heads. "What'll it be, folks?"

When Amber turned to grab a bottle from the backbar, she secretly sniffed the inside of her right forearm. It still smelled like Mike's after shave. She smiled and sighed at the woman she saw smiling back at her in the big gilt-tinged mirror.

38

WHAT'S IN YOUR WATER?

The call from Hewitt had come in at about the same time as the one from Mason, which Mace let go to voicemail.

"Deputy Mace? Hewitt here. I have some results for you. The results on the tests for both opioids and methamphetamine came back positive."

"I see. How about the sample from the river?"

"Same thing. When you asked for that, I decided to also test well upstream, near our facility there. That was also positive. I ran another in Murrieta Creek, but there the tests showed negative."

"Why would it be different?"

"Probably because there is no reclaimed water discharged into the creek. I suspect this is coming from flushed pills and urine. The drugs are surviving intact and passing right through the system."

"Is there enough to affect humans?"

"I can give you the parts per million numbers in my report. But the answer to that should come from the medical people."

"What can be done to get rid of it?"

"Best practices I've read indicate a combination of reverse osmosis filtration and UV light treatment works well."

"So, that's the plan?"

"Not yet. It's going to cost a lot. More than our current budget can cover. I'm going to have to get new funding from the County Board of Supervisors. They're going to want proof that this is a problem. That's where I need you to get involved and obtain testimony from the doctors. I won't lie to you, Deputy Mace. It's not going to be easy with this lot. They'll probably have a public hearing on it."

"Got it. That's unfortunate. I was hoping to handle this quietly. We'll have to make an announcement to get ahead of it. Get me the report and I'll check for doctors to help us."

"Doc Jones has helped us on a couple of occasions in the past. I'd start there. When you set the appointment, include me and I'll go along with you to explain our findings. I'll help draft the announcement and go to the public hearing too."

"I appreciate that. We don't want to create a panic. Very good, Mr. Hewitt. I'll be in touch. Thanks."

"Don't mention it. And since we're going to be working together, call me Steve."

"Sounds good. I'm Mike. Bye, Steve."

"Bye."

Mace's next call was to Doc Jones' office. Dixie answered, of course.

"Doctor Jones office, this is Dixie. How may we help you today?"

"Hi Dixie. I need to set an appointment with Doc for myself and a colleague from another county department, Steve Hewitt."

"Are you both feeling ill? We usually schedule individual appointments."

"No, nothing like that. This is a business call. We just need to ask Doc Jones a few questions about a project we are working on together."

"Sure. I remember Mr. Hewitt now. County Water, isn't it? Doc has worked with him before. How about Wednesday at 8 am?"

"That works for me. Please put it down and I'll double check to make sure Mr. Hewitt is available. And Dixie, I'll be returning your Beretta, so why don't you and I meet there a few minutes before the appointment?"

"That's great. I'll be here. Thanks!"

"One more thing, bring the Glock with you, unloaded."

"What, I uh..."

"Don't act like you don't know what I'm talking about. I know all about it, and the fact that you took it home before getting cleared. Don't worry. I'm not going to bust you for it. I just want the weapon."

Dixie knew she was cornered. She just didn't know how she got that way. Did Little Bob squeal? She felt nervous and unmoored.

"I'll bring it along. Sorry, Deputy."

"That's okay. I'll see you then. Thanks."

"You're welcome. Bye."

Mace was alone in the jail. Ray T. had gotten bailed out the day after they hauled him in. Daphne's Cleaning Service had just finished and left, so the place was sparkling. Wheezer was out running errands for Mace. No calls were coming in for once. Apparently, the good people of the county were at low tide crime-wise.

Mike leaned back and took a deep breath. He luxuriated in the peace and solitude. As he did, he reflected on his visit to Amber's house. A warm smile spread across his face, and he sighed. His reverie was interrupted when a young woman opened the door and said, "Good morning, deputy. I'm here to report a crime."

He jumped up, concerned, "Amber! What happened?"

"I haven't seen you in too long. It's a crime." She smiled. "I miss you already."

Mike walked around his desk and wrapped her in his arms. "Me too. I'm so happy to see you. I was thinking about you just now."

"Can you get out of here for a while?"

"I'm kind of stuck until Wheezer gets back. I sent him out to do a little shopping. He won't be back for a while."

Amber moved back a bit but held onto his hands. "Do you have any guests back there?" See nodded toward the cells.

"Nope, we currently have three vacancies."

She pulled away and started walking toward the door leading to the cells. "Come along, Deputy. And bring your handcuffs."

Mace locked the front door and flipped over the sign to read "Closed."

A few minutes later, Dixie was walking up to the jail to pay Mace a pre-appointment visit. She wanted to see if she was in trouble before he came to the office on Wednesday. She stopped when she heard loud moaning coming from inside and noticed the closed sign on the door.

"Sounds like Barney Fife finally grew a pair and learned how to properly interrogate a prisoner. He must be beating the hell out of poor old Ray T." Word hadn't gotten around that Ray had been released. Dixie turned around and headed back toward Doc Jones' office. She did her best to stave off the mild panic attack that was sending rapidly flashing red messages of alert to her confused mind.

Wheezer got back about a half hour later with bags in hand. He noticed the sign had been turned to closed and wondered where Mace had gone. He let himself in just as Amber and Mike came out of the cell area. "Hi Amber. How's it going?"

She flashed a big smile as she adjusted her shirt. "Everything is just fine, Wheezer. Really fine. You enjoying police work?"

"I love it. I was hoping to collar a few perps though. Mike, I got everything you had on the list. Where do you want all this stuff?" Wheezer noticed something was off about Mace's uniform but couldn't tell what.

"That's great. Just put it on the table in the back. I'll be right with you."

Amber headed for the door. "Well, have a great day, sweetie."

"I already have." Mike gave her a quick peck on the cheek as she opened the door. "See you Monday?"

"Count on it. Later, Mike."

Mace flipped the sign over after she had gone. His head was spinning a little. He went back to show Wheezer how to distribute the supplies.

"Hey Mace, why is there a set of cuffs locked to the bars in Cell 3?"

Mace felt his face reddening. "Oh, I uh, those got in my way when I had to move the bed for Daphne when she wanted to clean in there. Thanks for reminding me."

The deputy retrieved his cuffs and clipped them to his belt. He knew what an implausible reason he'd just given, but Wheezer just nodded and asked, "So, what's next, boss?"

"Let's put this stuff away. Then I want you to call Mason for precise directions to where he was fishing on the river and Murrieta Creek. You're going to go out there and take some photos."

"Cool! Sounds like some detective work. Should I take a gun?"

"Absolutely not." Mace rolled his eyes, and they got to work.

39

BOARD TO DEATH

"So that's the plan. We can hold a briefing with the board of supervisors before going public. I'll arrange the appointment. I'll start with an overview, drill down into the statistics, and share some history about drugs moving through water treatment facilities. Doc, you can present the facts on what concentrations could be expected to cause symptoms in people."

"Some people. Remember what I told you: everyone's tolerance and reaction is different. I will need to point that out. Otherwise, they will wonder why everyone isn't acting paranoid and aggressive."

"Very good, some people. Mace, you can share some of the behavior you've witnessed around the county lately. In addition to that, you probably have the toughest job—explaining how this information came to light. Suffice it to say, if you don't couch the story properly, we'll lose them the second you mention the word "ghost."

"Most prisoners I've interviewed have convicted themselves by sharing too much when they're telling their story. I'll keep it simple and general, with as little detail as possible. Hopefully they'll be more interested in what you two have to say."

"I think we are as ready as we can be. I'll make the call this afternoon. Doc, thank you very much for doing the calculations to determine if those concentrations in the water could affect some humans. It's good to be working with you again."

"My pleasure, Steve. Give my regards to Mrs. Hewitt and remind her it's time for her booster."

"Will do. Mace, I'll be in touch when we have a date for the meeting. Thanks for your work on this."

"All part of the service, Steven. So long for now."

Hewitt left the office. Doc turned to Mace, "Expecting trouble, Deputy?"

"Not really Doc. Why do you ask?"

"I couldn't help but notice you have a second pistol in your gun belt. I thought you might be prepared for violence."

"Oh no. It's just an unwanted weapon that was turned in by a citizen today. No big deal. In fact, I'm on my way to Big Bob's after this to drop it off. He helps us with disposal."

"Glad to hear it. Hopefully you'll be a lot less busy after we get the water issue solved. Don't be having any of Little Bob's ice cream when you go there. I can tell you've put on a few pounds since your last physical."

Mace laughed at that. "Yeah, it's all the gourmet food we get down at the jail that does it. Can't resist. Thanks, Doc. I'll let you know when we're going to meet with the supervisors."

"Just tell Dixie. She keeps the calendar. I'd never know what I was doing next if she didn't keep it all straight. See you soon."

Mace didn't share that the citizen who had turned in the weapon right before their meeting was Doc's own receptionist, Dixie. The good doctor hadn't arrived at his office when Mace walked in on her. She jumped noticeably when the deputy showed up and struggled to hold her composure.

"Good morning, Mace. I have the Glock right here,

unloaded and ready to go." She started to tear up a little. "Are you going to arrest me?"

"No Dixie. Calm down. I just want to set things right, even though what you and Little Bob did was very stupid. I brought your Beretta. You need to sign a receipt for me, and I need you to promise to be more careful. I want to see you on the next two Thursday mornings at the jail from 7 am to 7:30 for a refresher gun safety course. That way you can make it to work without bothering Doc. Understood?"

"Yes, sir. Thanks, Mace." She sighed and began to relax, knowing she wouldn't bear the embarrassment of having Doc see her hauled away in cuffs. "That's a relief. I was walking by the jail yesterday and I heard you beating up Ray T. I was terrified that maybe I was next."

"What? Beating up Ray T.? I would never do anything like that, Dixie. Ray was bailed out two days ago, so I don't know what you're talking about." But in that instant, it dawned on Mace what Dixie had actually heard. He scrambled for a cover story. "You probably heard those feral cats that have taken up residence behind the jail. They make a hell of a racket when they get going."

"Well, that's a relief too. I didn't want to think you would be involved in police brutality. You never seemed the type."

"I'm not. Anyhow, I'm going to take the Glock back to Little Bob and make sure he gives you a full refund. He'll be very happy to cooperate. Just so you know, he could have been arrested and lost his business."

"I'm sorry Mace. Really. I'll never do anything like this again."

"That's right. You're fine now. Why don't you go back and compose yourself before Doc and Hewitt arrive? I'll just wait out here."

Dixie did as he said and visited the restroom. She looked in the mirror and thought; *I don't even know why I did that. Is some-*

thing wrong with me? Everything IS fine. I should be happy now, not worried that people are out to get me. She pulled herself together and fixed her makeup where the tears had coursed through. She returned to her desk just as Doc walked in with Steven Hewitt in tow for their meeting.

"Everything is set up in the conference room, Doc. There's fresh coffee, water, and notepads on the sideboard. Let me know if any of you need anything."

"Morning, Deputy Mace. Thanks, Daisy. Hold any calls, please. Right this way, gentlemen." Doc led them to the conference room, and the meeting began.

The group would reconvene a few days later at the county offices. But today Mace had another mission and for that he went to visit Little Bob.

The bell on the door rang cheerfully as Mace entered, looking anything but cheerful as Little Bob emerged from the back.

"Good morning, Deputy. How are you? Time to replace that service pistol?"

"Hello Little Bob." Mace pulled out the Glock and laid it on the counter. "Recognize that?"

"Let me take a look at the serial number." Little Bob knew very well where that gun had come from, and his head started to melt as he started to worry. He made a show of checking and then looking up the number. "Ah yes, as I thought. That's one we sold a couple of weeks ago."

"Yeah, to Mrs. Dixie Cadwallader. You delivered it before the background check could have been completed, right?"

"Uh, well, yes. I think I recall that. I made a small clerical mistake. It's been so busy lately, and then the robbery. I'm under a lot of pressure."

"You're going to be under a lot more pressure if you pull something like that again. Do you understand me?"

"Yes sir. I'm sorry. Are you busting me?"

"You'll issue a full refund to Mrs. Cadwallader and put that back in stock as a return. Bring me a copy of paperwork when it's done, and that better be today."

"Will do. I'll get the credit written and I won't do this again."

"I know you won't. Okay, Little Bob. I'll see you later when you bring by the receipts. Bye for now." Mace turned to leave.

"Bye, Deputy. Thank you."

The bell tinkled again as Mace exited the shop. Little Bob looked up at the large stuffed owl his dad had installed on a high shelf across from the ice cream display years ago and spoke to it. "Why am I still in this lousy business, anyhow? I don't even like guns." The owl just stared disdainfully down at the shopkeeper.

The meeting with the supervisors was set rapidly when they learned there might be a problem with the drinking water. The intrepid trio was sitting in the reception area waiting to be called in.

Mrs. Murphy came out to retrieve them. "The board will see you now."

"Thanks Mrs. Murphy." Hewitt led Doc and Mace into the boardroom. The members were seated at a round table rather than their more formal places up on the dais. Mrs. Murphy followed with a notepad and recorder. Board chair John C. Swayze greeted the group on behalf of the board.

"Good morning, Steven. Glad to see you again. Welcome Doc Jones and Deputy Mace. Deputy, I think this is your first time meeting with us, isn't it?"

"Yes sir. The sheriff usually handles our communication with the board."

"Well, please let him know we all hope he is feeling better soon. Thanks for pinch hitting. If everyone can please take a seat, we'll get started. Mrs. Murphy will record the proceedings. Gentlemen, I think you know everyone here?" They all nodded, and the supervisors waved except for Dick Curtis, the curmudgeon of the board. Hewitt knew him as the man most likely to vote against any spending proposal. Curtis just looked down and scowled at his notepad.

"So, where is Jack?" Jack Williams was the County Public Works Commissioner. Hewitt answered, "He's on vacation, but he is aware of the situation. He is available by phone if you need him. He asked me to take this meeting for him."

"On vacation? He's smarter than I am. Since today's topic is water, would you like to lead off with a summary of the situation, Steven?"

"Thank you, John, and thanks to all of you for meeting us so rapidly. As I mentioned in our meeting request, we are here today due to a possible public health issue with our water supply. I have some packets to hand around. Mace, would you please get these started? Recent tests conducted by our department show an unusually high level of pharmaceuticals have been entering the water we draw from the Santa Quiteria River."

Jennifer Bluebird Collins, the board's sole member from the old hippie faction interjected, "What kind of drugs?"

"Opioids and methamphetamines, also known as crystal meth."

Everyone on the board sat up and focused more of their attention on what Hewitt was conveying. Curtis shook his head.

"Are these levels dangerous?" Chair Swayze was known for being a quick study and cutting to the chase.

"Yes, we believe they are. Doctor Jones is with us today and will speak about it in more detail shortly. First, I want to give you some insights as to how this works, and how our current water treatment facilities were not designed to be able to filter these items out of the drinking water supply."

The board was all ears and took copious notes as Hewitt explained the tables and graphs in their packets. He moved on quickly to the age of the filtration infrastructure. Then it was Doc Jones' turn to speak.

"Hello everyone. You all know me as Doc Jones, and as a doctor, I am accustomed to delivering difficult news to patients. Today we have difficult news. I took the parts per million data that Steven just shared with you and recalculated it to figure out the dosage of each drug one could expect to find in an eight-ounce glass of drinking water. While it isn't enough to produce an acute reaction in but a fraction of cases, over time, the drugs can have debilitating effects on many, but not all, humans."

Again, Swayze led with insightful questions, "Can you provide some examples of those effects, Doc?"

"Paranoia and delusion are likely to be the most common. Some of you may have noticed resulting behavior among your neighbors."

Dick Curtis spoke up. "Sure do. We see it every month at board meetings during the public comments."

"You may have noticed more incidents lately." Doc tried to not let Curtis drag down the tone of the meeting.

Jennifer Bluebird spoke up again. "Are those incidents what Deputy Mace has come to speak about today?"

"Yes ma'am. That is part of why I am here. Pages 17 and 18 in your packets provide a brief summary of some of the recent incidents, and page 19 is a graph that shows how those have increased over time. I'll walk you through three such incidents to provide a sense of what we are seeing out there."

The deputy described the candy dish tossing and fire incident at Lolita's house, the weathervane shooting at Stargazer's farm, and the big brawl at The Anvil.

Swayze looked at the other board members and said, "It looks like we have a problem on our hands." The others nodded in agreement and looked concerned. "So, Steven, how do we solve it?"

"We'll need to add equipment to provide reverse osmosis filtration and ultraviolet light treatment."

"Reverse who?" Supervisor Edgar Burns, a merchant from Groverton, wanted clarification. Hewitt shared what he knew about the process and the equipment. He concluded with, "Do you have any questions about that?"

Dick Curtis raised his hand. "What's all this going to cost?"

"As you all know, we'll need to work with Procurement to put out a Request for Proposal to get quotes. My initial estimation is forty to forty-five million dollars capital expense, and about another million a year in increased operating cost."

"Holy shit, Hewitt! You cannot be serious!" Curtis was apoplectic and red in the face. Doc kept an eye on him to see if he was going to have a stroke. His previous tests indicated Curtis was a good candidate for one.

Swayze rapidly stepped in. "Steven, I'll contact Procurement to let them know to expect your RFP this week and to give it priority. As you are aware, we'll need to have a public hearing at the board meeting. The board will need to hold an emergency special election to pass the bond measure needed to fund the project. Fortunately, that comes up in only two weeks. Members, we also have a PR issue to deal with. We don't want to cause a panic, but we are required to make an announcement."

Hewitt shared that the three of them had written a first draft announcement for the convenience and consideration of the board that was included in the packets. He also suggested that the information be kept under wraps until the approved announcement was published. Everyone agreed on that point.

Swayze asked, "We all know what to do. Do any of us have another question?"

Jennifer asked the trio, "Just one more. How did this information originally come to your attention?"

Mace thought, *Oh, boy. Here we go.*

"Two concerned citizens reached out to Chief Murphy. I happened to be at the firehouse when they came by."

"Why didn't she follow up on it?"

"I felt it was more within my purview to check it out."

"Fair enough. Who were those citizens?"

"Mason Cadwallader and a newcomer to our county, Chad Burr, who moved here with his wife Tiffany from Rancho Niebla Tóxica. They were fishing on the river and Murrieta Creek and noticed some bass behaving very aggressively. There are photos of the location in your packets. They suspected drugs in the water."

"Cool, cool. Well, I'd say we owe those two a debt of gratitude." Jennifer was smiling. She enjoyed handing out awards at board meetings.

Edgar Burns chimed in. "I know Mason. He's a good man and a great fisherman. He would know about fish behavior."

Mace drew a breath and let it out slowly. It appeared he had successfully ducked the topic of Marvin's ghost.

"Okay, folks." Swayze was done. "If that's it, let's adjourn and get to work. Thank you for your excellent presentation, gentlemen."

Jennifer walked up to talk to Mace on the side. "I hear you're dating the bartender from The Anvil. How's it going?"

"Oh, great. She's a terrific girl. We're really hitting it off."

"She's a terrific *woman*." Jennifer smiled and winked.

"Yes, of course. Sorry."

"I noticed your aura looked a little off when you were talking about Mason and Burr out at the river. Was there something else you forgot to mention?"

Mace braced himself. "Well, they had expressed that there may have been a supernatural element to their discovery."

"Yes, so I thought. There usually is, Sergeant Sunshine. There usually is. Okay. Keep up the good work and have a nice day." She beamed at him with a broad grin and looked deeply into his eyes, as if checking out what was in his soul.

"Thanks, Supervisor Collins. You too." Mace was uncomfortable and ready to bolt.

"Just call me Bluebird, Mike." She walked back to where the other members were chatting and said to herself, "There *always* is."

Thus ended the meeting to convey the bad news. From there on out, it was a matter of executing the solution and monitoring results.

40

A BRIEF INTERLUDE

Mace's picnic date with Amber arrived before the public hearing and formal board meeting. They both were grateful for a break from their activities with the general public and were over-the-moon happy to be doing something together.

Mace picked Amber up at her place and drove back to his.

"What is this place, Mike?"

"It's my house. The trail begins here."

"Great! Are you going to give me a tour?"

"Afterwards. If we go inside now, we'll never make it to the picnic spot."

Amber giggled at that. "That is a fact, Jack! I brought my hiking boots and a small daypack with some essentials. I hope you are bringing lunch." Amber was an experienced hiker. She believed you should always be prepared for the unexpected. Her kit included nothing less than a topo map of their area, compass, sunglasses and sunscreen, extra socks and a sweater, a headlamp, first-aid kit, flint and steel for starting fires, knife, and a couple of power bars. A toothbrush and a pair of undies were tossed in at the last minute. She was thorough.

"Lunch and everything else we'll need is in the back of the truck. We're good to go." Mace's pack included food, utensils, wine, and a blanket.

They set off on the well-trod footpath. It turned beautiful after only a few yards and dropped off into a small ravine formed by the river that disappeared somewhere upstream. Amber was surprised she had never heard of, let alone seen, this part of the Santa Quiteria. They hiked next to the river for almost two miles with their heads down to keep from tripping on the many rocks that served as cobblestones on their path. Then Mace stopped and said, "We're here."

Amber looked up to see the ravine had opened up. They were on the edge of a small, grassy meadow surrounded by pines and a little manzanita. A cliff wall soared up from the far end of the meadow and from it dropped an amazing waterfall. The waters dropped into a pond and exited a short distance from where they stood to reform into the river. The over-whelming beauty of the spot took her breath away.

"Oh Mike, it's so beautiful. Stunning, really. I had no idea there was anything like this around Big Squirrel. It is unbelievable."

"There are a few small waterfalls around the county. This is the only one that flows year-round. It does slow to a trickle in the winter, though. I knew you'd like it."

"I love it!" Amber was smiling and a little giddy. She was rocking up and down on the balls of her feet and pumping her fists at her sides. She truly loved the outdoors, and this was one of the best places she'd seen. And right in Mike's backyard.

"And Amber..." Mike took her hands in his. "I love you."

This was the second time she felt stunned in the last few seconds. She looked deeply into his eyes and the smile left her face for a moment as she said, "Awww, Mike. I love you too." Needless to say, that was followed by an epic kiss from which Mike, after quite some time, pulled back.

"Shall we forge on?"

"There's more?"

He continued through the meadow to an edge of the pond that was much closer to the falling water. "This is our picnic spot." He dropped his bag and laid out the blanket.

"What's for lunch?"

"You'll see." Mike pulled out each item with a bit of a flourish. He didn't usually engage in such showmanship, but this was an unusual moment. Amber laughed at each presentation. His basket included a lovely spinach salad with walnuts, raspberries, and tiny heirloom tomatoes. There was fresh baked French bread, a charcuterie board of meats and cheeses, a small bottle of Dijon mustard and another filled with mango chutney. He produced plates, utensils, linen napkins, and two wine glasses for the bottle of dry Riesling from the Alsace region.

"Holy smokes, Mike! Is this what cops do with their spare time? What a spectacular spread." Her cheery kiss landed on his cheek as he poured.

"This is what I do when I want to visit my favorite place with my favorite person."

"Awww, Mike. That's the sweetest thing anyone has ever said to me. I've already told you I love you. My gun is out of bullets."

"Let's reload."

The young couple luxuriated as they dined, gazing off at the water landing softly from above and rippling across the pond. A few last butterflies of the season floated gently through the meadow. "Look, sweetie, they're monarchs!" Amber was smiling joyfully and pointing. Turning back to the meal, she complimented the chef. "This is delicious. Did you make the salad?"

"Yep. I baked the bread too."

"No way."

"Way."

"It's all wonderful, and so are you. So, how'd your meeting go with the board? Did they freak out when you told them about Marvin's ghost?"

"No shoptalk today, alright? This moment is too good. I'll just say it went great. I didn't have to tell them about the ghost. One of them seemed to figure it out in a way, but she spoke with me about it privately after the meeting. I think the secret is safe with her."

"That sounds like Jennifer. She's good people for an old hippie."

"Yeah, she is."

"Smart too. Do you know she has a PhD in microbiology? She was a researcher for a few years but gave it all up to move up here and work on Stargazer's farm when it was still a commune. She's fun to chat with when she comes into the bar."

"Man! I could tell she was sharp when we talked, but I didn't know all that. You never know, do you?"

Amber looked over at him with a loving smile. "Sometimes you do."

And so it went. They had what Amber would later describe as the best afternoon of her life. They hiked back to Mike's place, and as the sun set, he gave Amber the tour. It didn't take long. The farmhouse wasn't much larger than her place. He made pasta for dinner and served it on small plates with a pinot noir.

"Hey buddy, if you're trying to get me drunk, let me tell ya', it isn't going to work. I'm a pro, remember?"

"I'll keep that in mind."

She spent the night. They made love and slept like logs afterwards. They were both wiped out but happier than either of them had been in ages. Sweet dreams of wondrous things to come softly descended upon them.

When Amber awoke, she found cinnamon rolls on the kitchen counter with a note. It read:

Thank you for the best day I have ever had. I had to run off to work, but I'll be back in plenty of time to take you home so you can get ready for your shift. I love you, Mike. P.S. the waterfall is called "Butterfly Falls" because of the monarchs that pass through the meadow this time of year. I forgot to tell you.

She heated up one of the rolls and walked around the house. She ran across the one-eyed goldfish in the living room. "Popeye! It's so nice to meet you! How did I miss seeing you last night? Oh yeah, that's right. I was busy. Well, you are cute, aren't you?" She saw a little jar of food and a tiny spoon next to Popeye's tank. She scooped a bit up with the spoon and dropped it in the tank. Popeye swam to it and started gobbling it up. "Aww, you were hungry."

A little further down, she found a photograph of a somewhat younger Mike in a graduation gown. He was holding his criminology degree and was flanked by two older people, presumably his parents. "You were always a hunk, weren't you? Your parents look adorable. Can't wait to meet them. I will, right?" She kept inspecting the place, imagining all the changes she was going to make. She found the thermostat next to a closet and set it to 72. She had slipped on one of Mike's flannel shirts when she got up, but that was it, and she was getting chilly. The furnace kicked on but didn't produce much in the way of heat. Amber thought, "That's one more thing I'll fix here," and laughed to herself.

Amber went back into the living room and found firewood next to a hearth made of stones from the property. She built a cheery fire. She went back to the bedroom to collect the blanket from the bed and a pillow and wrapped herself up on the living room sofa, where she promptly fell back to sleep.

She woke up later to a ringing phone that was not her cell phone. Looking around, she spotted an old-school black phone on a small desk in the hallway. She picked up the heavy receiver. "Hello?"

"Good morning, sweet girl. Did I wake you?" It was now almost three o'clock, but still late morning for the bartender.

"Yeah, but that's okay. I should get ready for work."

"No problem. I'm on my way. See you soon."

"Drive safe. Bye, big guy."

She caught a whiff of herself in the plaid shirt as she hung up and grimaced. "Ugh. I reek! Let's hope the water heater works better than the furnace." She found the shower and cranked it on. Steam was rolling out in just a few seconds. "Excellent!" Amber dropped the shirt on the bedroom floor amongst the rest of their clothes and jumped in. The warm water felt delicious, relaxing, and invigorating at the same time. Amber started singing. She had just started a tune that was popular long before she was born called *Tonight you belong to me* when Mike rolled in.

He heard her rendition reverberating through the old wooden walls when he opened the front door and started chuckling. Making his way to the bathroom, he flipped open the shower door.

"Son of a bitch!" Amber jumped partway up to the ceiling. "Mike, oh, you scared the crap out of me!"

"I didn't know you could sing too. You are truly multitalented. Really, you have a lovely voice. Mind if I join you?"

"No way. I'm still shaking from your Psycho impression. Besides, I have to go home to change and get ready for work. How about a raincheck?"

"You got it. Anytime you like. Will you sing to me in the truck?"

"Get *out* of here!"

"I'm going, I'm going." Mike laughed as he went out to the living room. "Looks like you found the firewood. Nice, isn't it?"

Amber yelled back from the bedroom. "Very cozy. Good thing too. Your furnace is crap."

"I know. I've been meaning to give Mason a call. Just haven't gotten around to it."

Amber emerged from the bedroom in her hiking outfit from the day before.

Mike said, "Haven't I seen you somewhere before?"

"Let's go. I don't want to be late."

"I remember. I don't want to be responsible for Slim having a heart attack. Got all your gear?"

"I'll just leave the pack here, okay?" Amber was wearing an unusually sheepish grin.

Mace smiled. "More than okay."

They jumped in the truck and took the short drive down the hill. Mike walked her to her door.

"Well, here we are. Amber, I know it's soon, but there's something I want to ask you. Amber, would you..."

Amber quickly put an index finger to his lips. "Hold on, big guy. I am loving the period we're in right now. I want to savor it just a bit longer."

Mike looked a bit crestfallen. "Don't worry," Amber continued. "I feel exactly the same way. I was dreaming about it all night. Ask me in about a month, okay?" His expression brightened, and she kissed him for quite some time. "Gotta go. Watch out for the bear. I love you, Mike, more than anything."

"I love you too, sweetie. See you tomorrow?"

"You'd better!"

She closed the door behind her, and Mike turned to leave. *I knew it was too soon. God, I'm a jerk.*

The door opened again, and Amber grabbed Mace by the collar. "Hold on there." He turned to see her grinning from ear to ear. "Screw what I said before. Ask me your question right now."

Holding her hand in his, Deputy Sheriff Michael Fitzgerald Mace dropped to one knee and said, "Amber, will you marry me?"

She screamed and cried and answered, "Yes, yes, yes! Of course, I will. I love you so much."

They shared another long kiss. Mike said, "I love you too. I'll be thinking of you during your shift."

Amber yelled, "We're getting married!" The bear knocked into the new steel bear-box she had installed and that he was trying to open when the couple came out to the porch. He then ran off into the woods.

Mike and Amber laughed, and she said, "Okay, now really, go home. I need to suit up for work."

"So long Mrs. Mace-to-be."

"So long hubbie-to-be." And into the house she went.

Jaycee jumped up and down and screamed when Amber quietly announced the news at work to her and the boss that night. Slim did something he had never done before and would never do again: he gave Amber two nights off with pay, including her share of the tips. Then he bought everyone in the house a round of drinks, another first. They all toasted "To Amber and that damned deputy of hers!"

41

WHY SOME PEOPLE PREFER ZOOM MEETINGS

T he announcement and public hearing notice had been carefully crafted by Steven Hewitt of the water department, Doc Jones, and Mace. It was signed by County Board of Supervisors Chair, John C. Swayze and sent out by Mrs. Murphy who had it published in The Acorn Times, Desdemona County's weekly eight-page paper, posted at public buildings, and broadcast on the local K-UGH radio station. It included a short blurb regarding the solution they'd be voting on tonight.

Hewitt arranged for truckloads of bottled water to be delivered to all the towns and placed for free distribution to the public as an interim step until the filtration and treatment upgrades were operational.

An unusually large number of citizens had arrived for the Board of Supervisors meeting. They were nervous in spite of the well-written announcement and wanted both answers and someone to listen to their concerns. A box was filled with public comments forms.

The board was all present. Mrs. Murphy was recording the proceedings for later transcription. Her other job would be to time and politely end each public comment as the clock ran out. The editor/publisher/reporter/photographer of The Acorn Times was in the audience interviewing some of the attendees and madly jotting notes.

Hewitt, Jones, and Mace occupied the first three seats. Mason, Dixie, Chad, and Tiffany sat in the back. Mason and Chad were interested to see what the board had come up with and particularly if they would mention Marvin's ghost. Marvin's widow, Lolita, was in the middle of the room, completely unaware that Marvin was involved in the water issue. She was also unaware that her former and very deceased husband was farther back in the room, hovering invisibly and silently near the doors.

On the other side of Mace was Chief Murphy, who made it a point to attend every board meeting as long as nothing was on fire somewhere in the county. Little Mother sat next to the fire chief in the place where the sheriff used to sit before being struck with agoraphobia. He was at home watching the live stream of the meeting.

The public comment section of the agenda followed the safety announcement by Chief Murphy, the roll call, and the declaration by Chair John C. Swayze that they had a quorum.

"That brings us to public comments," Swayze announced. "I see we have a lot of names in the box tonight, so we'll get going. I want to remind all speakers that you will each be given a maximum of two minutes to make your comments. Mrs. Murphy here will run the timer and advise you when your time is up. Please stop at the point and take you seat. When I call your name, please come to the microphone in the front of the room. Let Mrs. Murphy know if you need assistance." He began by calling the first name. "Penney Fumagalli."

Penney walked up to mike and smiled. She turned and waved to other attendees and then back to the board on the dais. "Hi,

I'm Penney Fumagalli, and I want to say that adverse publicity about the water announcement is not good for business. Who is going to want to move here if they hear we have crappy water? It would have been better to keep it a secret." Again, she turned to the crowd, "But just in case anyone one wants to sell their home and move somewhere with good water, we at Palatial Real Estate stand ready to make it easy, fast, and profitable. We'll get you top dollar for your house." She smiled, waved, and threw in a little curtsey before leaving the mic to return to her seat.

Dick Curtis leaned over and whispered to Jennifer Bluebird Collins, "It's going to be a long night." Jennifer nodded with a calm Mona Lisa smile and leaned back in her chair.

Swayze said, "Thank you Ms. Fumagalli. Next up is Fred Mertz."

Fred Mertz, aka "Stargazer" stepped up to speak. "Hi everyone. On behalf of all of my brothers and sisters, I wanted to express concern over the bottles of water that are being handed out. Those are single-use plastics that get into the environment and fuck, sorry, I mean, mess up the planet. Bluebird, you know what I'm talking about." Board member Jennifer Collins smiled and nodded again. "They say you can recycle them, but everyone knows we aren't set up for that in Desdemona County. Those bottles take like five hundred years to decompose in the landfill, man. You don't want to be pushing that stuff out into the universe. We're gonna be up to our butts in bottles. That's some bad karma there." The old hippies and some of the young people in the crowd applauded. One of them smacked and shook a tambourine.

"Thank you, Mr. Mertz." Swayze said. "Please folks, let's hold the applause or we'll be here all night." Some people in the audience quietly booed. "Okay, Lolita Smith Severin."

There were some twitters, chuckles, and a catcall from the crowd. Ed Burns, the supervisor from Groverton was caught on a hot mic saying, "Oh boy. Here we go." None of that fazed Lolita, who walked right up and started in.

"Good evening, Chairman John C. Swayze and all the members of the board. I am here to express an urgent concern with the proposal before you, and a strong recommendation to not adopt it."

Burns, who had switched off his mic, turned to Dick Curtis, "Can I just kill myself right now?" Curtis almost smiled, but quickly reverted to his locally famous resting bitch face.

Lolita pressed on. "I have it on very good authority that the claim that there are drugs in the water supply is a total hoax." Marvin's ghost began to change in color from cloudy white to green, blue, and ultimately into hotter shades of yellow, orange, and crimson. No longer simply hovering, he now began to rock back and forth violently. It was clear that his former wife's words had agitated the specter.

"The 'filtration' system that has been recommended to you is a tool of the deep state here in our beloved Desdemona County, designed to introduce tiny nanochips into the water and thus our bodies and our brains. Invisible to the naked eye, these demon chips can control our minds and be used by the deep state to turn us all from being free men and women to being docile sheep, ready to do their evil bidding!"

In the front row, Mace hung his head and shook it back and forth. Hewitt stuck to his practiced poker face. Doc Jones stared at Lolita with his mouth open. Little Mother grabbed Chief Murphy's arm and whispered, "What the fuck is she talking about?" Tenaya just smiled.

Lolita pressed ahead, "This is just like when they started fluoridating the water and it shrank all the men's testicles." The male members of the board all cringed in their seats at that one.

"You cannot in good conscience unleash this liberal monster upon us. It is incumbent on each and every one of you to vote nay, nay, nay, and save us from the evil that has beset our dear, sweet community. Thank you."

The audience sat in stunned silence as Lolita turned to walk back to her seat. Marvin began to scream and kick and pound on the doors behind him, a feat only the dead can successfully perform. Still, he went unnoticed. The vow of silence and invisibility he had taken prior to going to the meeting prevented anyone from seeing his ghastly and yet somehow ethereal meltdown. The doors did bend back slightly, unseen by everyone save a lone security guard standing outside them who looked back as they did so, shrugged his shoulders, and went back to watching "The Voice" on his phone.

"Robert Ziglar."

Little Bob walked up to the mic. "Hello, I am Robert Ziglar. Some of you know me as Little Bob, but we all know that doesn't adequately describe me. Anyhow, I want everyone to know those drugs didn't get into our water by accident. They were put in there by terrorists or worse! The good people of Desdemona County are vulnerable to attack. We only have our excellent deputy, Deputy Mace, to protect us since the sheriff took ill. I also want everyone to know that we at Big Bob's Gun Shop and Ice Cream Parlor have been preparing for this moment and are standing by to help. We have to defend ourselves. If we don't, the terrorists win! Remember, the best way to stop a bad guy with a gun—or drugs that they are dumping in our water—is a good guy with a gun, or two or three. We are offering 20% off on all ammo purchased with a pistol or long gun for the next three weeks as a public service because we love our community and Big Bob's believes in giving back. Thank you."

Dixie could be heard from the back yelling, "Damn right, Little Bob, you tell 'em!" Mason looked down at the ground, and Tiffany giggled into her hand.

Mace looked at Doc Jones. "Great, Doc. That's just more

business for you, me, and Mort," Mort being Mort Soul, the mortician with a funeral home in Big Squirrel. "How am I supposed to be able to tell the good guy with a gun from the bad guy when I enter a situation? They'll both have weapons." Doc grimaced and shook his head.

"Thank you, Mr. Ziglar. Next is Audrey Griswold."

Ms. Griswold approached the mic. "I want to know, what's all this filter stuff going to cost us taxpayers?" Dick Curtis couldn't restrain himself from saying loudly, "Amen, sister, amen!"

"John Doe." Swayze looked around the room and spotted John Doe, otherwise known at The Anvil as the woodchuck, "Lefty," who had punched out Stargazer in the big brawl. "Please make your comment now."

"Look, we don't want temp jobs installing filters and black lights. I agree with Mrs. Severin. This drugs in the water thing is a hoax. We want our old jobs back. The jobs we had at the lumber mill. Those were good paying, union jobs. What are you guys going to do to bring the mill back?"

Supervisor Jennifer Collins noted that she was being referred to as one of "you guys," but let it pass. She sympathized with the woodchucks and wanted to get them well paying green jobs by attracting an American solar panel manufacturer to Groverton. She had secretly been negotiating with two of them for the past few months and felt they were getting close to being able to make a choice. There was no way she was going to lift a finger or vote to try to bring back the lumber company.

"Missy Colander." Missy Colander was one of the two elderly women who lived with Stargazer at the farm.

"I am Missy Colander. I am a farmer just outside Big Squirrel. We've had some trouble with hostile people lately, shooting up our poor weathervane and what-not. But this isn't the right solution. Mistreating the water isn't nature's way. It's like those vaccines. We never get them because they aren't natural. Our immune systems are. It isn't nice to fool Mother Nature. You won't like the results. We can help you raise enough water hyacinths to filter the water without all of the man-made structures and harmful UV light. All we are saying is, give plants a chance. Blessings and peace." Missy flashed the peace sign and sat back down next to Stargazer and her sister farmer, Moonbeam. Moonbeam had been sitting still, hands faced upwards on her knees, with her eyes closed, smiling as Missy delivered her comments, looking for all the world like the Buddha incarnate.

"Patti Gentry." Postal Pattie rose.

"As most of you know, I deliver the mail in Desdemona County. I can tell you: people and their dogs have been a lot more aggressive lately. It's getting scary out there. My job is critical, not just to me, but to all of you. We need this problem fixed asap. Please vote yes and make it happen. Thank you."

And so it went for the next two hours. At long last, a weary Board Chair Swayze said, "That completes the public comments, thanks be to the Lord. Mr. Jack Williams, County Public Works Commissioner, has just returned from attending a series of informative seminars in Hawaii and would like to take the floor. Mr. Williams, please come to the mic."

"Thank you, Chairman Swayze, and our esteemed board. Having been traveling on important county business, I haven't had a lot of time to master the subject, so I would simply like to call on Director Steven Hewitt, County Department of Water, to share the relevant data."

Hewitt approached and ran through a PowerPoint slide show that covered and graphed what their tests had shown, along with remediation steps taken by other utility operators around the country. He, in turn, introduced Doc Jones, who shared his calculations on how the level of drugs in the water could be expected to produce symptoms in some, though not all, people.

Swayze intoned, "And please share with everyone what some of those symptoms are, Doctor."

"Delusions and paranoia."

"Have you seen a rise in such cases lately?"

"Yes. In fact, I may have witnessed some examples here tonight."

Curtis once again whispered to Jennifer, "He's got that right! Total freak show." Supervisor Collins rolled her eyes, sighed, and focused on the speaker.

Chair Swayze thanked Doc Jones and called on Deputy Mace.

"Deputy Mace, how did you first find out about the possible presence of opioids and methamphetamines in the water?" The chair knew but wanted the citizenry to also be in on it.

"It was reported to me by Mr. Chad Burr and Mr. Mason Cadwallader, both of Big Squirrel. They noticed fish acting in unusual ways and were suspicious. I believe I saw them here earlier." Chad and Mason squirmed in their chairs, but Tiffany and Dixie were both beaming with pride.

"Mr. Burr and Mr. Cadwallader, we owe you a debt of thanks. We always say, if you see something, say something. But not many do. Please stand up and be recognized."

The two men reluctantly and awkwardly complied as the board and audience applauded them.

"Okay, moving on to Item One. Mr. Hewitt, I understand you have a winning bid from your Request for Proposal and would like to have us put the acquisition to a vote?"

"Yes, that is correct. The complete proposal is in your agenda packets. It is forty-five million dollars to be secured from an emergency bond measure that is included within the proposal. A special election has been scheduled to hopefully pass the bond measure next week."

"Thank you. We have all read the proposal. Are there any questions?" An exhausted board had none.

"Do I have a motion to approve the proposal?"

Supervisor Edgar Burns answered, "I so move." Jennifer Collins seconded the motion.

"Ayes?" There were four in favor.

"Nays?" There was one from Dick Curtis. In the end, he was for it despite the cost, but was afraid of his extremist neighbors, some of whom wanted to secede from Desdemona County and form their own "Jackson County," named after Andrew Jackson.

Half the crowd booed. The other half cheered. The triumphant triumvirate of Hewitt, Jones, and Mace just felt relieved. Mason and Chad felt embarrassed to receive many pats on the back. Marvin returned to being his gently smiling, gossamer self and floated outside through the doors.

Once the less interesting items two and three were handled, Board Chair Swayze adjourned the meeting. He looked at Hewitt and said, "Godspeed, Steven. Get it done."

The editor/publisher/reporter/photographer of The Acorn Times ran to his car to get back to his office and write up the story. He went to press that night as the paper would come out the next day. The story was already old news by then. Only one person wouldn't already be aware of what was said and done at the county supervisor's meeting. That was Phineas T. Burton, the man who had robbed Big Bob's Gun Shop and Ice Cream Parlor. He had jumped bail as soon as he was released the day after his arrest and fled to northern Utah, where he changed his name, joined a militia group called "Bacon Boyz" and disappeared.

A week after the board meeting, the people of Desdemona County passed, despite all the huffing and puffing at the public hearing, the measure to fund the water project.

42

TWENTY PERSON MARCH

Having failed at getting the bottled water sent back to the distributor by the County Board of Supervisors did not dissuade Stargazer. He applied for and was granted a Parade and Peaceful Protest Permit by Big Squirrel Mayor and Grand Pooh-Bah, Kelvin Nader himself, it still being a small town. The document was on a dark parchment and bore the mayor's red wax seal. Kelvin Nader prided himself on being a class act and didn't do anything the easy way if an elegant way was available. Stargazer also felt the vibe in Big Squirrel was more amenable to his protest than Groverton would be, and more people might join in. The event was scheduled for that Saturday at 1 pm.

Stargazer, Missy, and Moonbeam started furiously hitting the phones, inviting all the other old hippie types to join them on the march and to tell a friend. That started a chain reaction, and pretty soon almost everyone in the county had received a call about the protest.

Deputy Mace and Chief Murphy were alerted by Nader, as was Doc Jones, just in case. Dixie got the call and responded with, "Ha! That's great! God bless Stargazer. I might join in on that one."

Tenaya Murphy called the intrepid editor/publisher/reporter/photographer of The Acorn Times, who published a special edition—a one-page flyer—to notify the community of the upcoming march. The fire chief and editor had worked hard to keep in touch and help one another. She informed him of what was going on, and he helped push her press releases out to the public. He also ran the piece on his social media and website, which meant people might actually see it. Once again, the Times got scooped by word of mouth, this time due to the farmer's phone banking, and everyone knew about the march before the story came out in the media.

Mace told Amber about it over a late breakfast at Mother's Café. Chief Tenaya Murphy was also there, wolfing down pancakes at the counter while engaged in what looked like an intense conversation with Little Mother, whom she had just informed about the upcoming protest.

Amber looked concerned. "Are you expecting any trouble, Mace?"

"Nah. It won't amount to much. There will likely be about twenty of so of the old hippies, those that are still ambulatory, that is. My guess is that they'll poop out after a block or two, then just sit in a circle and chant for a while. The mayor called Murphy and me there just to keep an eye on things. The chief will bring the ambulance along, so she'll be the one to see some action, if there is any."

"Well, I hope she doesn't. I like those people. They're kind of charming in a weird way. I have to admit, I'd already heard about the march from Slim."

"Slim? How'd he find out?"

"Everyone comes to The Anvil, and Slim knows them all. He got a call from a gal in the Rotary Club in Groverton, who had heard about it from Supervisor Collins, who had heard about it from Moonbeam, the mushroom farmer. They have some kind of phone chain. I think it goes back to the old days when they used to do a lot of stuff like this march. I hear the newspaper is putting the story out tomorrow."

"Well, we'll probably have a few curious onlookers, just like at accident scenes and fires. Maybe I'll wear my sexy crowd control vest."

"Oooh. I don't want to miss that. Is that all you're going to wear? Anyhow, Slim wants the protest to succeed."

"Really? Why?"

"He has a huge stock of bottled water that's been taking up space behind our pantry for a couple of years. He bought it on a deal, but he can't sell any of it because nobody wants water at The Anvil. He was looking forward to unloading it when he heard about the drug problem in the tap water. Slim figured everyone would want to buy his bottled water. But the county giving it away shot down his big plan."

"I don't see the supervisors backtracking on the free water, but you never know around here."

"Yeah. Well, root for the hippies. I need Slim happy. I figured I'd get up early and attend the protest. I have a folding chair. Maybe I'll make a sign to wave."

Little Mother showed up with their order. "There ya' go. Got ya' an extra pancake in there, Mace. Have to keep our lawman well fed. How are you two lovebirds, anyhow?"

Amber beamed as she looked up at Little Mother. "Really, really awesome. Never better."

"Took the words out of my mouth." Mace was glad he could latch onto Amber's pronouncement. All he was going to say was, "fine."

"So, when's the big event?"

"We haven't set a date yet. Probably soon though. I need to

nail this guy down before he meets our cocktail waitress and runs off with her."

"Jaycee? No way, Amber. Nobody looks better in hiking boots than you." Mace was trying to keep up, but just wanted to dig into his pancakes.

"You two better invite me. I love weddings. So romantic."

"When are *you* getting married, Little Mother?"

"Ah, probably never. Why would I when I can still play the field?" Maisie smiled and winked at Amber. "You two need anything else, just call me. Enjoy."

"Thanks, Little Mother." Mace hit his plate like a Mike Tyson jab and started to chow down.

"Whoa, easy does it there, Mike. You must be hungry."

"I'm starving. I've really been running since the board meeting, even with Wheezer helping. He's a good kid. I think I forgot to have dinner last night."

"I'll fix that once we're married. All part of the service."

"You know, you should just move into my place right now. Why pay rent when you don't have to? We can play like we're married already."

Amber smiled and picked up her Denver sandwich. "That's not the worst idea I've heard today. You really want me there?"

"Of course! Did you think you'd still live in your house when we do get married? Give notice and I can move your stuff tomorrow. It'll be fun. I'll get to see more of you. I love waking up next to you."

"Aww. Same here. You can't sleep at the jail anymore if I do though."

"Promise. I don't want to miss a single night with you."

"It's a lot longer walk to work from your place."

"I'll buy you a bike."

"You say the sweetest things. It's a deal."

"Good. Now I'm going to finish these pancakes. They're delicious."

"True, but Little Mother's Denver sammie is to die for. I need more coffee." Amber looked over to wave at Little Mother, but the café owner was back into her yakfest with Tenaya at the counter. She waited another minute then held up her cup and pointed with a cheery grin. Maisie smiled, gave Amber a thumb's up, and grabbed the pot.

While Maisie refilled Amber's coffee, Mace asked her facetiously if she was planning to board up her windows in case the protest got rowdy.

"Nope. Most of those old farts can't even bend over to pick up a rock let along throw one through my windows. I think we'll be just fine."

The approved parade route, established by Mayor Nader and his city council of one, showed a starting point on Mulberry Street by the firehouse and proceeded onto Main, ending at the park. That made it easy for Chief Tenaya to follow the marchers with the Big Squirrel Fire Dept. ambulance. She had assigned that duty to her paramedics, of course, and planned to follow along in her fire chief's car.

Stargazer, who wanted to maintain good relations with the town, had drawn the route on the back of an old concert poster that was probably worth hundreds of dollars. He held up the drawing to show it to the crowd, which had grown way beyond the twenty or so old hippies predicted by Mace. It now appeared that close to two hundred people had shown up to march and yell. Had most of them come from Big Squirrel, there wouldn't have been many residents left to look on. But people had turned out from all over Desdemona County and from all walks of life.

Even the woodchucks were there. Lefty had rounded them all up and reported to Stargazer upon arrival, who looked a bit concerned. Lefty explained their presence, "So, Stargazer, we wanted to join you today because what's bad for the environment is bad for the logging business."

Stargazer puzzled at the irony of that statement, coming as it did from a man who used to earn his living clear-cutting hundreds of pines at a time and clogging up the various tributaries of the Santa Quiteria River, including Mason's treasured Murrieta Creek. But he'd been around this block a few times during his life as a protester, and he knew that politics did indeed make strange bedfellows, so he welcomed the help from his one-time adversary.

"Well, welcome fellow traveler! We're happy to have you along to stick it to the man. You're not gonna punch me again when we're done, are you, Lefty?"

"No way, Stargazer." Lefty hung his head. "I'm really sorry about what I did that night, buddy. I get a little down about having such a crap job these days compared to what I used to do at the mill, and seven or eight beers don't exactly help my mood. I was taking it out on you, and that's not right. I hope you can forgive me."

"Of course, I forgive you, Lefty. The wheels of the universe are greased with forgiveness, man. Look at this crowd. This is going to be totally far out!"

The two of them looked out on the surprisingly large throng gathering behind them. Mulberry Street had never looked so full. The old hippies were at the front of the pack. Some held picket signs, and Moonbeam swung a brass incensor to and fro, filling the air around her with lavender-colored, sweet-smelling smoke.

Behind them was an assortment of plaid flannel and camo covered woodchucks, one of whom carried a small chain saw for an unknown purpose. Past them was an odd assortment of Desdemona County residents, some of whom felt strongly about not promoting the use of plastic bottles. Others were there for something fun to do.

Stargazer held up his big map and called for attention.

"Ladies and gentlemen! Ladies and gentlemen!" Clearly, nobody heard his old, weak voice in all the hubbub. Mace, who was standing by, handed him the bullhorn he had dug out of his SUV when he saw the size of the crowd. The deputy had set it on "talk" as there were other buttons for various siren and alarm sounds.

Stargazer took it and immediately pushed one of those other buttons accidentally. A blaring horn noise like an old air raid alarm went off and continued in an endless loop. At least everyone stopped what they were doing and looked toward their protest leader. Mace took the bullhorn back and returned it to the talk setting. He pointed to the button and handed it to Stargazer.

"Thanks, Sergeant Sunshine!" When he said this, it was broadcast by the bullhorn to the entire crowd. Everyone laughed and repeated in unison, "Thanks, Sergeant Sunshine!" Mace returned to his sideline position, shaking his head.

Missy took the poster and held up the route map for everyone to see so her fellow farmer and roommate could better deal with the bullhorn. Stargazer resumed. "Ladies and gentlemen, thank you for coming out today. We are all here to stop the destruction of our land with single-use plastic bottles. There is no Planet B!"

Again, the crowd yelled back, "There is no Planet B!"

"It is important that we stay on the route that Mayor Nader laid out for us to follow. We will go forward here along Mulberry Street until we reach the corner of Main and then we will turn left toward the park. The march ends there, but we can continue our protest as late as 4 o'clock."

The marchers interjected with "4 o'clock," and many laughed. Apparently, people were really there to have a good time, not just protest. Stargazer took no offense at that and forged on.

"That's cool. Remember, this is a peaceful protest. Above all, take care of each other out there. Now, let's march!"

The marchers cheered and snaked ahead down Mulberry. Mace took a position on their right flank, near the middle of the queue. Semi-retired Deputy Mark McPherson was on the left, near the front by Stargazer, Missy, and Moonbeam. Missy had rolled up the concert poster/map, tied it with twine, and carried it on her back where it looked like a quiver for carrying arrows. She took the bullhorn from Stargazer and started a chant, instructing the crowd behind, "What do we want? Ban plastic bottles! When do we want it? Now!" She provided the questions, and the crowd called back the answers.

They marched past the fire station and down the block to Main. Johnny's Fishing Gear and Bait Shop stood at the corner. There was a large handwritten sign in the front window that read, "20% off on fishing gear for protestors. Today only!" One of the woodchucks dropped off the route to go shopping inside.

The Clampers had joined in and came with their ridiculous little cars. Some wore the normal red shirts and blue jeans. Others were dressed as clowns. They tore up and down both sides of the marchers and circled around, laughing hysterically. They had no idea there was a protest. They had heard it was a parade, and they never missed one of those. One of the Clampers in clown make-up almost hit Deputy McPherson who yelled, "Watch it! I can give you a ticket, buddy!" The clown honked his ooga horn and sped off in another direction. McPherson laughed in spite of himself and continued to march along.

Hundreds of onlookers flooded the sidewalks on both sides of the street. When the march reached Mother's Café, the old hippies were the first to see a group seated in lawn chairs out front. Slim was there with Jaycee from The Anvil. Amber was next to Dixie, Tiffany, Chad, and Mason. Little Mother and her cook were standing in front of the door in their white uniforms.

Amber had a picket sign lying on her lap with the lettered side facing down, out of view. It looked like an improvised, de facto reviewing stand, all the more so as they each had a deck of 6x9" cards with numbers on them. Marchers treated them that way too, turning to salute the members at Mother's. As each group walked by, the "reviewers" held up the card with a number they felt reflected their performance and appearance ranging from 1 to 10.

The hippies chanted and banged on tambourines as they went by, and incense could be smelled up and down the block. The woodchucks followed. The guy with the chainsaw fired it up periodically and held it over his head, giving it a couple of revs before bringing it back down and flipping it off. He repeated this continuously throughout the march. His fellow woodchucks waved fists in the air and yelled, "No plastic in the forest!" each time he performed his noisy act. That move got his group an average of 9 from the reviewers, though nobody was bothering to keep score.

Next was an assortment of semi-concerned citizens, mainly from Groverton. Those included merchants, teachers, a plumber who waved a sink plunger overhead, and others including Herb Gardner, gun aficionado, who limped along with the group. Herb was carrying his black powder musket that he fired into the air every so often, causing marchers and onlookers to duck instinctively, except Deputy Mace, who walked upright and gave him the stink eye from near the back of the parade. Fortunately, Herb had not put any musket shot in the gun before shooting it. He would stop to reload after each blast and then limp rapidly to catch up. Kids looking on from the sidelines were fascinated with his process that included using a ramrod to push everything down deep in the muzzle. Herb was proud of being able to execute the entire move in just under one minute.

Some kids from the Groverton High band were there in

green and gold uniforms. They repeatedly played the school fight song, sounding a little off as many of the usual instruments were missing. Their instructor marched alongside, smiling and waving to the crowd. The abbreviated band was being led by three flag girls in green dresses and white go-go boots, each holding a very long pole with a large green and gold flag near the end. They waved these and occasionally would toss them into the air, wait with open arms, watch them fall into the street, and go chase them down to repeat the move a few yards down the route.

One such errant flag came crashing down onto the reviewers in front of Mother's Café, followed by a red-faced flag girl. Tiffany handed her the flag and the girl repeatedly babbled, "Sorry, sorry, sorry!" as she retrieved it. The group gave the flag girls and band a unanimous 10 mainly as a result of the near impalement.

Big Squirrel Mayor Nader and his wife rode behind the band in a black 1924 Studebaker roadster that he maintained just for such events. It was driven by his lazy son, Thad, who was thirty-two, still lived at home, and had to be paid to drive in the parade. A banner hung on each side of the vehicle, emblazoned with a picture of a bottle of water and the words "Ban the Bottle!" A smaller brass plaque on the rear end of the vehicle was engraved with the words, "Mayor and Grand Pooh-Bah, Kelvin Nader and Family." Mayor and Mrs. Nader waved at the onlookers like Queen Elizabeth once did. Onlookers admired the car and Mrs. Nader and tried to ignore Kelvin.

Mayor Nader was a showboat and self-promoter to be sure, but he got a bad rap. He also cared deeply about the town and its delightfully diverse, if not downright eccentric, citizenry. That said, the good people of Big Squirrel had re-elected him to a third term in the last election, if only because they feared what would happen if Councilman Warner, who ran for the office every time, would take over. Warner wanted to modernize everything, even changing the title to Mayor of Big Squirrel, dropping the Grand Pooh-Bah element. The electorate felt that was a sacrilege. Even the younger folks felt the existing title added a certain panache missing from other local governments. Among his notable supporters were Slim Jim, Chief Murphy, Little Mother, and Mason and Dixie. They stood and applauded as the Studebaker stopped to allow Nader to salute them in front of the café reviewing stand. He received an average score of 9, with which he was well pleased.

Mace finally arrived before the café, accompanying a group of equestrians from various ranches. A guy in a skunk costume followed the horses with a pushcart and shovel to help keep the streets of Big Squirrel tidy. He missed a lot as the Rotary Club who were next could and did attest as they performed an awkward version of the Texas Two-Step around the remaining piles.

Amber stood when she saw the deputy, handed her score cards to Tiffany, and held up her picket sign. It said in large block letters, "I love you Mike Mace!" She waved the sign and pumped her fist in the air to catch his attention. She ran out and grabbed him with her free arm and planted a huge kiss on him. He felt embarrassed for just a second, then let that go and kissed her back. Amber dropped her sign and wrapped her arms fully around Mace, who was holding her tight.

The reviewers stood, cheered, and clapped madly. The cowboys assumed the applause was for them and took off their ten-gallon hats with which they waved back. The skunk guy did a little jig over the shovel that he'd placed sideways in the street. A flask dropped from a hidden pocket in his costume and clattered on the cobbles. He picked it up, took a long swig, and put it away, thus explaining his lack of poop shoveling accuracy.

Amber walked along with Mace, his arm around her shoulders. They were trying to get ahead of the local retro-punk band that followed called The Electrodes. Snot, the bleach blonde, heavily tattooed front man, was hollering a song about a girl named Britney who allegedly had shot him as the guitarists played wirelessly into a wheeled amp towed on a heavy chain that was wrapped around the waist of the bassist. As it turned out, they were overly confident in their ability to play while walking in a protest march, and the high decibel noise was a cacophony that sent small animals scurrying and young children crying.

The horde inched ahead, with everyone having a splendid time. Some of the old hippies got winded and dropped off on the sidelines, but they were picked up by some of the Clampers who told them to stand on the rear bumpers of the absurd little cars they'd been spinning around and to hang on for dear life. So, everyone was able to make it to the park, which was the terminal point on the parade route.

First to arrive was Stargazer, his ladies, and the remaining old hippies who had stopped chanting several blocks back. Lefty was right behind, leading the woodchucks, one of whom carried a shopping bag from Johnny's Fishing Gear and Bait Shop and two new fishing rods.

The woodchucks looked as wiped out as the hippies. They weren't in the same condition they had been when they were lumberjacks working for the mill. It dawned on some of them that had been many years ago.

Lefty joined Stargazer and the women who were seated on a step in front of the gazebo. They were so tired, they didn't notice a small PA system set up inside the gazebo. "Phew, that was a hike, eh Stargazer?"

"Yep, a slog. I'm parched. I've got cotton mouth something awful, and I left my Nalgene back on the farm. Bad planning on my part, dude."

Lefty looked over to the right side of the gazebo. One of the water distribution boxes had been set there by the county, filled with thirty-two-ounce bottles of Tesker's Pure Alpine Spring Water. He pointed a thumb at them and looked at Stargazer with a smirk that silently said, "Don't those look refreshing about now? And they're right there for the taking."

"Oh man, don't tempt me. That's like seven years' bad luck, that is." But the old farmer's resolve was weakened by thirst at that point. "Oh well, a man's got to know his limitations, right?" They walked over to the box.

Stargazer picked up two different bottles, one from each side of the crate, and asked, "Mit gass oder ohne?"

"What did you say?"

"Oh, sometimes something will trigger me into speaking some German I picked up there when I was in the army. It means, do you want yours with bubbles or without?"

"You were in the army? I'd have never guessed that."

"Yeah, man. I was drafted. Most of my friends burned their draft cards and resisted, but I decided to go and have a little adventure. They assigned me to tanks, and I spent most of my time looking through two wire fences at a crew in a Russian tank that was pointed straight at us, as we were at them. It isn't a comfortable position, but I muddled through. Got a lot of leave and went into town most nights. Picked up some of the language from a few of the townie girls. That was fun."

"Wow! Well, thank you for your service."

"You don't have to thank me. I wasn't exactly volunteering for anything. When my tour was almost up, I decided to stay in Europe. Once I got my discharge papers, I backpacked all over Germany, Austria, part of Italy, and ended up in Switzerland for a spell where I got a job at a dairy. That was where I first dropped acid, back when not many folks were really aware of it, and it was still legal. Changed my whole outlook. You should try a psychedelic like acid or shrooms, Lefty. I swear you'll see things you never noticed before."

"I've thought about trying those magic mushrooms,

Stargazer. People say they help with anxiety. This might be just the nudge I needed. You know where I can score any?"

"Well, it just so happens I do, Lefty. Yep, I sure do."

They walked back to where the women were sitting, bringing an assortment of the two types of bottled water. Without any hesitation, they both grabbed one and started chugging it down. Stargazer and Lefty laughed and joined in.

"Lefty, I don't even want to think about what kind of karma I just hurled out there, but damn if that didn't hit the spot. You want another?"

"Hell yeah. Let's grab a bunch. We still have to walk back now that Ray T.'s offline for a while."

"Maybe the Clampers will run us back."

"Those dudes are lucky Mace doesn't slap 'em all with DUIs."

"Sergeant Sunshine. He's cool, man. He knows they aren't going to kill anyone in those little go karts, even if after a couple of shots."

"Could still be a mess. We'd have to get that guy in the skunk costume to clean It up."

The horde of "protestors" gathered around the gazebo, chanting "No more plastic" while picking up bottles of water from the box. Suddenly, the screech of loud feedback got everyone's attention. The entire County Board of Supervisors was on folding chairs up in the center of the large gazebo. The mayor and his wife were seated next to them. Board Chair Swayze was standing at a floor mic that fed into the portable PA system.

"Greetings citizens of Big Squirrel and Desdemona County. We are here today to let you know—we hear you! The people have spoken, and your board of supervisors is ready to act."

A small cheer and applause followed. Missy looked at Stargazer and asked, "Did we win?" Moonbeam sat with her eyes closed, smiling and rocking slightly from side to side.

"Not yet, Missy."

Swayze went on, "As of today, this board is resolved to commission a study to determine the feasibility of adding plastic recycling equipment to our waste management system!"

The crowd didn't cheer. They didn't applaud. They didn't boo. They simply stood in silence, staring at the stage. Twitters started to be heard coming from the back. Then laughing. The laughter built and flowed in waves to the gazebo.

Swayze stood shocked at the mic, turned, and looked back at his fellow supervisors. Jennifer Bluebird Collins teared up and broke into laughter, as did Mayor Nader and his wife. Soon they were all laughing, save Swayze, who turned back to look at the crowd. When he got it, he started to laugh too, a deep belly laugh that reverberated right through the PA system.

Everyone knew the pronouncement was bullshit, including the board that wrote it. And everyone got a good chuckle out of it. Even babies were giggling in their mothers' and fathers' arms.

Then Swayze left the gazebo with his entourage to mingle with the people. The Electrodes took over the stage, set up, and started blasting. Some kids stuck around, along with a couple of older punk fans, but most everyone else began to leave for home or other venues. The most popular choice among the protesters and politicians was The Anvil. Slim, Jaycee, and Amber had already figured that out and headed out early to get everything ready there.

Mace thanked McPherson and Wheezer who had joined them when the marchers reached Main Street and sent them home. They both went to the fire station to change into civvies and headed for the tavern.

Mace stuck around to make sure everything was cool around the park, which it was. He stepped back and surveyed the scene. The absence of the tainted tap water in everyone's diet appeared to have caused peace to break out after only a few days. Disparate parties forgot their differences and focused on what they had in common, which was often a love for this place and the people in it. The crankiest folks left were mainly the super-hydrators, including a fair number of runners. They seemed to be going through some mild withdrawal symptoms, and a few sought help from Doc Jones. All in all though, a welcome calm had descended on the two main towns and outlying county. The deputy sighed and smiled. He truly loved Big Squirrel and all its weird inhabitants, especially one in particular.

He headed over to the fire station to wash up too, but he would be staying in uniform that night. As he walked by one of a few recycling bins, he noticed they were overflowing with empty Tesker's Pure Alpine Spring Water bottles.

Mace looked in on The Anvil about a half hour later. It was an official patrol visit as the place was slammed with revelers and had a history of small problems, but mostly he just wanted to sneak a peek at Amber.

Everyone was there. Laughter and country music from the jukebox filled the air, and the suds were flowing. A few couples had moved a few tables aside in the middle of the room to allow dancing, an activity for which The Anvil was not permitted. Mace looked the other way and moved over to one side to look around.

Slim was working the bar with Amber. He was wearing his lucky apron with The Anvil Tavern logo, an anvil with the name of the place hammered into it and the words below that read "Free Beer Tomorrow!" Of course, it was never actually tomorrow.

They looked admiringly at Jaycee, who had her hair in a ponytail, was wearing black short-shorts, a white blouse, and a pair of white skates on which she was circling through the tables, carrying trays of drinks.

Slim gave Amber a glance and said, "Wow!"

She replied, "Yeah, wow! I had no idea she could do that!"

"Me neither. Damn, she is good!"

"Sure is! And technically she's wearing black & whites."

"Gives the place kind of a formal touch, don't it? Amber, can you skate like that?"

"Forget it, Slim. No room behind the bar. That's Jaycee's gig."

When the speeding cocktail waitress rolled by Mace, he just looked and said, "Jesus."

She was delivering a round of drinks to a large round table occupied by Lefty, Mrs. Lefty, two other woodchucks, Stargazer, Missy, Moonbeam, Supervisor Jennifer Bluebird and her husband, Everett, Tenaya in her civvies, and Little Mother. There were ten beers and one Cosmo. The cocktail was for Stargazer, much to everyone's surprise except Moonbeam who sat with her eyes closed and smiled. Jaycee said to the group, "Would anyone like water?" Simultaneously, the group yelled, "NO!"

"Didn't think so." Jaycee laughed and spun off to take an order at another table.

Mrs. Lefty was chatting with Stargazer. "I couldn't believe Ray T. shot up your weathervane and dumped a horse's head out at your farm. I ride with him all the time, and he seemed fine. Goes to show that you never really know people, do you?"

"Oh, Ray T. is alright, Susie. He was probably all wound up from the speed in the water. He came by to apologize the other day. Said he felt terrible, didn't know why he did it, and was very sorry."

"I'll bet he's sorry," Jennifer Bluebird chimed in. "The judge slapped him with a hefty fine, twenty hours of community service, and told him to pay you and Miller's Feed & Seed for the damages."

"Yeah, he asked what he owed me. I said kindness to all would do, but he insisted on a number, so I gave him one. He handed over cash on the spot. He's a cool dude. Just got a little twisted up for a while."

"Well, I'm glad he's driving again for one," said a relieved looking Mrs. Lefty. "We may need his services tonight!"

"I don't think he can fit all of us into that SUV of his. Although, it would be fun to try." Lefty was laughing slyly.

Mrs. Lefty patted his one remaining hand and said, "Oh, Lefty. None of the ladies want to squeeze in with you, dear."

Tenaya said, "Good thing some of us can walk home." The woodchucks stared at her. They'd never seen her out of uniform before. She looked a bit too elegant for The Anvil in a cream-colored mini dress with matching heels, topped off by a short charcoal jacket.

"You got that right, sister!" Mother lifted her beer mug in a small toast. "But can you make it in those heels?"

"I can if you can, Maisie." Tenaya smiled. Little Mother was wearing her sneakers.

When Chad and Mason, accompanied by Tiffany and Dixie, walked in, the tavern erupted in cheering. There were pats on the back from many of the patrons as they made their way to table 3, where Jaycee had pointed them. "Way to go guys!" "Thanks, Mason and what's your name!" "We love you!" They had moved from an average guy and an unknown stranger to local heroes in a couple of short weeks.

Jaycee rolled up after making another delivery. "Hey guys! Glad you're all here. The mayor says whatever you're having is covered by him, so I don't even need to open a tab for you."

Mason sat up quickly. "In that case, I'll have a couple of steaks, medium rare, Jaycee."

"Mason, you know we don't have steak. How about a couple of fish tacos? I know you love those."

Tiffany piped up, "How about a pitcher of Sierra Nevada and a pitcher of Campfire Stout, Jaycee? And I'll have the fish tacos too."

"Got it. Dixie?"

"I'd just like a salad." Everyone laughed. "Just kidding. I'll have three of those tacos. No, four."

Chad said, "I'll have the same. Three tacos, no salad."

"Great, I'll be right back with your beer."

"Thanks Jaycee. Love your skates!" Dixie turned to Tiffany. "How can she do that? That's amazing!"

Mason looked over to where the mayor was sitting and waved. Nader gave him a thumbs up and smiled. "Guess I'll have to vote for him next time."

"Look at this, Dixie," exclaimed Tiffany. "We're married to a couple of celebs."

Dixie laughed.

"I just feel bad that Marvin isn't here to enjoy the free beer too," Chad said. "I mean, he was the one who told us about the drugs in the water."

Mason glanced around. "Keep your voice down, Chad. People don't want to hire a crazy man to fix their furnace."

"Or handle their finances," said Tiffany, looking at Chad. "I for one am very glad he isn't with us tonight."

"Oh, I think it would be fun. I ain't afraid of no ghost!" Dixie was thinking she would enjoy seeing Marvin again, especially now that he was dead.

"Dixie, you'd wet your pants and shoot him if he showed up."

Dixie chortled. "Screw you, Mason. Hey, speaking of Marvin's ghost, anyone seen Lolita today?"

Chad pointed to the far end near the service bar. "Isn't that her, sitting up at the bar?" He'd noticed her when they first came in, and also how Slim Jim seemed to head her way to quickly chat each time they had a short lull in orders.

"Yep. That's her alright," Mason confirmed.

Tiffany said, "She looks cute tonight. Maybe the bottled water perked up her mood."

Dixie looked toward the service bar. "That or the glass of chardonnay Slim just refilled."

Slim asked Lolita, "So, you're feeling better now?"

"Yeah, Slim. I don't know what got into me. I'd been acting nuts since Marvin died. It's embarrassing to think about."

"Well, don't. You had gone through a lot. Plus, what got into you was probably the opioids in the water. I've told you before, never drink water while I have wine."

"Ha! That's good advice, Slim. I'll keep that in mind. Thanks for being sweet."

"I'm just happy to see you here. You look beautiful tonight, by the way."

"Thank you, kind sir! It's been a long time since I've received a compliment from a gentleman."

"You deserve it, kid. Uh oh, gotta get back to work." Slim noticed Amber was rapidly pulling bottles and mixing. She had just received an order that Jaycee gave her from Table One, where the Groverton Women's Club was seated. They all ordered craft cocktails one of their members had seen on TV and talked up at their last meeting.

The Clampers were at table 9 in various stages of clown costume and their regular apparel. They were a little later to arrive than most of the crowd as they carefully loaded their tiny cars into a trailer. They hadn't agreed on a designated driver, so it would probably sit just outside The Anvil parking lot overnight.

Jaycee got a tray of beers to the Clampers table using her miraculous rolling balancing act. "Here you go, gentlemen. Will there be anything else?"

"Yep, how about some of your onion rings?" The rest of the Clampers shouted agreement.

"Coming up. Would anyone like water?"

They all shouted, "NO!"

"Yep, I'll have those rings up soon."

Things settled down just long enough after the Table One order was complete for Amber to see Mace looking at her from his spot on the sidelines. She smiled and blew him a kiss, all while continuing to pour a Bud. He blew her a kiss back.

One of the woodchucks was returning from the restroom and saw the exchange. "Well, ain't that sweet?" He then pretended to gag.

Mace gave him a deadpan expression. "Move along, Paul Bunyon. Nothing to see here."

Former lumberjack Paul Frazier, whom everyone called Paul Bunyon, laughed, blew Mace a kiss, and moved along.

Mace figured things were mellow enough at The Anvil that he could head out to patrol the town. He wanted to wave goodbye to Amber, but she was once again getting slammed up at the bar. He walked out to the parking lot and waved at Ray T. who was sitting in his SUV, waiting for a fare. *Good that he's here. Hope I don't have any DUIs tonight,* Mace thought. Ray waved back and rolled his window down.

"Hi Mace. Hey, thanks again for not coming down on me too hard. I'm doing better now."

"You're welcome, Ray. I'm happy to see you're staying out of trouble. Have a nice night."

"You too, Deputy." Ray rolled up the window and checked his app to see if anyone wanted a ride.

Mace got in the SUV and drove back to the park to see how things were there. The Electrodes had packed up and moved on, as had their audience. Mace wondered where they had ended up. There was one old couple walking their basset hound through the park, and that was it. They waved at Mace as the dog stopped to sniff, the 27th time he did so on that walk alone.

Mace drove on and finally decided to head home and stand by there. Things were quiet all around Big Squirrel except for The Anvil, and he wanted to feed Popeye. His place was close enough that he could be back in town in two minutes if anything came up. He drove by Amber's place on his way home. It didn't look like anyone had moved in yet. He shined his floodlight over. The bear came out, looked at the light, and ran off into the woods. Mace laughed and drove up the hill. *That girl needs to move in with me right away.*

43

SO, WHAT HAPPENED ALREADY?

C had and Mason went fishing most Saturdays after the protest. Mason shared more secrets about how to figure out if the fish were there before dropping in a fly or lure. Chad's casting improved to the point where he could move his line sideways upstream in Murrieta Creek under a canopy of heavy growth that hung just over his head.

Being local heroes did wonders for their businesses. People who had put off servicing their air conditioners called Mason to come out just for the opportunity to meet a celebrity. Even Tenaya asked him to submit a bid to replace the HVAC system at the firehouse. As it turned out, it was the only proposal, as two others from outside Desdemona County had been rejected by Procurement.

Chad's clients looked at him and his recommendations with new respect. It seemed at times that all of Desdemona County was lined up in front of Chad's place, looking for wealth management, tax preparation, or stock tips. The Acorn Times dubbed him "The Wizard of Big Squirrel." He invested most of his additional earnings but used a major part to put some upgrades into the house and get a custom restoration done on his Citroen that brought it up to fresh-out-of-the-factory mint condition. He was invited down to Burbank to appear on an episode of Jay Leno's Garage.

Tiffany, not being a celebrity, built her business the old-fashioned way—through hard work, savvy marketing, and a wee dose of luck. Having Dixie rounding up clients for her with Doc Jones' approval didn't hurt either. After only a couple of months, she had enough work to bring in a second therapist named Katie Kato from Culver City, helping to offset her rent and pay half the salary for Jen, the receptionist. Jen herself took courses in therapeutic massage and started practicing in a converted walk-in closet in the back of the office, bringing in even more business.

When they had time, Dixie and Tiffany enjoyed breakfast together at Mother's Café, where Tiffany usually ordered the Denver sandwich.

"You know, Dixie, when Chad first suggested moving to Big Squirrel, I had major reservations. But it turned out to be the best decision of my life, other than marrying that goofball."

Dixie held her hands across the table. "It was the best decision for my life too. Otherwise, I wouldn't have met my BFF. I love you, Tif."

"Awww. I love you too, sweetie."

"I hate to break up this love-fest girls, but your order is here. Tiffany, here's your Denver. And Dixie, here's your oatmeal. How's that diet going anyhow?"

"I've lost fifteen pounds, Little Mother, and ten of those came off my ass. So, not too bad. It helps that I actually like your oatmeal."

"So do I kid, but don't tell anyone. There's no margin in it at all. You two want water?"

"NO!" the ladies screamed together. Everyone laughed and Little Mother went back to refill some empty cups along her counter.

"Tiffany, I'm thinking of hanging it up."

"What? Not your job at Doc's. You run that place and half of mine."

"No, nothing like that. The Roscoe. I'm thinking of selling my Beretta. Now that things have calmed down around here, I feel it may be unnecessary. Besides, I don't know if you've heard, but I've had a couple of bad experiences with guns lately."

"Everyone's heard about it, Dixie. I think that's a great idea. I don't want my BFF shooting her eye out."

"Aww. It's in my safe at home. I'm going to take it to Little Bob next week to sell on consignment. Or maybe he'll buy it outright."

"I love it," Tiffany said. "You know how to take care of yourself pretty well without it. I'll go with you if you like."

"Super! We can get some ice cream there afterwards."

"It's a date! Let's eat. My sandwich is getting cold."

The two friends chowed down and went to the register to pay.

"Thanks girls," Maisie said. "Don't forget, we'll be closed next week for vacation."

"Don't you mean honeymoon? We're so looking forward to the wedding this weekend. You and Tenaya will look adorable!"

"You think? I sure hope so, for what those dresses set us back. I'm glad you'll be there. It should be a hoot."

"Wouldn't miss it. Break a leg, Little Mother!" Dixie was grinning from ear to ear. The BFFs walked out and headed back to their offices.

"Don't you think they're cute, Dixie?"

"That could have been us in another life, Tif."

"Really? Nah, I snore. You'd have shot me by now."

Doc Jones wondered what all the laughing was about when the girls reached the office complex.

Little Mother and the fire chief had come out a few weeks

before. Well before that, they had shared their love with their families, who were accepting for the most part. They had kept their love affair a secret for over two years, sneaking off for vacations and long weekends here and there. Or so they thought. When Chief Murphy gathered her fire fighters together to announce it, they all responded together, "No shit, Chief!" and laughed.

She stood in shock, then started laughing with them. "Well, not much stays secret in this place, does it?"

The crew gave her a lot of pats on the back and calls of "Congrats Chief!" filled the fire house. The paramedics pulled a couple of bottles of champagne out of the cooler in the ambulance and broke out paper cups for everyone. Chief Murphy didn't ask what the bottles were doing in the ambulance.

One of them proposed a toast, "To the best damned fire-fighter on the planet! Yay Chief!"

Everyone yelled "Yay Chief!" It was the first and last time Tenaya ever cried in front of the men and women of The Big Squirrel Fire Department.

It was a good thing there weren't any fires right then. The singing and yelling were so loud nobody would have heard the alarm.

Everyone around the county reacted very positively around the county except Dick Curtis, who said to his fellow board members, "This better not prevent her from doing good fire-fighting."

It was Jennifer Collins who responded to him, a bit out of her normal character, "Dick, don't be such a DICK!"

Most folks knew and liked or even loved Little Mother and Chief Murphy and were simply happy for them. That's why the couple decided to throw their wedding in the park in Big Squirrel and invite the lot of them. As a result, they wouldn't be able to pop for food and an open bar, but Desdemona folks were always happy to bring their own, so long as there was a reason to party.

The wedding would be covered by The Acorn Times with a front-page article. It would be, after all, the Desdemona County event of the decade.

That night Dixie opened her safe and, making sure it was unloaded, put the Beretta in her purse. She planned to take it to Big Bob's Gun Shop and Ice Cream Parlor the next day at lunch and get it sold. She stroked it lovingly in the bottom of the purse. "I'm gonna miss you, little buddy. We've had some special times together, you and me, haven't we?"

"Who the hell are you talking to, Dixie?" Mason was grinning in the doorway right behind her.

"Holy shit, Mason! Don't do that! You scared the Pemmican out of me. I think I peed my pants a little."

"Sorry sweetheart. Can't say I'm sorry to see that thing go. I always figured I'd be your first human victim."

"You sneak up on me again like that and you will be, gun or no gun."

Mason swept her up in his arms. "I love it when you talk like that." He kissed her with more passion than he had in years.

"Aww, Mason, I'd have dumped it a long time ago if I'd known there'd be such a nice reward."

He took her by the hand and led her down the hallway. "Come on, kid. We have a date." They turned into their room and fell into bed.

The next day at lunch, Tiffany and Dixie walked on down to sell the Beretta to Little Bob. But when they arrived, they found the shop was closed, the windows boarded up, and a sign on the door that read, "Closed for Renovations. Come back in two weeks. Sorry for the inconvenience."

"What now, Dixie?"

"What the hell is this?" Dixie walked up closer to the door.

There was pounding coming from inside. The door was slightly ajar, and dust filled the air inside, lit up by beams of sunlight streaming in from the street. She grabbed the door and slowly opened it all the way. The little bell rang. Tiffany came up behind her to watch and put a hand on her shoulder as they peered into the dusty gloom.

Little Bob looked up from a long wooden shipping crate he had been nailing shut. "Hi ladies. I'm sorry. We're closed."

The place was a mess. The gun racks were empty. Packing materials were strewn all over the counter. More wooden crates were stacked up in the middle of the floor. They all had large "FRAGILE" stickers on every side. The Charlton Heston poster that had been above the door was missing. The pistols that usually were stocked under glass in the counters had all been removed. A menagerie of taxidermized animals and birds lay on a bed of straw in one of the long crates. The shelves upon which they once perched were stacked up in a corner of the room. There were cans of paint, rollers and trays, and some bolts of fabric near the shelves. An enormous carton stood behind all of that with a picture that looked something like a Russian samovar. It was bound in strapping tape. The label on the carton was addressed to Big Bob's Gun Shop and Ice Cream Parlor.

All that remained was the register, the ice cream display, and the "Loopy's Circus Cones" sleeve standing on the counter.

Dixie stepped over a pile of wadded up paper in the doorway and walked in with Tiffany in tow. Her mouth hung ajar, as did Tiffany's.

"What the hell's going on here, Little Bob?"

Robert Ziglar rose up to his complete five-foot five-inch height.

"Well, Dixie, I'm out of the gun racket. Business dropped like a sack of potatoes after everyone stopped drinking the water. And that robbery freaked me out. You know that guy is on the loose somewhere? Yep, he jumped bail. And don't get me started about all the paperwork. I've had enough. That was my dad's business, not mine. I'm changing my business model. In a couple of weeks, you'll be standing in the brand new "Robert's Gelato and Boba Tea Emporium."

"Who is Robert?" Dixie asked. Tiffany pointed over her shoulder at Little Bob.

"Me, Dixie. I'm Robert Ziglar. I'm also out of the Little Bob business. New shop, new me. I sure hope you'll come by for a gelato and tea."

"I sure will, Little, I mean, Robert. But how are people going to know it's your place?"

"They'll probably figure it out when I'm standing behind the counter. I'll also be advertising online and in the Acorn Times. I plan on having a big grand opening in about a month or so. It will be fun."

"I'm looking forward to that," said Tiffany. "I love Boba Tea."

"Is that the stuff with those icky little balls in it?" Dixie scrunched up her nose and grimaced.

"Tapioca. They're good and fun. You should give it another try when this place opens. Do you have any gelato in yet, Robert?"

"Nope. That's still ice cream in there. I have a bunch of recipes from my mom. She was Italian, from Genoa, and made it for us kids. I'm going to make all the gelato right here in the old stockroom. Freezers and a stove are coming tomorrow. You can have ice cream cones if you like, on the house. I have to clear it all out."

"Thanks, Robert. That would be really nice. Do you have any pralines and cream?"

"I think so. Dixie, what would you like?"

"How about chocolate mint?"

"Coming up." Robert went behind the counter to make their cones. "Here ya' go. Bon appétit!" He produced a stack of little black cards. "Here. Take one of these. They're for my loyalty program called 'TEAriffic Friends.' Catchy, right? Once you buy nine teas or gelatos, you get your tenth for free."

"That's cute, Robert. I wonder if that would work for physical therapy?"

"You don't know until you try. So, what brings you ladies by?"

Dixie reached into her bag and pulled out the Beretta. "Actually, I came by to see if you wanted to buy it or sell it for me on consignment."

"Gosh, I wish I could, Dixie. That's a fine little gun. See those long guns in the crates? I sold them all to a dealer in Colorado. The pistols are going to a place in Milwaukee. So, I'm already done with it. I know a dealer in San Berdo that might be able to help. I can call him if you'd like."

"Could you, Little Bob, uh, Robert? You're the best." Dixie gave him an awkward hug over the counter. She dropped the Beretta back in her purse. "Well, that's lunch. Good luck with the new business, Robert. We'll sure be back. Thanks so much."

"My pleasure. I'll call you at the office if my friend wants to buy your gun. Give my regards to Mason."

"I'll be back too, Robert," Tiffany said. "And I'll bring Chad. He loves gelato!"

"Great. Tell a friend! Take care ladies."

The girls stepped over the paper and walked out the door.

"Well, if that doesn't beat all," Dixie exclaimed. "That place was a gun shop before I was born. Looks like Little Bob may have gone hippie on us."

"I think it's going to be great. And good for him for embracing change. Things never stay the same, and they shouldn't. Change is good."

Dixie nodded. "Yeah, you're right. I can't blame him for getting rid of the guns. I'm getting rid of mine."

"See? That's good change, Dixie. I'm so proud of you!" Tiffany smiled.

Dixie took a closer look at Tiffany and started to laugh.

"What's so funny?"

"You, Tif. You've got an ice cream mustache!"

Tiffany wiped her mouth with her napkin. "Oh hell, thanks for telling me. That would have looked good back at the office. We'd better get going."

"Yep, we have a one o'clock. I have to get back too."

"Good thing we have lunch to go."

44

BUT WAIT, THERE'S MORE

Hewitt's procurement awarded the water jobs to a local contractor, The Tweedle Brothers, Dwayne, Daryl, and their associates. After they finished installing the reverse osmosis (R/O) systems at the two treatment plants along with the UV system at the one upstream, tests showed everything was working as hoped. The systems went online after a celebratory event held by the board of supervisors that nobody attended except the editor/publisher/reporter/photographer of The Acorn Times. Supervisor Edgar Burns remarked that the upstream facility didn't stink like he imagined it might. Hewitt shook his head and prayed the event would end soon.

Further testing showed all was well, and in fact, the water was cleaner than ever before, at least during modern times. An announcement went out that tap water was once again safe to drink. The citizenry took to the news slowly and with trepidation. But ultimately people found they had various reasons for spurning bottled water, the greatest of which was cost now that the county subsidy had run out.

Mace and others could see that things were improving rapidly. The word started to filter out to other water districts in semi-rural areas around the state and country, mainly because Hewitt spoke about it at a couple of industry confabs. And in those places that made the investment to rid themselves of water-borne opioids and meth, the results were similar.

The ripple effect was felt in surprising ways. Crime rates went down, but that was expected. What wasn't predicted was the nationwide precipitous fall in engagement for conspiracy websites, particularly among users that lived in small towns. As advertisers lost interest in them, some of those sites went dark, never to spew again. Political elections showed a shift as well. Extremist firebrands ended up replaced by calmer, more moderate, and compassionate representatives in those areas.

R/O and UV light manufacturers were elated and went on a hiring spree. The economy was picking up steam so quickly that Chad was able to put together a consortium of investors who bankrolled a startup solar panel manufacturing company in Groverton for which Jennifer Bluebird Collins was grateful as her deal fell through. Almost all of the woodchucks got jobs there, joined a union, and ended up with better pay and benefits than they had when they worked at the lumber mill.

One who did not go to work there was Lefty. He followed up with Stargazer to learn how he could try some magic mushrooms. The old farmer arranged for Lefty and Mrs. Lefty (who wanted to join in the fun) out to the farm for a safe tripping experience, supervised by himself, Missy, and Moonbeam.

The couple lay under blankets on sofas in the living room after ingesting a specially infused tea prepared by Moonbeam. Stargazer watched over Lefty while Missy held Mrs. Lefty's hand across the room. Moonbeam sat with her eyes closed cross-legged in a chair, smiling, rocking, and softly humming.

Before it was over, Lefty had a vision of a tall, radiant one-armed woman in a flowing white gown, beckoning for him to follow. The woman took him to an easel with a canvas, a small table holding paints and brushes, and a chair set up on a grassy hillock overlooking a verdant valley below. She began to paint the scene with her single hand.

Afterwards, Lefty took classes in plein-air painting and spent many mornings and afternoons traipsing around Desdemona County engaged in his new hobby. He was a bit slower than other painters but saw with a keen eye. He displayed some of his favorite works at an arts and crafts fair held in the park in Big Squirrel.

An art writer for the paper in L.A. took a liking to his work, interviewed him, and published photos of Lefty and his works in the news. He got calls from galleries following that. Mrs. Lefty managed his business affairs and ultimately the onetime lumberjack found himself doing quite well selling his beautiful impressionist outdoor scenes. His works, which heavily featured trees, sold for tens of thousands of dollars apiece.

When they moved into a lovely new home in Big Squirrel with room for a large studio that Penny Fumagalli sold them, they held a housewarming party. Stargazer and the ladies attended and gifted the artsy couple a box holding a long, white, clay smoking pipe made by Stargazer himself. There were runes carved into the side that gave it the appearance of a scrimshaw. Stargazer translated them as saying, "May peace follow you like your own shadow." There was also a little cloth bag inside of which was some potent weed grown by the ladies at the farm, and an incense burner with patchouli oil scented incense cones. Lefty found he loved the smell, though Mrs. Lefty wasn't so sure. The last item was an expensive Dunhill lighter. Stargazer explained, "That's the kind James Bond uses." Once again, the old man surprised Lefty with something that seemed, at least at first glance, to be out of character. But it wasn't. Giving away a material treasure to a friend was part of Stargazer's nature. The couple accepted the gift by clasping hands and saying, "Namaste."

Also not in the news, Slim Jim and Lolita started dating. Their first date was at The Branding Iron Steakhouse. When they arrived, Tex asked Slim if he was checking out the competition. Slim said he just wanted a good steak since they didn't have them at The Anvil, and Lolita said, "It's our first date."

Tex said to Slim, "See, that's the difference between your establishment and mine. People come here to celebrate things like their engagement. People go to The Anvil to drink after their divorce is final." Slim parried with, "I can't deny it. Maybe that's why I'm more successful than you." They all laughed at that.

Slim told Lolita over dinner that he always wanted a hot, younger woman like her. "That's me!" Lolita said even though she was five years older than him. They both knew that but didn't care.

"This is really fun, Slim. I'm so happy you asked me out."

"I agree, Lolita. May I add that you look radiant tonight?" She did. The pained expression and worried brow she'd been wearing for months had disappeared. Her color had come back. She'd decided to go with smokey eye makeup that night. It may have been a risk, but Slim loved the way she looked.

"You may indeed! Thanks. I love compliments. I sure didn't get any during the dark period."

"Well, you're going to get plenty from now on, if I have anything to say about it."

The couple got to know one another better and found they were really hitting it off. That needle moved up when they went out on the dance floor after dinner and Lolita did a funny little tango of sorts, where she circled around Slim. He was laughing hard, but he also found it kind of sexy.

When they got back to Big Squirrel, Slim walked Lolita to

the door and gave her a perfect goodnight kiss. They agreed they both wanted to go out again soon, and Lolita walked inside for the night. She closed the door, looked up at the living room ceiling, and with an enormous smile screamed, "I'm back!" Indeed, she had returned to the land of the living.

45

THE EVENT OF THE DECADE

Guests started arriving in the park in the early morning. People wanted to make sure they had a seat as nothing limited the number of attendees that might show up. There was also no absolute set time. Formal invitations only went to family and close friends, and those said simply "After Lunch." Most folks interpreted that as iish. It had all the makings of a Big Squirrel event.

Roadies were setting up a sound system and running tests. Nobody knew who they worked for, but there was a large black tour bus parked nearby. Another crew was installing an arch on the gazebo stage and covering it with flowers of many colors. Black wooden folding chairs were being strung together with rainbow-striped crepe paper ribbon draped across the seat backs by family members and friends who'd volunteered to help set up.

White tablecloths covered tables on both sides of the main aisle, featuring guest books, photos of the happy couple on their previously secret dates, and floral arrangements. Nearby stood an enormous wooden crate filled with Tesker's Pure Alpine Spring Water, with choices of flat and sparkling.

Slim Jim, Amber, and Jaycee were busy setting up a no-host bar off to the side near a circular patio that would serve as a makeshift dance floor during the reception. Between the bar and patio, a small round table would soon hold the wedding cake.

A wood carver arrived and began to set up an ice sculpture depicting two swans in a neck embrace next to the cake table.

Mace, wearing a suit, was seated as close to the no-host bar as possible, joined by McPherson and Wheezer. He saved a seat next to him for Amber. Tiffany, Chad, Dixie, and Mason would arrive in Ray T's Ride-Share SUV and join them.

Penney Fumagalli and her rather morose looking husband headed straight to the front and sat right behind the row for family members. She immediately started handing out her business cards to her neighbors. The agent smiled, posed, and waved to everyone in the crowd like a Kardashian. Somebody a few rows back yelled, "Sit down, Penney!" and she dropped into her seat. "Why I've never!" she exclaimed to her husband.

"I've warned you before, Penney. Can we just pretend we're people and enjoy the wedding?"

The folding chairs filled quickly and were surrounded by latecomers who were forced to accept SRO status. Everyone heretofore mentioned was in attendance, except of course for Phineas T. Burton, who was training somewhere in Idaho, and the sheriff, who was at home watching via a security camera on the bank across the street from the park.

The editor/publisher/reporter/photographer of The Acorn Times who was also officially invited there as the wedding photographer, ran about getting shots of everyone and everything.

Stargazer was at the back of the stage in a tux and top with a flowing cape that made him look like Doctor Demento except that instead of a bowtie he wore beads and a silver chain from which dangled a huge crystal. There was a smiling man in the moon made of silver sequins on the back of his cape. He walked to the front of the gazebo around a baby grand piano that had been moved in and stopped behind a floor mic. Snot, the lead guitarist and front man from the Electrodes, stood up on the audience-right side of the stage and played a screeching riff on his Telecaster to get everyone except those in Standing-Room-Only to sit down and shut up.

Snot next started to play a sweet and perfect rendition of Pachelbel's Canon in D Major, much to the amazement of his three girl "fiends" who sat behind him on the stage.

Tenaya's brother and Maisie's sister led the way to the gazebo. They were followed by Tenaya's little niece as flower girl, and Maisie's next-door neighbor's son as ring bearer.

Next came, to huge cheers from the audience, Tenaya and Maisie dressed in identical white and very revealing Vera Wang gowns, holding hands and waving. Both wore flower-bedecked headbands with ribbons that trailed down their backs. Few noticed that Maisie was wearing her white sneakers and Tenaya, her black steel-toed work boots due to the length of their gowns.

The couple climbed the stairs to the gazebo stage and stood before Stargazer, whom they had asked to officiate. He was able to do so as a fully and legally ordained priest of The Church of the Latter Day Dude. Stargazer saw "The Big Lebowski" as his personal book of revelations rather than a film, and he saw it close to fifty times. He raised his arms wide and high, and the crowd went silent.

"Fellow passengers upon Mother Gaia! Today we shall witness a most blessed joining of two children of Big Squirrel. They shall be joined in love and peace. Marriage is a force, a form of energy that, like light, permeates the universe and raises awareness not only for the married from whom it springs, but for all who encounter them along the journey. Two thus joined, though they may separate for a time, will be drawn back together by the bond they share that is love, time and again, for eternity AND BEYOND!"

Stargazer paused a few seconds for effect and then resumed. "Now is the time for us to hear from each of what shall form a newly bound pair. Tenaya, please begin."

"Maisie, I didn't love you at first sight. It took several seconds. Once I did, I knew. I also really needed someone who could cook."

Maisie mugged for the crowd and said, "Aha, that's why you proposed!"

"I can't imagine spending my life with anyone but you, sweet child. Nobody else understands me. Nobody else lights my soul on fire. I love you and pledge myself to you today and for all the days that follow."

The crowd collectively said, "Awww." Stargazer teared up. So did Snot and his girl "fiends." "Maisie, it's your turn."

Maisie stared up at Tenaya through her librarian glasses. Up as Tenaya towered some seven inches above her. "I have loved you my entire life, though I only met you five years ago. I knew you were the girl for me when you came into my café and put away the Blue Plate special in only four minutes. Nobody had ever done that before. And you spoke to me in a way nobody ever had before. You made me feel like a treasured jewel instead of the owner of a greasy spoon. I am yours now and forever."

They turned to Stargazer, who exclaimed, "Wow, man! I mean—ring bearer! Bring forth rings!" The little ring bearer did as he was bid. Stargazer took each one out, placing one on Tenaya's finger and the other on Maisie's. They would later secretly swap them so that they had the correct ring without embarrassing Stargazer.

"Maisie, do you accept Tenaya to be your wife?"

"I do."

"Tenaya, do you accept Maisie to be your wife?"

"You're damned right I do! I do, sweet Maisie. I do."

"Then by the powers vested in me by the goddess Gaia, and the Dude who abides, and the State of California, I pronounce you wife and wife! So, kiss already!"

They embraced and kissed like nobody was watching. The crowd cheered. Herb Gardner fired his black powder musket into the sky. The crowd, Maisie, and Tenaya ducked. The couple continued to kiss with abandon as Snot played his Telecaster as the Goth girl "fiends," danced jaggedly.

Finally, Maisie and Tenaya walked down from the gazebo and waved at the crowd as they made their way to the back. They passed through the firefighters lined up on both sides of the aisle in dress uniforms holding swords aloft over their heads. When the couple made it to the end, they passed by onlookers and made a bee-line for the bar. Jaycee served them, as Amber had bolted to sit next to Mace during the ceremony.

"Mace, wasn't that the most romantic thing ever?" asked Amber. "How is our wedding going to top this?"

"Easy. You're going to be the bride."

"Awww, Mike. I love you." They kissed with the same abandon as Maisie and Tenaya had moments earlier. Separating only slightly from her fiancé, Amber said, "I gotta get back to the bar. Slim can only take the money. Jaycee and I have to do all the bartending. Come by and I'll comp you a daiquiri."

"Like hell you will. I'll be drinking Sierra Nevada."

Everyone grabbed their chairs and walked them over to the patio, where they placed them around it in concentric circles. Many had brought bottles of wine and growlers of beer. Others got something from the bar. Soon, everyone was in place for the next stage.

Maisie and Tenaya walked up behind the cake, admiring the lovely ice sculpture by its side. The cake was an enormous three tier Sacher torte that oozed rich chocolate. Tenaya had sprung for that, recalling the cake fondly from a trip she took to Salzburg the summer after graduating from high school.

Maisie cut a slice and tenderly fed it to her bride. Tenaya cut a slice and laughed as she threateningly held it back like a football. She then just as gently fed Maisie, who ended up with a chocolate mustache anyway. Tenaya kissed it away as they both giggled, and Snot played Vivaldi concertos on the gazebo stage. His girl "fiends" had moved down to the bar where they were showing their fake IDs to get served beer. Mace spotted them but looked the other way. Amber, however, told them to take a hike.

Many in the crowd opened little boxes they'd been carrying and dug into slices of cake they had brought themselves, knowing there wouldn't be enough for the masses in attendance.

The music stopped, and the crowd looked up at the gazebo. Chad and Tiffany stood at the mic. Tiffany smiled and took the lead. "Little Mother and Tenaya, congratulations on your marriage. This is our wedding gift to you…"

Jeff Stickney walked out with his band behind him, bowed, and sat down at the piano. The crowd went nuts. Chad leaned into the mic and yelled over the cheering and applause, "Ladies and gentlemen, the incomparable Miss Melody Gratch!" Maisie started jumping up and down, holding Tenaya's shoulders. The cheering grew louder. Stickney waved Snot over and invited him to sit in and jam with them, an invitation Snot happily accepted. The pianist pointed to a chair the drummer had set up with charts on a music stand and a playlist taped to the floor. Snot smiled and eagerly settled into his place.

"Hello everyone, I'm Melody, and this is Jeff and the band with your very own Snot on the guitar. Hahaha! Is everyone having a great time?" More cheering. "Congratulations, Maisie and Tenaya! We love you. This one is for you both on your wedding day."

The brides walked to the center of the patio and held one another, ready to dance. The band played, and Melody crooned, "The Way You Look Tonight." The onlookers smiled and swayed while watching the happy couple with affection.

Amber ran up to Mace and kissed him. "I'm going to sing that to you at our wedding." She turned around and ran back to work the bar. Mace admired her figure as she ran away in her flowing burgundy dress. "That's the most beautiful girl in the world."

McPherson replied, "I had no idea you felt that way about me, Mikey."

They both laughed, and Wheezer looked at them curiously. Mace smiled at him, "He's just bustin' my balls, kid."

At some point, they decided to go through the garter-tossing ritual. Maisie sat on a chair in the middle of the patio and Tenaya reached up to pull out a white garter that she tossed into the crowd. It was caught by Steven Hewitt, who immediately tossed it further into the crowd.

They exchanged places. Maisie lifted Tenaya's dress danger-ously high and pulled down the black garter on her right leg. It got stuck on her work boot. Maisie struggled to release it to no avail. Tenaya reached down to a strap with a leather holster on her other leg and pulled out a small Bowie knife. She used it to cut the garter, releasing it into Maisie's hand.

Maisie threw the broken garter over her shoulder. It landed in the outstretched palm of Mayor Nader's wife. She faced away from her husband and smiled at Doc Jones while waving the prize. Doc looked embarrassed and quickly walked away, pulling his wife with him.

Tenaya removed the chair, and everyone resumed dancing, mingling, and drinking. Children ran around the park laughing and singing with the band. Some of the woodchucks started a crap game behind the gazebo. Others played cornhole near the bar. The old hippies danced in a circle on the lawn and smoked rune-emblazoned clay pipes all fashioned by Stargazer. Supervisor Collins was with them, dancing madly, with a look of sheer ecstasy on her face. The smell of patchouli oil permeated the air around them all.

Melody took a short break as Stickney played on with the band. At one point, he pointed at Snot to take a solo. Snot laid one out that sounded like it had been played by Wes Montgomery. Stickney looked surprised and impressed. He gave the kid a big thumbs up.

Maisie and Tenaya made the rounds, mingling like crazy. Usually Tenaya hated doing that, but something about doing it with her new wife in this place at this time made it fun. The people were so happy to see them and so happy for them. It really was a love fest.

Slim cut out from the bar, found Lolita, and walked her out to the dance floor. After a couple of fast dances and one slow one, Lolita looked up at him. "Don't you love weddings, Slim? There's nothing quite like them to get you in the mood, you know what I mean?"

"I think so, sweetie."

They snuck off to a cluster of tall bushes near the Mulberry Street exit and disappeared into it.

Marvin was sitting invisibly way up on a high branch in an oak tree on the far side of the lawn, swinging his feet with the music. It was from his lofty perch that the ghost observed all of these proceedings unfold with glee. When he saw Slim and Lolita walk off to seek some very public privacy, he sighed, looked up to the heavens, and smiled. "Ah, my work here is done. I'm off," dramatically swinging an arm out. And with that, Marvin disappeared into the ether with a whooshing sound that ended like a softly popping cork.

Below the tree, Mort Soul the mortician heard it and felt a mild disturbance like a passing draft. A sense of déjà vu gave him goosebumps. He'd heard that sound more than once during his long career. He frowned and looked around. Finding nothing, shrugged his shoulders and walked over to the bar.

Melody Gratch returned to the stage and started singing, "We'll meet again." The crowd sang along and swayed. Maisie and Tenaya stopped, kissed, and started dancing again.

Amber had a dance with Mace, then said, "I have to help Slim and Jaycee break down the bar so we can go open The Anvil. I have a feeling this party is going to continue into the night over there. By the way, have you seen Slim? He disappeared a while ago and I haven't seen him."

Matter of fact, the observant deputy had noticed Slim and Lolita stealing away earlier. "Uh, yep, I think he and Lolita had some personal things to take care of. He should be right back."

"Good. Love you!"

"Love you too!"

A quick peck on the cheek would suffice for now. Amber darted off to the temporary bar to have Jaycee start packing surplus while she handled customers.

The happy couple appeared at the mic in the gazebo, and the band stopped playing. Melody announced them. "Ladies and gentlemen, Mrs. and Mrs. Murphy!" Maisie was all too happy to lose her maiden name "Wilco" as the kids in school used to tease her by calling her Roger. The crowd applauded.

Tenaya spoke into the mic first. "Hi everyone! We are so grateful to see you all here. You may not have seen our parents yet as Maisie and I wanted to walk each other down the aisle, so here they are." Maisie's mom and dad were on their right, and Tenaya's mother was on the left. Mr. Murphy had passed ten years before. The crowd cheered, and the parents bowed.

Little Mother took the mic next. "I hope you have all had fun!" More cheering. "If we missed saying hello to any of you, drop by the café or the firehouse when we get back in two weeks. But now we have to make a flight out of LAX to our honeymoon, so it's time for us to say so long."

Somebody yelled out, "Where you going?"

Tenaya answered. "Kauai for some hiking, snorkeling, and skinny dipping. The precise location is classified, so don't try to follow! Now keep the party going here in Big Squirrel." Melody and the band improvised a rendition of Aloha Oe as the girl "fiends" lined up next to one another and mimicked a hula. Cheers and laughter followed as the couple descended the stairs and walked to a waiting limo.

When they looked back to wave, they saw that the fire crew had used their hoses to create a water arch over the gazebo behind them. The setting sun struck it just right and exactly as they had planned, changing the arch into a glowing, flowing rainbow. The newlyweds both started crying and smiling. Tenaya called out, "That's against regs, you knuckleheads!" She waved and laughed as her crew waved goodbye.

The driver stopped at the firehouse so they could grab their bags and change into traveling clothes. They left their wedding dresses in Tenaya's office and took off for LA.

A grinning Slim finally showed up at the bar with giggling Lolita, who was smoothing her very rumpled dress. Jaycee scoffed. "Nice of you to join us, boss!"

"We had some quick errands to run."

"So I see." Amber laughed. "Jaycee has us half-packed back there, and I'm pouring a last few before I hang the closed sign."

"Great job you two!" Slim turned to the line and called out, "Last call, ya'll. Meet us at The Anvil if you want to keep going." He gave Lolita a kiss. "See you at The Anvil?"

"Heck yeah. What a fun day, huh?"

"The best ever!" He moved around the back to help Jaycee as Lolita moved into the throng to chat with Dixie.

The Anvil team wrapped things up, loaded everything in Slim's pickup, and took off for the tavern. About a half hour later, they opened the joint for business. The bar and tables filled rapidly, and the juke box blared. Jaycee once again donned her skates and made the rounds.

Slim saved Lolita's stool at the bar which she soon filled. Amber made her a mango daiquiri as Slim stood behind Lolita with his hands on her shoulders. He bent down and kissed her ear. Lolita looked up at him. "Aww, you sweet man."

Amber laughed and said, "Get back to work, Slim! We're gonna be busy tonight."

Mason, Dixie, Tiffany, and Chad sat at a table right in front of the bar and got a pitcher of margaritas. Tiffany started their version of the conversation that dominated all the tables. "Wasn't that a lovely wedding?"

"Sure was, Tif. And I enjoyed that it was a little different than most."

"I loved that, Dixie. It was really fun. Stargazer is something else!"

The woodchucks took their usual table, as did the old hippies. When Snot walked by with the girl "fiends" in tow, one of the woodchucks in a yellow and black plaid flannel shirt stood to shake his hand. "You were great today! You know so many genres. I didn't think ya' had it in ya'. I mean, I figured you had *something* in ya' seeing as your name is Snot and all, but not that much talent. You rocked!" The woodchuck smiled, and they shook hands. Snot affected a poorly done London Cockney accent and replied, "Why thank you very much, sir. Thank you very much. That's mighty fookin' kind of ya', in't it?" The woodchuck stared at the guitarist like he was a creature from an alien planet as he and the girl "fiends" walked off to find a place to sit.

Stargazer hung his cape and top hat on one of the pegs by the entrance and looked remarkably regal in his tux.

Mace arrived and sat with McPherson and his girlfriend, Maggie Mae. Wheezer had joined the firefighters, at least those who were not on duty that night. Mace caught Amber's eye up at the bar, and she blew him a kiss. He blew one back in a more circumspect manner than before. McPherson noticed anyway and said, "Oh Jesus." Maggie Mae hit him on the arm, "I think it's sweet. You could learn a thing or two from Mace here, you old coot."

Mayor and Grand Pooh-Bah Nader went up to the bar and whispered conspiratorially with Amber. When he turned to face the crowd, Amber picked up a cloth covered mallet and struck the gong they kept in the backbar for getting everyone's attention. Slim gave her the stink-eye and wondered what was going on.

The mayor began, "Good evening, everyone."

There was a collective, "Oh no," from the patrons, accompanied by catcalls. Somebody yelled from the back, "Not another speech!" Mrs. Nader cracked up back in her seat and tried to keep a straight face.

The mayor ignored it all. "As most of you know, I am Kelvin Nader, Big Squirrel Mayor and Grand Pooh-Bah." More no's and calls to sit down ensued. The mayor continued. "I need to do something that's overdue." More yelling. "Like resign?"

Nader motioned to Amber again, who reached behind the bar and pulled out two brass plaques, each one emblazoned with a large, gilded key. "I would like to present these keys to our city to a pair of heroes and our saviors, Mason Cadwallader and Chad Burr. Would you two please join me up here?" The jeering turned to cheering and applause as an embarrassed couple of fishermen stood and took the plaques while shaking the mayor's outstretched hand.

The editor/publisher/reporter/photographer of The Acorn Times came up to snap photos and jot down the mayor's proclamation in his tiny notebook.

"I wanted to present these tonight before I forgot again, Chad and Mason. We'll never forget what you did for our community."

The pair turned to face the patrons, who applauded again. The mayor added, "Oh, and guys... we all know you heard about it from Marvin."

The crowd laughed like mad.

Mason and Chad turned to face one another. "I didn't tell him, Mason!"

"I didn't either, Chad."

"Then who did?" The guys turned to look at their wives. Tiffany smiled, shrugged, and said, "Not me."

But Dixie was looking around the room guiltily. She looked up at Mason and mouthed, "Sorry, honey!"

The guys shook their heads but laughed and sat down. Lefty stood up and yelled, "Who ya' gonna call?" The entire tavern yelled back, "Ghostbusters!" and broke into a loud, sloppy version of the theme song from the movie.

Slim looked at Lolita, worried that this reference to her dead husband would set her back. But she was laughing and singing along with the others.

Tiffany, with tears in her eyes, looked at Chad, gave him a big kiss and said, "I'm so proud of you, sweetheart!"

Dixie kissed Mason and said, "I'm proud of you too, ya' big palooka, and I am so, so, sorry." She started to cry when he replied, "I love you too. Don't worry. I knew you'd blab sooner or later."

Dixie reached down to retrieve a handkerchief from her pink purse on the floor. She put it on the table, reached in and —POP! That was the very loud sound of the Beretta going off. The slug blew out the bottom of her purse, went through the table, and into the floor below, finally stopping in the soft soil underneath. Dixie withdrew her hand and fell back in her chair, staring at the purse.

The crowd stopped singing and ducked. Mace drew his weapon. Everyone looked around to see where the shot came from. When smoke started to rise from Dixie's purse, people in the crowd spotted it and started to laugh. Soon the whole place saw it and erupted in raucous laughter. Mace holstered his pistol, walked over, and without a word, removed the gun from the still smoking purse, pulled the clip, and walked back to his table, shaking his head.

Slim glared at Dixie, who looked over at him, her face redder than a hothouse tomato. He then did a facepalm, winked at Dixie, and started to laugh. He yelled over, "I'm putting that on your tab, young lady." He shrugged at Lolita and kissed her again.

Someone yelled "I ain't afraid of no ghost!" The crowd laughed again. Mace blew Amber a kiss, and Jaycee skated out with another round of beers. It was business as usual in Big Squirrel.

EPILOGUE

T.E. Morrow, assigned to Portal #7,890, leafed slowly through a slim booklet bound in a grey cover. That was all that was on his small desk except for a cube that held a single pen. The guide was wearing a drab grey suit, white button-down Oxford dress shirt, and a green and navy striped tie. Morrow was thin without appearing gaunt and of medium stature. He had salt-and-pepper hair with a slightly receding hairline. It was impossible to tell his age. He was totally unremarkable. He looked over his wire-rimmed reading glasses at his guest. "So, Mr. Severin..."

"Please, call me Marvin."

"Okay, Marvin, tell me, how were you able to stop visiting Lolita?"

"I realized in the instant after she threw the candy dish into the TV that I was holding her back from life. She needed to move on. I saw that she would never move forward with me still there. Lolita needed a chance to be with somebody more, uh, corporeal. That understanding didn't make it any easier, but it did provide me with motivation and strength with which to accept letting her go."

"So, are you saying that staying with her as long as you did was a selfish act on your part?"

"Well, yes. It was."

"I understand. What made you tell the fishermen about the drugs in the river?"

"Somehow, I just knew about the drugs. I told Mason and Chad about it as a way to help Lolita, and others, without being a presence in her life."

"That was a nice thing to do, Marvin."

"Thank you."

"What would you have done differently if you'd had the chance?"

"I would have given her more time before getting serious and asking her to marry me. I always felt that I may have robbed her of her youth. She was much younger than me. I felt guilty about that from time to time when I was alive."

"She loved you more than anything, Marvin. And you loved her. Like they say, when you know, you know. She knew too. You shouldn't beat yourself up so much."

"I know that now."

"Good, good." Morrow placed the open booklet on his desk and turned a few pages as he read on. Finally, he came to the last one where there was a space with a dotted underline. The guide picked up the pen from the cube and signed his name and title, T.E. Morrow, Spirit Guide.

"Well, I have fine news, Marvin. Your papers all appear to be in order, and you have been approved to move on up. Congratulations."

Marvin felt a compulsion that was impossible to resist and started singing the theme song from *The Jeffersons*, an old sit-com, "Ah we're movin' on up to the..." He stopped when Morrow stood up to shake his hand.

"Sorry. Thank you, Mr. Morrow."

"Quite alright, Marvin. You've earned a bit of joviality, wouldn't you agree?"

"Yes, I would."

"Do you have any questions?"

"Why do you do this? I mean, why are you still working?"

"My ex's place is next door to mine. The system is wonderful, but it isn't perfect. Plus, I love meeting people."

"I see."

"I will be taking you only to the point of departure. After that, you will need to walk alone to your destination. Don't worry. The path is easy to follow, quite smooth, and has a very gentle upward grade near the end. You'll find it is shorter than it looks at first. You've already done all the hard work. Someone will be there to receive you when you arrive and help you get settled into your place. We'd best get started."

They walked ten steps and stopped, surprising Marvin. "Here we are." Morrow pointed to a cream-colored path that stretched on to a horizon of sorts. The path was surrounded on both sides by grass dotted with Spring wildflowers.

The two spirits faced one another, and Morrow extended his hand once more for a final shake. "Enjoy the journey. You did very well. Goodbye, Marvin."

Marvin turned and found that Morrow had placed something in his hand when they shook. He looked at it and turned it over. It was a key attached to a heavy brass fob. Dark letters were etched into the fob. They said, "Engine #1 Big Squirrel Fire Dept." Marvin smiled, looked ahead, and followed the path, softly whistling *The Jeffersons'* theme song.

As the spirit that had been Marvin Severin, beloved husband of Lolita Smith Severin, and arguably the best teacher of Groverton High, went down his path, Morrow watched him and thought that the way Marvin walked reminded him of another guest who had passed through Portal #7,890 not long ago, a Mr. Chaplin.

Morrow returned to his desk, where he found his next guest already seated.

46

ACKNOWLEDGMENTS

I would like to thank Deborah Garner for her help in editing this story and providing the cover art. Had she not offered corrections and advice, I would have had to change the title to *A Dog's Breakfast*.

Thanks to Art Gallegos for sharing his technical expertise and wisdom regarding water treatment processes.

Thank you to Molly Arehart, a delightful daughter-in-law and artist, for providing internal art.

Finally, thanks to my wife of many decades, Tammy Williams, who put up with me as I typed and laughed each day of writing.

Made in the USA
Middletown, DE
20 May 2023